TEST FLIGHT

A quiver passed through the chill of the maze as Control gave them the five-second call. At one second to null the clearance code came over the link as Cargo gave the order to go.

They hurtled down three kilometers of lightless tunnel before bursting through to the glittering violet sky. The wind assaulted them, buffeting the batwing's gently curled structure. Cargo didn't fight it. He banked toward the mountains and felt the turbulance flow under the craft, lifting and propelling it still faster. In the distance he saw a thunderhead rolling over the foothills and urged the craft to meet it.

The wind was crazy here, switching back and creating low-pressure pockets. They fell suddenly through one, descending in a stomach-turning plunge until another gust caught them up again. Cargo didn't hear himself laugh.

He opened the craft to top go, plunging toward the ominous cloud at burn speed. He could feel Ghoster's efforts to keep them just below yield, to control maximum gees in the turn. And he smiled at Ghoster's efforts as he began to loop upward into vertical, belly to belly with the storm. . . .

Cyberstealth

S.N. LEWITT

ACE BOOKS, NEW YORK

For Mickey and Lynn Lewitt
in loving memory

Chapter

1

The high plain of Vanity that played host to the batwing base was something out of an underdeveloped hell. Outside the perimeter the horizon remained untouched by the intrusion of intelligence.

A million and one bases in the universe have a million Spin Streets just across from the perimeter. In some places the Spin Street isn't much, a couple of bars, a cheepo arcade and a few overage hookers decked out in hot magenta and chromium-yellow chains of heat-colored titanium. A million bases have a town a short ways from Spin Street, a real town with houses and schools and maybe a deli. At Mnueser base the town had the best bakery in the whole damn void. They made a chocolate fudge pie that could induce insulin shock in the unwary.

Cargo sighed and studied the empty plains. The wind whipped the long grass from here to the horizon on every side. A howling bitch to fly endo, the real test of skill. In the moonlight there was no color. Everything had bleached into gray and shadow, what of everything there was to see. Which wasn't much. No town, no Spin Street, even. Just the compound behind the embedded Eye beams of the perimeter and a single living guard whose duty was to clear grass and dust from the beams at regular intervals. Maybe all the rumors about the Directorate weren't so crazy after all.

Ghoster was the one who had suggested that they put in for the batwing. That was over a year ago now, way before they left Mnueser Base for Azar where the carrier they were stationed on, the *Torque*, had put in for repairs. Mnueser was one of the largest and most advanced bases in the Collegium, and

it was there that they had seen their first and only stealth-
fighter.

The base, like Kraits and carriers, was double hulled titanium. Burn colors glowed all over, as if someone was afraid
to leave one centimeter of surface unmarked. Teams of artists
did the first burns, maintainence groups the second. After a
while kids had used graffiti torches, burning slogans of gangs
like "Kill Walkers, they're already dead," in electric blue or
violet on all the orange and pink and hot yellow surfaces leading to Spin Street. In that jumble of color the black batwing
stood out like a sliver of the void.

It was Ghoster who ended up popping annies with the
stealth crew who wore their wings painted out matte black.
The Akhaid had to be pulled out of a bank of African violets
and have his head dunked in a basin of refresh gel more than
once before he got sober. Cargo had made an old family rec-
ipe to remove the hangover, something the Bishop had taught
him the first time he and Two Bits had gotten that drunk in
front of their patron.

At least it wasn't coffee. Coffee made Ghoster so high he
had to be peeled off the cloud cover.

"Are you trying to kill me?" Ghoster had screamed after
gagging violently on the first swallow of orange juice mixed
with raw egg and hot sauce.

Cargo had smiled. "Looks like you're yourself again. What
were you taking? Greens?" Of all the legal analog drugs available, greens left the worst head. At least in humans.

Ghoster had snorted and then looked away. Finally he had
curled up in Cargo's favorite easy chair, moaned, and dropped
off to sleep.

It was the middle of the night before Ghoster was coherent
again. He had shaken Cargo awake. "They're looking to be
short," the Akhaid had repeated over and over again as Cargo
struggled to open his eyes.

"What's short?" Cargo mumbled, half asleep.

"The batwing. That's what I wanted to tell you." Ghoster
didn't stop shaking Cargo to talk. "If we put in for the transfer
now, we're practically guaranteed they'd take us for the
Hand's Day class. You know damn well we've got the best
record of any team on the Torque. And the Torque's got a
double-Alpha rating. Besides, the guys told me that Four-

ways, head of their personnel section, was going to be here next week."

Cargo's eyes flew open. There was murder in them. "You woke me up in the middle of the night to tell me *that*? You have a death wish? You wanna live on the Wall?"

"I didn't want to forget. Come on, think about flying those batwings. The Stealth-eleven-fifteen. The one that's down in Hanger Nine. That you dragged me to see yesterday and the day before that." Ghoster would have gone on but he was interrupted by a ragged snore.

Stuck now in Vanity's excuse for a base, Cargo was going to say something disparaging to Ghoster, who didn't even have the good sense to be ashamed. Then a movement caught his eye. Black on black, it was a slip of shadow between the stars. He pointed, not sure he'd seen anything at all, but Ghoster followed his hand and became silent.

Batwings were silent, stealthcraft, made for slipping unnoticed from exo to sky. They came in low and slow, spirit walking across the dawn until they slipped out again. It was the batwings they had come for, dignity and challenge against the fast Kraits that glittered all the colors of burned titanium. Batwings were as black as the Wall. Watching them dance endo made Cargo taste desire.

Masked by the wind, by the empty horizon itself, the stealthcraft rose and flickered against the backdrop of the sky.

"Don't you just and truly want one?" he asked Ghoster after the batwings had disappeared, merged into the night.

The Akhaid looked at Cargo with alien ears pulled down in a way no human could imagine and his nostrils flattened in a manner that for a human would indicate disgust. He could have been expressing a number of reactions, but whatever it was it surely wasn't approval. Not at all. That much Cargo knew. Then he turned his back and walked toward the bar that had been their destination.

The wind howled and bit through to the flesh. Cargo knew his mother would say that the screaming in this wind was caused by the souls of infants who had died without names. He didn't believe in that crap, and what's more he didn't think his mother did either.

Against the sky stood only one lone outpost that offered some of the amenities necessary to sustain a training regimen. And if Stolie's was the only representative of what the Collegium offered to affiliates, Cargo was damned sure he would have defected to the Cardia long ago. Rumor had it that they, at least, had the sense to provide off-base transportation to recreation centers. Of course, rumor also had it that the bat-wing was the hottest assignment in the whole goddamned Service. Seeing the batwings chasing each other across the sky, Cargo decided that there were sources of information less accurate than rumor.

Inside, Stolie's bar seemed unnaturally quiet, even if there were only fifteen or so beings, human and Akhaid mixed, there. He would have expected more, even though the place was ugly. There were more chips in the imitation wood veneer than there was veneer left, and the torn cushions on several chairs hadn't been mended. Still, it was cheap. More important, there wasn't anyplace else to go.

He'd hoped to find a game of khandinar in progress, play a few rounds and get to talking, maybe pick up a little scuttle-butt. The fact that there were no cards in sight struck him as more than a little odd. "Khandinar?" he inquired generally.

A tall blond man in civvies turned from his station at the bar. "Now that is the first civilized thing I have heard this evening," he said. "Here I am, stuck way out in country even God has forgotten, where a being can't even get a decent drink. Not a bartender who can make a mint julep for twenty light years any direction, or I'd be pleased to offer you one. Now, what're you called and can I buy you a beer?"

"I'm Cargo," he said, trying not to notice Ghoster's expression. "And a beer would be fine."

The stranger nodded and smiled evilly. "Cargo, is it? So we're getting transport personnel who haven't even danced vac? You're in maintainence then? Or repair?" A glass appeared at the speaker's elbow with a thick, foamy head. He pushed it toward Cargo.

Cargo wouldn't touch it. He sneered. "You heard about Azar?" he asked softly. "Me and my Eyes, we were decorated for that."

The blond's smile never wavered. "I don't believe I've had the pleasure. Why don't you tell me and make up for my lack of erudition?"

Cargo met the stranger's gaze as a challenge. Even Ghoster would have to understand. If he backed down now he wouldn't get any respect for the entire time they were training on Vanity. This guy didn't look like the type who let anything go, ever.

"No one'd expected Cardia at Azar," he began. "We were out on routine patrol, Two Bits flying lead and me on his wing, when they burst out behind from the Community cylinder. There were four of them, two for Two Bits and two for me.

"I was in tight mode and the whole thing was vis. That Krait maze didn't like if at all, either. They don't trust vis and honestly I can't blame them. And this was pure and simple surprise.

"I knew where my two were and where they were heading, so I stayed where I was and waited for them. And just as they came around and committed to the pass I gave her all the juice I had left and shot up the center. Two Bits took one of them with a CP bolt there, or I might have ended up on the Wall. Anyway, he left the second one for me.

"I spiralled under him so fast that if we hadn't been exo the hull would have gone violet. Just as that gomer was making his pass I cartwheeled under him. We were pulling more gees than I want to remember and the exhaust of the Krait was spewing crud ray to top go. We wheeled around under that gomer just as the exhaust ducts hit double time and caught him on the high.

"Now if there's one thing I can't stand, it's a being who doesn't play fair." Cargo fixed the blond pilot with a pointed stare before draining half his beer. "We had two and they had two and we should have split the odds. But these Cardia dancers hadn't shown more than null decency since we'd engaged. Now these two had turned on Two Bits and I was massively p.o.ed. I decided that I was gonna get satisfaction even if I ended up on the Wall.

"Since they were ignoring me anyway, I just paraded right by those gomers in waltz-time with Eyes on them. Ghoster, he's my Eyes, got off two shots so clean even my mother would have approved. It was like nursery school.

"Only one of the damned Cardia had gotten off a shot first. I never would have believed it if I hadn't seen it realtime."

Cargo finished the beer and called for another. He tried to avoid seeing the whole thing in his head, the same way he had after the hearing when the shrink told him to focus on the future. He couldn't help reliving that moment now any more than he could then. Two Bits was dancing vac, coming out behind the Crafters and disappearing behind the Colony. No one could make it work from that angle, that distance. Only he had seen it himself, the flash and then Two Bits' Krait burst open like a timelapse chrysanthemum. All yellow and red against the void.

"At least I got those two. None of them was going to live and take credit."

The blond stranger had the decency to admit defeat. "I apologize," he said choosing his words carefully. "Only Cargo *is* a strange call sign for a fancy dancer, you know."

The second beer had gotten warm, but Cargo drank it anyway as a peace offering. Besides, it was wet and talking made him thirsty. I talk too much when I tell that story, he thought. Combat is different. There's no time to think dancing vac. Kraits are faster than flesh can control, the gomers the same that way. And the maze, that nondimensional interface between the computer, pilot and Eyes in cybermode and the mechanics of the craft itself, didn't completely trust any of its elements.

"What's your call sign again?" Cargo asked the guy sitting across the table, drawing geometric figures with his fingers between the crumbs on the table. He was so blond that he looked nearly unhuman in the dim light.

"Do you know what the difference is between a pilot story and a fairy tale?" the stranger said softly. "A fairy tale begins 'Once upon a time,' and a pilot story begins 'There I was cutting exo.'"

"You say I'm not telling the truth?" Cargo asked. He had decided he didn't like the blond, whoever he was. The man was definitely pushing him.

"You're in the new stealth class, right? So I'm going to find out at eight-hundred hours. I can wait." He smiled before he stood up and left, a cold little smile that made Cargo wonder if he was going to live that long.

"Let's get out of here," Ghoster rasped in Cargo's ear.

"I haven't played a single game yet," Cargo protested. "I haven't found one single person to play one friendly round and it's still early."

He would have protested further, but Ghoster's fingers were squeezing his elbow like a vise. Not that he knew all that much about Akhaid expressions, but he knew enough to recognize Ghoster's flattened ears and slightly open mouth as either fury or disgust. He didn't want to deal with either of them. Alien Ghoster might be, but he was still Cargo's partner. And, more important, he was the only person Cargo really knew on Vanity. For a moment he reconsidered the wisdom of coming here.

Ghoster didn't let go until they were outside. There wasn't another being in sight except the guard at the base perimeter. And even if there were, the wind blew in deafening gusts so that it was difficult to hear a person less than an arm's length away. Plain rock glittered in patches under Vanity's twin moons that were bright enough to obscure the stars. Cargo could see Ghoster's face clearly enough in their light, his pale bronze skin dulled and darkened. He'd seen him like that only twice before, and both times he'd been certain the Akhaid was going to kill him.

"You promised that you'd never open your mouth about it again. You promised it was gone, had never happened. You shouldn't have done it while I was there." Ghoster's whisper matched the harsh wind of Vanity.

"You saw I didn't have any choice," he replied.

Ghoster made a sound in his throat that Cargo caught under the howling wind. Then his face went smooth and blank, though Cargo could see the tension throughout the alien's body.

"This time," Ghoster said, enunciating very clearly, "I will pretend that it has not happened. But only because we happen to be the best team there is and I'm not willing to give that up. Not yet. But don't push your fabled luck. Even your luck won't hold that long."

The Akhaid turned gracefully and strode across the grass back to the base. Cargo swore at his Eyes under his breath as he watched his partner leave.

So far as he was concerned he hadn't broken his promise. He'd left out the points Ghoster didn't want anyone to talk about, that Cargo had promised him had never happened. In truth, he'd never said a word about them. He didn't blame Ghoster, either, even if Two Bits had been like a brother, almost, only better because a brother would have tied him to home. It wasn't the Akhaid's fault that some Cardia gomer had sent Two Bits to the Wall. Besides, guilt wasn't a major part of Akhaid culture. Cargo couldn't understand why Ghoster was so all hot and sensitive about it.

Besides, Ghoster couldn't blame Cargo for the investigation. Some fruit-of-the-loom, manure-breath, math brass decided that the only possible way Two Bits went to the Wall was friendly fire. And that meant them. No one else was out there at the time. Not in that particular sector. Not in range.

Being accused burned more than anything. They finally came up with null when they looked at the Krait tapes. The investigating board couldn't disprove it from the camera evidence, but there was nothing that looked like confirmation either. What the board didn't know was that Two Bits had been Cargo's oldest friend.

Cargo did not speak of that investigation because he had promised Ghoster, had decided that if they were going to work together then it had to be forgotten completely. Besides, there was still the batwing waiting, and that had all been Ghoster's idea anyway. It had been his partner who had been seduced by the elegant black stealthcraft. Cargo had been perfectly happy driving a Krait once upon a time, before he had seen the mellifluous curves of a batwing cradled in its hold.

Anyway, the whole investigation had been insane. He knew completely to the core of his soul that he had nothing to do with Two Bits' death.

He wanted to return to the bar. It was cold out, the biting cold of a brisk wind that had not abated since they'd arrived that afternoon. Stolie's might not be his first choice, but the only other possible alternative was to go back to quarters, and he wasn't ready for that yet. The memories were still dark enough that he wanted only bright lights and laughter and more beer and maybe a couple of rounds of khandinar even with a low ante. He wanted Spin Street, only there wasn't one, and Cargo cursed what there was.

Quarters on Vanity were only marginally worse than the entertainment situation. The celofabbed units were flimsy and the sound of the wind cut through everything. The windows hadn't been resealed since the shacks had been thrown together, so cold drafts permeated the space. Even the extra blankets provided weren't enough to keep Cargo warm.

The wind howled through the crack between window and wall over his bed, but Cargo told himself that he'd gotten used to that. He only wished it wasn't so cold. A distant hiss and a few half-hearted flickers of the plate near the floor indicated that the heating was on, although he couldn't feel any effects. He put his hand over the panel. Nothing.

It was hard for him to sleep when it was too cold, and even harder in a strange place. The smell of Vanity, raw and slightly moist, kept him awake. Cargo cursed the decision to come, and cursed Fourways more than that.

It was Fourways who had encouraged Ghoster to go through with the transfer to this miserable excuse for a base. The *Torque* might have been as cramped for space as any carrier, but it had a great cook, a decent rec deck and no infernal howling cold.

And they'd had a fair share of excitement on the *Torque* as well. Not that they had ditched the long patrols, ten, twelve hours on end, straining the Krait's fuel reserve to stare into the everlasting void. But there had been those short, brilliant moments when the gomers had pushed a pace dancing vac, when even thought wasn't fast enough to keep up with the action.

Still, he couldn't deny the fact that the batwing was really the elite. He wasn't stupid enough to imagine that the transfer would mean higher pay, better accommodations or a cush posting. Vanity was uncomfortable as hell but somehow Cargo found it all very reassuring. All the money, all the innovation, had gone to the right place. This was hard evidence that the batwing was on the cutting edge. A group's importance was almost always in exact reverse proportion to the amenities of their base. Mnueser had been scruffy and peeling around the corners. Vanity was held together by match-welds, medical adhesive and obstinacy.

All this transfer meant was a chance to use the best craft ever designed, for the most challenging tasks. For Cargo, that was enough. He suspected that Ghoster had known that all along.

When the transfer orders came through nearly eight months later they were on the *Torque* and already underway for Azar. Not that that stopped them from some serious partying, although the *Torque* didn't have quite the recreational variety of the Base and Spin Street and the town beyond.

The group threw the party on the rec deck. Members of their own group bought the first round. By the time all the toasts had been drunk, two artificial trees and seventeen fake birds had been dismantled and scattered over the floor in a game of Smash.

Two Bits had still been alive that night, Cargo remembered. He'd won the first two rounds of Smash and was buying a third. He was more maudlin than annie blind when he staggered over and threw an arm around Cargo's shoulder.

"Remember," he said clearly, his words soft and even and perfectly formed. "Remember what the Bishop said. About the pilgrimage to the Black Virgin."

Cargo nodded slightly, trying to keep the room from spinning around too rapidly. No matter how gone he was, he couldn't forget the lectures every week, along with the end of every conversation and call. He'd even made a vow to the Bishop that someday he'd go to the Black Virgin and make the pilgrimage to the shrine on Earth of Ste. Maries-de-la-Mer. He had made the vow before *marhime* had been decided, but wasn't sure if that made it invalid or only uncomfortable.

Two Bits had pulled a chain out from under his collar and fastened it around Cargo's neck. "To keep you safe from the Evil One," he muttered.

Cargo had looked at it later. It was a pilgrimage medal of Ste. Maries de-la-Mer. Two Bits had hinted that he had gone, although he'd never come straight out about it. Cargo understood that perfectly well. Not only did the Church disapprove of using the medals as magical charms, Two Bits and Cargo did too. But so far as Cargo knew there wasn't a Krait jockey in the whole of the universe who didn't have some form of magic. There was the one who always had to do the checklist in reverse order and the one who had to put on his left glove first or else. And the one who carried his grandfather's pocket-knife and the one who always had to have a picture of Ali Tyronne secured in the cockpit.

So he took the medal and he'd never taken it off, not for a moment. Like every other pilot he had to carry his sacred luck.

On his first morning on Vanity, he fingered the medal slowly. It meant that Two Bits had been his brother. Cargo respected him for it, and at the same time was horrified. Sometimes he wished that his old friend hadn't always felt compelled to follow him everywhere. Into the navy, into combat flying, even to the *Torque*. Cargo tried to tell himself that it wasn't his fault, and besides, he'd always looked after the

guy like the younger brother he was. Two Bits had never
come to any harm for following him.

Anyway, the next morning they'd arrived near Azar and
Two Bits and Cargo had drawn patrol.

Ghoster had already finished breakfast when he arrived.
The Akhaid was sitting over two mugs of coffee and shoved
one at Cargo when he sat down.

"What the hell are you doing?" Cargo hissed, infuriated.
That was all he needed. Not, he swore again, that what the
Akhaid did was his business. Except in the maze, and a training maze tended to be thinner than what they were used to in
the Krait. It was hard enough to touch the alien in mode as it
was, to have to face the fact that Ghoster wasn't perfectly
human in a funny wrapper.

Ghoster closed his eyes lazily. "Decaf," he whispered.

Cargo started. "Sadist," he replied. "That isn't funny."

"Yes it is. Now, I suppose you have already seen today's
schedule?" Ghoster asked softly. Cargo was grateful that he
waited until they were halfway through the coffee, and he had
thawed out enough to think at all. He shook his head.

Ghoster's ears relaxed against his skull, and his eyes got
wide. At least he wasn't still angry at Cargo for last night. The
decaf probably evened things out by Ghoster's logic. We manage pretty well, Ghoster and I do, Cargo thought. Better than
a lot of teams he'd seen. But then that was one of the reasons
they had been selected, or so rumor had it.

"So what's on the sched that's so interesting?" Cargo asked
lightly.

Ghoster didn't answer. Cargo didn't expect him to. The
Akhaid always liked to keep him in the dark about little
things. Things that didn't affect them directly if he screwed it
to the Wall, that was. For an Akhaid, Ghoster had a pretty
well-developed sense of self-preservation. Cargo wondered if
he'd ever Walked. He'd wondered that regularly since he'd
met the alien, but knew better than to ask. He and Ghoster
were a damned fine team, and he wasn't going to jeopardize
that. Neither was Ghoster.

Ghoster left the table to get them both a second cup. Cargo
glanced up toward the door and mentally made a face. The
blond guy from last night was leaning casually against the
unpainted concrete wall, staring across the mess hall. Cargo

took a quick recce and was relieved. The wings on his uniform were shiny, not the matte black awarded to full stealth fliers. It was those black wings that had given the group its name. No, whoever he was, this guy was just as new as Cargo.

The blond met Cargo's eyes and sauntered over until he was standing across the table, a plate of chops in hot sauce in his hand. The smell nearly made Cargo gag. He smiled.

"Cargo, right? Mind if I sit down?"

"Whatever you like."

Ghoster slipped back into his seat. Noticing the visitor, his whole face drooped in a single motion. Cargo opened his mouth to make introductions, but Ghoster shook his head very slightly. He understood. The Akhaid was still humiliated by his storytelling of the evening before. Cargo figured that if he could have done it gracefully Ghoster would have sat on the other side of the room.

"Now, there is one thing you've got to learn," the stranger said as he emptied the pepper shaker on the table over his chops. "You just do not lie very well, my friend, and that is a fact. Now, last night for example, you should have told me about how those gomers blasted your buddy down to electrons. And then how you got the last one on a long shot. Damn. If you're ever gonna make a spook you stick too close to the facts. But I do give it to you, it was a fine thing to try before we even got started."

Ghoster appeared on the verge of being sick.

"You never did tell what you're called," Cargo said. Maybe he'd been too hasty to judge this person last night. Not because he liked being what the stranger said, but because the man's face was open and smiling. There was something appealing that Cargo couldn't exactly place, as if the stranger were subtly asking him to join in a joke.

Suddenly the stranger's smile broadened. "Well, that's fine. You didn't come back and let me have a go at you, and I did have a story that would do my namesake proud. Best I could do was keep my identity all matte and dark."

"So far you're doing a wonderful job," Ghoster said dryly. He obviously still wasn't happy about what his partner had done. Cargo felt a tinge of guilt watching Ghoster take out his frustration on the stranger, who was merely available but hadn't deserved it.

The stranger turned. "Now, unless ole Cargo here was lying better than I had suspected, you are Ghoster. Now don't tell me I'm wrong."

He seemed very satisfied with himself, and Cargo hated to admit that he had reason to be. They still didn't know who he was, and he was alone. Cargo wondered where his Eyes was, too. One of the reasons the batwing had recruited Cargo and Ghoster in the first place, at least according to Fourways, was because they were such a good team. It was something he knew personnel looked for, the ability to cross species prejudice and really interface.

Ghoster and Cargo stared at each other, excluding the stranger. "I don't care," Cargo said airily. "First session starts in ten minutes. I think I can wait that long to find out who he is."

"Maybe we ought to start over now," Ghoster said. "I wouldn't want to be late."

They both rose precisely together. The stranger laughed. "Stonewall. I'm called Stonewall. How about if I come over with you? All shinys together."

He hadn't heard the term before but he understood it straight off. Of course. Their wings were still shiny, hadn't been painted out the matte black of a batwing. Not yet.

Stepping out into the brilliant morning, Cargo understood for the first time why the place had been named Vanity. Even though the wind was cold and ripped through fabric and flesh, its constant movement brought the plains alive. Whipping the long varicolored grass, the near gale turned the ground cover from red to yellow to mottled blue with patches of purple, while black volcanic boulders stood glittering above the kaleidoscope movement of the shaggy turf.

He had to blink against the glare, unprepared for this display after the dimly lit interiors. Against the brilliant grass, even the dirty beige concrete buildings of the base seemed part of an esthetic plan.

The Center was impossible to miss. Unlike the rest of the base, it had been built with some thought to tradition, to stability. Red brick rested solid, deep in bedrock. The message was clear. Here, at least, things weren't thrown together. They were considered and weighed. They were here to stay. Or for the duration, whichever was longer.

Stonewall's Eyes met them at the front entrance. He, or

she, Cargo couldn't really tell with Akhaid, was still blinking with sleep. Staring was impolite but Cargo couldn't stop looking. This was the most unusual Akhaid he had ever seen.

"This is Steel." Stonewall did the introductions.

No wonder where that call sign had come from. Cargo had seen Akhaid in about all the colors they came in, from almost silver to polished obsidian. Their skin had a slighly metallic cast and was vaguely reptilian with quasi-scales that looked cold and perhaps slimy but weren't, and their eyes didn't have any whites—but otherwise they were basically hominid. Not that Cargo would ever say that to Ghoster. The Akhaid would take it as an insult, he figured. At first he'd found them disconcerting, disorienting, although he'd certainly seen plenty growing up. His mother had nearly as many Akhaid customers as humans, which proved only that gullibility was a universal trait.

Still, Steel was unusual. His skin was about the color of a good knife blade, and with about as much sheen, the gray dull enough that Cargo wondered if he was sick. Or she. It was a problem.

The room they'd been assigned was clearly marked. It obviously served double duty as a briefing room since the display table was set up with a frontal interface. The white walls were covered with several brightly colored schematics of satellites, planets, colonies and batwings. Across the front a carefully lettered sign read, "Welcome to the Second Directorate."

The briefing table was a newer model than Cargo had seen, individual screens set in the overall fluid display instead of separate patches, and the collars covered in clean soft fabric. Yellow collars for Akhaid, blue for humans, the table had obviously been set up to link across instead of side by side.

Cargo snorted lightly at the setup. He preferred to share a screen with Ghoster, at least in the early stages of checking out new equipment. It was easier to compare exactly what each of them was really doing. He had to acknowledge that this was more realistic, however—at least if the batwings were anything at all like the Kraits.

Without thinking, his hand went to the pill patch in the left sleeve of his uniform. Damn. After two weeks on transport and signing in yesterday he'd forgotten to fill up on Three-

B's. He deserved to be damned to all-rotten hell. On the *Torque* he would have been fined at least a week's pay for that, and a yellow line would have gone into his personnel file.

Stonewall and his Eyes were already seated across from each other. Two other teams were also getting settled, one an Akhaid pilot and human Eyes, neither of whom Cargo recognized. The last pair, Plato and Glaze, had spent a couple of weeks on the *Torque* en route to a new posting at Columbine. He watched as Plato, the human he remembered as a Krait pilot, swallowed a handful of the pills he had forgotten.

It took only a few minutes for the Three-B's to open the altered DNA chip nestled in the base of the skull so they could slip into cybermode, linking with the computer system and Akhaid counterpart. Much as he was embarrassed by his own omission, Cargo knew he couldn't hold off any longer. He slipped in between Stonewall and the human he'd never met.

"Got some extra Threes?" he asked Stonewall casually.

"I believe I might. I would dearly hate to please Fourways so well as letting him catch one of us unprepared." Stonewall's expression hinted at a smile as he handed over the tiny red pills.

"Thanks. I owe you," Cargo said softly.

Then he wondered about Stonewall's comment. It seemed innocent enough that their class had to stick together. Cargo wondered if Stonewall really thought Fourways was looking to catch one of them out, to kick someone down. During the three dinners that he had eaten with Fourways on the *Torque* he hadn't gotten that feeling at all. The head of cyberstealth recruitment and training had been very formal and aloof, but that could be perfectly ordinary.

What Cargo had found far more noteworthy was that, despite his matte wings, the man had not tempted them with any of the specs of the stealthcraft. At the time, Cargo figured it was all classified out of his reach. And that was a perfectly logical assumption. Ghoster had agreed that it wasn't strange at all. Only thinking back on it now, Cargo realized that Fourways hadn't told them much of anything, really.

Fourways stepped through the door at precisely o-eight hundred and took a seat directly under the sign. His bearing was slightly stiff—unnatural—which had made Cargo com-

ment on the *Torque* when they had first met. Ghoster had
suggested that he could be covering for an old injury, and
Cargo had to agree that was possible. He was older than he
should be at the rank of Commander, Cargo thought again,
unless it was possible to go that completely gray prematurely.
From what he knew of Fourways' racial group it wasn't likely.

Fourways looked them over individually and then dismissed the class in a single glance. He turned his attention to
the liquid display that lit the center of the talking table where
the schedule for the next few weeks was illuminated in yellow-orange. No wonder Ghoster found it funny.

"Naval intelligence is divided into six directorates," Fourways began very softly. "The first is intelligence, and that is
the primary purpose of the entire organization. Intelligence
means gathering and analyzing data. That data is our product,
our real mission. It is the job of the First Directorate and does
not concern you. You are under the jurisdiction of the Second
Directorate. Make no mistake about that. You are no longer
with any fleet or affiliated with any ship or fighter group."

Cargo noticed that Plato had gone white. The Akhaid had
reacted to that statement, too, eyes wide and ears pressed forward. Only Stonewall remained unmoved. For himself, Cargo
had to fight the urge to leave the whole mess. This wasn't
what Fourways had told him in the recruitment meeting. Then
his understanding was that the batwing was like an elite
fighter wing that specialized in cyberstealth technology and
intelligence targets. At the time it had sounded a lot like any
other military unit, albeit with a specialized task. Flying constellations just didn't seem like it would be that different from
flying gomers. A little more or less challenging, maybe, that
was all.

Just the sound of the title "Second Directorate" brought to
mind some organization of lurkers and spooks, underhanded,
somehow not quite clean. Nastily, the thought welled up in the
back of his mind that it was exactly where he belonged. Being
marhime, he was probably unusually suited to whatever the
Second Directorate was.

"The Second Directorate includes the entire division of
Covert Operations," Fourways continued. "The cyberstealth
group is one subdivision within that framework. As such, you
are all now subject to the same career training that anyone else

in the Directorate receives, with the exception that you will also check out in stealthcraft."

Cargo read through the course listing. Subjects like identifying and spreading disinformation, masking operations, sabotage, hand weapons, Cardi technology and vulnerability and covert communications appeared on the screen one after another. The list left him somewhere between fury and murder. To make a pilot play with those things was to dip him in slime.

For a moment that got caught in the fold as the Three-B's started to take effect, and Cargo wondered if he'd made the right decision. Those old Kraits, burned to look like some whore's junk jewelry, were very tempting just then. Here, on Vanity, the only colors he'd seen were the grass and the sky. The gaudy magenta and electric blues were gone, banished to a harder, brighter place.

Ghoster kicked his shin and brought him back. Fourways was already on another topic. The coffee which Cargo had drunk that morning threatened to burn a hole in his stomach as he tried to concentrate.

This time Fourways was explaining how the real function of stealthcraft was to knock out enemy ELint satellites, orbital missiles and the like. He heard a soft whistle and saw Stonewall nod with satisfaction. There couldn't be anything more challenging in the known universe than to try that, to go up against a constellation of orbital intelligence, targeting and attack units. This was what Fourways had said, this was what they had come for, Cargo acknowledged.

He didn't set out to be a spook, but this was worth it. It was dangerous, more dangerous than anything he'd done so far in a Krait. And Fourways hadn't even mentioned endo yet, flying sky.

The wind rattled the heavy glass and a cold draft invaded the room. Endo. What would it be like to take on that gale, to cut from vac to atmosphere in something a little more sensitive than a pig? The thought became a beautiful jewel, a single clear point of satisfaction in Cargo's experience. The Three-B's were starting to penetrate the blood-brain barrier and affect him. There was something distinctly pleasurable as the drug began to key him into mode. At times he had wondered whether his courage was no more than chemical keying on the

Krait. Then it was time, and he fastened the blue collar as the link opened.

Cyborg mode was the highest freedom of existence. The interface was established in his mind, and he had only to direct the barest thought or image to have it answered. This one continuous, seamless link had given him access to all the information, all the power, he could desire. Not that he was physically unaware in mode, but that his consciousness was expanded to include the system to which he was linked. It was glorious, addictive, and every time Cargo interfaced he was more and more deeply enamored.

The system, however, wasn't perfect. Cargo hadn't touched his personal file since he'd been on transport. Modes were carefully guarded, and only a few nonmilitary uses were approved. Even if he'd wanted to get in he hadn't had access.

A soft voice in his head asked if he wanted his messages. Cargo wondered who had had time and permission to send a message through mode, and he swore at the machine mentally in four languages.

"There are no data under those headings," the mode answered.

Cargo gave up and requested his messages. The first was the usual from the Bishop. Ever since the old man had gotten mode access he sent a message at least once a week. Probably more as an excuse to use the feature than anything else, Cargo thought, knowing how it would delight the Bishop to play with such a toy.

In the next the tone changed sharply. Fourways' voice was clearly displeased, ordering Cargo to report alone after the day's instruction had ended. Pressing his palms together, Cargo considered requesting a replay. He couldn't think of any reason Fourways would seek him out so soon. Alone, with orders through mode where they couldn't be accessed by anyone else, it had all the marks of a reprimand. Only Cargo hadn't done anything at all yet. It wasn't possible.

He turned it over in his mind for a moment. "I am sorry but I have no further information on this subject," the computer informed him.

Cargo debated with himself only briefly and then decided that worry was uneconomical. Using time and adrenaline wouldn't accomplish anything.

Instead, he thought about the batwings, and instantly he was immersed in enough information to keep even him happy. Fourways was forgotten as Cargo attacked data with relish, challenging the mode to keep pace. He was startled when the link interrupted with a time reading and a reminder that the head of the training program was waiting in his office.

Chapter 2

Fourways was waiting behind his desk when Cargo arrived. It had taken Cargo some time to find his office, which turned out to be on the second floor of the Admin Center, not that anyone had told Cargo that. Besides, Cargo smelled trouble as clearly as he smelled the stench of Vanity's decaying weeds swept up by the wind.

Fourways was leaning back in a battered slant chair looking at something on his display screen, ignoring the scuffing of hard soles on harder tile. He remained silent, staring, for at least a minute before he turned to acknowledge Cargo. The desk was a pitted barrier between them, its once gray surface as scratched and stained as a planetside battlefield. A straight chair of about the same vintage stood to on the other side but Fourways didn't invite Cargo to sit.

The office alone told Cargo enough. The neatly labeled files, all closed, the perfectly clean desk, even the angle between the screen and the wall were all beyond what military custom and practice demanded. Old and beaten up these things might be, but they were so precisely placed that Cargo was sure his superior was slightly obsessive. It made him vaguely uneasy, like watching a thunderhead roll in and waiting for the deluge.

"Cargo," Fourways muttered, staring at the wall and not at his subordinate. Then he swung his eyes around to pierce Cargo like a pair of guns. "You know we almost canceled your reservation during the Azar investigation. I was for it. I don't want you here. I don't trust you. I got overruled by some ass-kisser who doesn't know the first damn thing about intelligence but saw the Mirabeau name and that was that. So I'm stuck with you, and if I have any say in the matter you won't get one task as long as you're in my command. Or maybe you think no one should ever have discovered the Six. Everyone knows where the Mirabeau stand on that."

It took everything Cargo had ever learned not to shout, to grab Fourways by the collar and demand what he meant by that. He'd been prepared for something unpleasant, but this was beyond anything he had ever anticipated. Fourways' barb had been well beyond what was considered acceptable baiting. No one questioned the importance of the Six, even if the Cardia thug-leader Ki Shodar had destroyed the evidence. Not even the Mirabeau had protested, although it took more discipline than Cargo thought he possessed to stand still and listen to shit about the Bishop.

Suddenly the office and Fourways' thunderclap came together, and he remembered where he'd seen this type before. It had been the warden who'd warned the Bishop off, hated the name Mirabeau. They weren't commanders, not in the real sense. No one would follow them. Cargo managed to keep his face impassive. "What in my record makes me untrustworthy, sir?"

Fourways made a steeple with his fingertips, looking down at them and then back up. "Besides Azar? I don't like people who get investigated in the first place. I particularly dislike people who get cleared for a lack of evidence. But more than anything else, I hate people who have fuzzy backgrounds. Do you understand what I mean, Cargo?"

He spoke soft and slow, letting each word fall like a separate and individual threat.

Cargo stared pointedly at the bare wall just over Fourways' head. Only the rigid habit of formality came between him and murder. It was the warden all over again. "No, sir, I don't understand. What do you want me to do, sir?"

Fourways smiled almost genially and ignored the sarcasm. "Don't try to play innocent. I want you to resign and rejoin your old group," he said in an almost conversational tone. "I've seen a copy of your Marcanter birth registration. I don't know where you got the friends you do, but you wouldn't be here without help. As a matter of fact, given our general policy about people born on Cardia worlds, it's rather amazing that you weren't deported at the beginning of the hostilities.

And there's the matter of your second birth certificate on the Sahl-Goodun Colony. And we can't forget the fact that you have some powerful friends. An ex-Trustee, no less. One rather well known for being soft on Shodar, unfortunately. However, the Fourth Directorate is already alerted. And the Fourth Directorate has been suspecting trouble with the Cardia for awhile. Beyond the present hostilities, that is. That's their job. If there's anything on you, they will catch you immediately, and I will be more than pleased to help them. I hope you understand the full implications of this. Dismissed."

Cargo saluted carefully before he left. Out in the hallway he leaned against the wall and gasped for breath. The wall was cool and he pressed his forehead against it, trying to slow the fear rising. Just like combat. Someone once described it as hours of boredom punctuated by moments of raw terror. Nothing any gomer had ever done had made Cargo know the raw terror Fourways had induced.

Damn that bastard! he thought. The Bishop understood about the Marcanter registration, but it was the Bishop's name that was causing trouble in the first place. Cargo had encountered this only very rarely before, the individual who assumed that the Mirabeau name meant he was worthless. It never occurred to them that he must have impressed Bishop Andre Michel Mirabeau with more than song and a request for a handout.

Cargo had a strong urge to put his fist through Fourways' face, but the last time he'd used that solution he'd been locked in solitary for a week. Instead, he headed outside into the wind that hadn't stopped. Walking into it as sharp uncut blades of grass wrapped around his legs and bit into his ankles, he directed the anger.

"Anger makes you lose sight of the goal," the Bishop had said. "Your own will kill you if you let it. Use your head, not your glands."

Cargo had claimed cultural immunity when they did his first security check, with the Bishop as guarantee. No one had ever questioned the word of an ex-Trustee of the Collegium. Cargo always assumed they wouldn't dare. It should have been in the personnel file, triple starred and under the Inter-Cultural Affinity shield.

Besides, even if he *had* been born on Marcanter it hadn't been enemy territory then. He was old enough to remember the Luxor Incident, the images of the vacationers anticipating only a few overpriced weeks on a play planet who had been held as hostages and then executed. The Cardia Group had been on the edge of secession for a long time, and the Trustees of the Collegium had hardly believed that they had nothing to do with the Luxor Band. The more the Cardia Group protested, the harder the Trustees held the line, and the Group needed very little to make good its threats. The Cardia had declared independence, taking with them fourteen worlds that included two of the most highly industrialized in the entire Collegium. It had been a serious blow.

The Collegium declared that the population of various Group planets and colony habitats were being forced into political extremism against their will, and it was up to the Collegium to uphold the rights of those individuals whose choice had been abridged.

Cargo had been thirteen years old at the time, and clearly recalled watching his parents listen to reports from the Collegium on the viddie and saying it was some Gaje thing and didn't concern the Rom. They had left the room and he had gone on watching, remembering the face of the leader of the Cardia extremists, Ki Shodar. Even now that pale, whiplash look was the personification of pure evil to Cargo. Maybe that was one of the reasons he was so convinced that he had no other choice than to volunteer for the front lines. Every time he was in combat he was attacking that evil saddened expression.

The wind in his face cooled Cargo down. It was good to walk free across the fields. Although he was inside the base, there was far more open land than developed area. He concentrated on the sensation of being alone under the glowing violet sky and forced himself to consider Fourways as just one more bypassed slime-brass bastard who got off on intimidating inferiors. Today's interview couldn't have been solely for his pleasure. Fourways couldn't do anything once Cargo had completed training anyway; he was only responsible for the recruitment and training phases of the batwing. He counted null in operational assignments.

Out in the open where he was free again, Cargo thought about what he had been told that morning. As a member of the batwing he was expected to become a fully functional operative in the Second Directorate. Having a birth certificate from a Cardia world could be a real advantage. He hadn't really considered all the implications.

Cargo struck out without choosing a direction. It was good to walk, to be free again from the confining walls and restrictive life of the base. Cargo acknowledged that he had chosen that life—but just now, just this moment—it was newly foreign once again.

The wind was so loud that it would be impossible to hear anyone coming from behind. It acted like a wall of sound that kept out even the chatter in his own brain. Then a light touch on his right shoulder jolted him, calling him abruptly from only his awareness of wind and color back to the place of logical thought.

Plato stood with her back to the stiff breeze. Caramel-colored tendrils of hair reached out to Cargo as if they were snakes. "Go for a drink?" she asked.

In the brisk wind Cargo wasn't sure she heard his reply, but his intention was obvious. They struck across the uncut field toward the gate and Stolie's. It was impossible to talk while they fought the raising gusts that carried their voices away from each other. The relative quiet inside Stolie's was pure relief. Although it was still light outside, the place was comfortingly drizzled with shadow, and people spoke in soft tones.

Plato preferred tequila to annies, but Stolie didn't stock it. Cargo was impressed. He'd never had tequila. He told himself that probably Plato wasn't really that sophisticated and was just trying out one of those spook games Stonewall enjoyed.

There was no reason to miss out on any of the fun, so he asked for pepper vodka. The Bishop had served it once, and even the old man thought the stuff had more snob appeal than cough syrup, but was otherwise indistinguishable. Cargo tried not to be too obviously pleased when the bartender looked disgusted and made some comment about shiny tastes being bigger than their salaries. Cargo and Plato both settled for beer and a table near the wall.

"You know, I don't really know how to say this, but Fourways, well, he's been asking me strange questions," Plato said hesitantly.

"About me?" It was the only reason he could believe anyone would question Plato. Fourways had made it very clear just who was not particularly welcome in the batwing, and Cargo had met Plato once or twice before. She'd been with a different group, but they had overlapped a rotation together on a carrier and part of a weekend liberty. Not that Plato could tell Fourways anything about him at all.

She laughed. She threw back her head and laughed with her eyes squeezed shut until she had to wipe the tears away. "About you? Are you crazy? Or maybe Fourways is. Paranoid, I'd guess. No, he asked about me, mostly what I'd done during two years with no records. Not that it's his business. So he asked you, too. I wonder if he got everyone in our class."

"And I thought I was special," Cargo replied caustically.

"Yeah, right, right after me and Stonewall and Scatter and all the Akhaid, too. I'd have thought I wasn't that dumb anymore."

Cargo shook his head. "No, not dumb. Arrogant. Like the rest of us. The Akhaid, too, I'll bet."

Smiling half bitterly in the dim light, Cargo really noticed Plato for the first time. He'd met her and they'd talked before, but he had never really looked at her, never recognized the mixture of habitual command and irrational faith that made him think of the Bishop. Even her eyes were large and wide and as innocent and unclouded a gray as the Bishop's, enough so that Cargo wondered fleetingly if they were perhaps related.

Then he told himself that was stupid and stared at her untouched glass instead. Condensation dripped down the side making tracks against the gold liquid and collected in a neat puddle where the wooden veneer of the table had suffered mild damage. The foamy head had disappeared, leaving only lacy reminders near the rim. He thought about it seriously, not noticing that his own glass was in exactly the same condition.

So Fourways was just playing games with all of them. Cargo wondered if he did that with every class, or if they were special. Maybe a little of both. He'd figured Fourways for a sadist, and Plato had only just confirmed the matter.

Then the implication of what she had told him about herself hit. Two years off the record, two years that Fourways had no right to ask her about. Two years that had contributed absolutely nothing to her personnel file. Plato had Walked.

Carefully, not trusting his own reactions, Cargo picked up his glass. At least paying attention to the beer could mask the leading edge of his revulsion.

Cargo had seen his first group of Walkers when he was fifteen years old and in the company of the Bishop. The old man had taken him and Two Bits and Manuel and Yojo to the Collegium stadiat for the games. The crowd had been so thick that the Cathedral sled wasn't able to pull up to the entrance and they had had to go in on foot.

The pickings were good enough to make Cargo's fingers itch. There were more rich and middle-class people than he had ever seen in one congregation before, not counting the time he couldn't slip in to Mr. James Allen Covington's inaugural banquet. The men and women both wore chains around their necks, bangles on their wrists and rings with stones. Some of these were real gold mixed in with the gaudy titanium pieces the younger ones wore slumming. The most fashionable wore long silk scarves, with real gold tassels and embroidery, tied around the left thigh. Cargo had coveted one of those scarves, bright and gaudy and rich.

He had turned away, forced himself not to consider what a pickpocket's hands could do in that crowd. But he had promised the Bishop, a sacred promise. Cargo even half suspected that if he told the old man of his desire for one, the Bishop would give it to him as a gift. There had already been so many gifts that Cargo didn't ask.

In this great crowd a gap appeared. At first it seemed to be nothing. Then, as they approached the stadiat gates, people who had been heading in one direction or another had gathered around, stopped and stared. Those in back raised on tiptoe and held the shoulders of those in front trying to get a view.

Cargo darted through the crowd. There was a corpse on the ground. He had seen the dead before, laid out in the morgue and washed and laid out again in the most expensive coffin the undertaker could provide. He had seen other dead, too— Lulu's fat baby who had died in her sleep. Lulu had held the tiny body in a red blanket and rocked her and talked to her and wouldn't let the priest bury her.

This one had died of starvation, lying in the dirt like a sleeping skeleton. He could not tell from the face if this had been a man or a woman, but quite definitely this had been no alien. What served as clothing was hardly sufficient protection in the early spring chill, but Cargo recognized immediately that several years ago the outfit had been very expensive and very fashionable.

Next to the corpse sat a person who was exactly like the dead one except for the fact of still being alive. The living one was also wearing the tattered remnants of what had once been a fine outfit, also indistinguishable as to sex or age. What Cargo found most fascinating is that the live one was the only person in the entire assembly who was not looking at the corpse. The live one was staring at the dirt as if he or she didn't know anything had happened and wouldn't care.

Someone gave the living one a half-eaten sandwich. The person took it without a word and ate with real hunger. Then the living one stood up and walked away. The crowd parted to let this being pass. No one wanted to get too close to the stench.

Cargo waited until the sled had lifted to return from the games before he asked the Bishop, and it was the Bishop who told him with the same sadness he used to speak about Cargo's habit of stealing.

"Walkers," the Bishop said. "They took it from the Akhaid ritual of adulthood. Perhaps it suits the aliens. They need certain emotional and hormonal adjustments to become mature, physically as well as spiritually. But it wasn't meant for us. I can't say I understand humans who do it. I haven't studied it in any depth. Perhaps you would care to?"

Cargo had declined. The image had stayed with him, came back whenever he saw those vacant creatures walking or sitting on the side of the road. Always they seemed without will, as sentient as a mote of dust in the void. They repelled him, but they fascinated him too. There was something about their complete divorce from humanity that he found darkly alluring.

"It's not that I'm unwilling to talk about it," Plato said softly. "It's the point of the thing. No one asks about it."

Cargo nodded gravely, agreeing partly to reaffirm his own propriety. He wanted to ask but there was no way to do so. Instead he began speculating to keep from digging into Plato's past. "Then he really did go after both of us. I wonder if he got Stonewall too. And Scatter, is that his sign, the Akhaid?"

Plato laughed. "Yes. I've been wondering about that all day. Scatter, I mean. Where he got it. I'll have to ask Glaze."

A thought occurred to Cargo, and he whistled through his teeth. "I should have thought to ask if Fourways called in our

Eyes, too. I mean, is he just being ornery, or is there some pattern behind it?"

Plato shook her head. "We don't need any more information to make a perfectly rational generalization. I've never known anyone in charge of any training program whose first order of business wasn't to make their trainees as miserable as possible. I was a flight instructor for awhile, and I swear we used to sit around the instructor's lounge and figure out ways of tricking students into failing."

The beer had gone warm, and Cargo didn't want it anyway. His stomach was still too raw from the encounter with Fourways. Instead he thought about Plato's theory. It made perfect sense, he had to admit. And he was dead sure it was perfectly wrong.

Wrapped in his own universe, he noted when the door slammed shut once or twice only subconsciously and ignored it. The noise level had gone way up with the new arrivals.

"I seem to be the very last one here," a familiar voice cut through the clamor in Stonewall's oddly pleasant accent.

Plato turned before Cargo did, but they both ended up staring, grinning at the way Stonewall raised his glass to them slightly before leaning on the bar. He rested one hand on the gleaming black rail and perused the crowd. Cargo followed Stonewall's gaze not only to Plato and himself in one corner, but to Ghoster and Steel in another. They had a glass bowl of annies between them, blues and lavender and soft pink. Cargo closed his eyes. One thing he knew about annies was that the softer the color the more potent the kick.

Stonewall smiled out over everyone, strangers who obviously had prior claim as well as his own shiny class. "Now how do you like that? My very first day here and my two best buddies make off with all the ladies and leave me lonesome. Back home I'd have gone off and got drunk someplace where nobody knew me, but now Vanity is not exactly the hub of the manifold. Vanity does not offer me the choice, and so I am forced to watch what I would prefer to avoid."

A good majority of the beings currently in Stolie's laughed. Stonewall was hamming it up ridiculously. Cargo had the sudden terror that if he got drunk he would sing, and poor singing was something Cargo experienced as physical pain.

Stonewall took a long drink and set the glass down beside him. "Given the situation, I am forced to find some alternative form of recreation." With that, he poured the remaining beer from his glass over the nearest table. Someone else decided to help out and poured a second glass out, only Stonewall happened to be trying to spread the contents evenly over the scarred surface and managed to get drenched. He smiled broadly. Then he backed up and took a flying leap, landing square in the middle of the table and sliding to the edge. More beer was thrown down and someone else followed. Stonewall, soaked through and laughing, stood by and watched.

"Splash!" one of the participants yelled when another didn't quite make the table.

Cargo noticed that Stonewall had moved and was now sitting with several of the beings who had earlier called him a shiny. He resented that a little, that they'd been there such a short time and already Stonewall had broken the insularity of their class. He got up, uncertain whether he wanted to join Stonewall or interrogate him.

"You're not going to play?" Plato asked, her voice heavy with disgust.

Cargo shuddered delicately. There were certain practices he had no wish to unlearn, and Splash violated most of them. "I prefer cards," he said firmly.

Plato laughed again, that rich, ringing laughter that Cargo remembered from the one night liberty they had spent in Spin Street. It seemed too big for her, he thought, and it startled him again.

"I should have remembered," she said brightly. "Eight-deck khandinar, right? I never did figure out how you managed to keep count. I kept hoping I'd run into you so I could ask."

There was something infectious about her pleasure that he couldn't resist. He couldn't stop the smile that responded to hers, couldn't help noticing that all the tension of Fourways' interview was gone. Thanks to Plato. "Counting isn't the problem," he whispered conspiratorially. "It's knowing when the other party is cheating."

"Don't you mean it's knowing when the other party is about to catch you cheating? I saw what you were winning that night," she countered brightly.

He was glad Plato found this as hilarious as the memory of their night in one of the cleaner gambling establishments outside of Mnueser Base. He pretended to be insulted. "I never cheat at cards. It's my only vice. Besides, I'd always meant to ask you," he queried in return, "why you played dice. I thought it was crazy going for chance over skill."

Plato shook her head. "I don't have much skill. I've got a better shot at winning on pure luck than trying to count cards," she said, shaking her head. "But that still doesn't explain why you were leaving. Unless you were getting another beer. I could use another. If you're not playing Splash, that is."

Cargo hesitated, thought, and then sat back down. He squinted in the dimness across the table. Plato wasn't exactly a stranger, but she wasn't what he'd precisely call a friend of long standing, either. He wasn't sure if he wanted to try to tell her what was only a half-formed suspicion nagging at the back of his head. He pushed the temptation aside. "I just thought we might as well get out before it got too out of hand. Next they'll probably do the Wedge, and I'm not crazy about that, either. I mean, it isn't bad when you're drunk and it's after midnight. But I just can't see playing late-night games before dinner."

Plato nodded sagely. "I agree. Speaking of dinner, it's about that time. And if this place is like every other base I've ever been on, the food's better if you get there early."

Before they could move, two tall figures appeared beside Cargo's chair. He'd heard them come, even made out a word, maybe two, that they were saying. Now that Ghoster and Steel had made their presence know, there was nothing to do but invite them to sit down.

"We were just going to dinner," Cargo said.

Ghoster ignored that. "Steel and I have wondered something," Ghoster plunged in. "Some time today we were both interviewed by a being called Double. It seems that Glaze was, too. I don't know about Scatter. We haven't seen him since we left class."

"Who is Double?" Plato asked softly. "Which species?"

Steel looked over both of them. Cargo felt as if he had just been inspected and handed over to the dissection team.

"First, answer," the alien interrupted coldly. "Were you also subjected to some form of intimidation, or was this only practiced on those of my race?"

Cargo looked at his hands. It was safer than meeting Steel's eyes. He knew this being, had known others of this type before who always first personalized and then assumed the worst about every situation. For a moment it occurred to him to feel sorry for Stonewall. Privately, Cargo was sure he could never work with a being like Steel for fifteen minutes, let alone the years needed to forge a good team.

"No, we were discussing the same thing. Fourways saw everyone of my race in our class that I have spoken to." It was Plato who had answered in excellent Atrash, the most wide-spread Akhaid language.

Cargo was a little surprised and then shook it off. She'd Walked. That was an Akhaid ritual and there were probably books and philosophical discussions before taking the first step. He had the grace to feel some shame, he who had been so proud of his own poorly accented and ungrammatical ability in Ghoster's language. Only Plato had probably learned properly with a tutor tape and daily practice, where he had picked up what he could in the street. At least he was pleased to see Steel blink very slowly, an expression which for Ghoster meant confusion and grudging acknowledgment.

"Your courtesy is understood," Ghoster said, returning to the Indopean commonly used among them. Steel didn't seem to want to say anything more. "This becomes far more interesting, then," Ghoster continued calmly. "We must assume there is something more than harassment value."

"We weren't sure about that," Cargo said. "Maybe it is just testing, troubles, pure and simple. Maybe they're trying divide and conquer."

Ghoster nodded. Steel looked a little surprised, but Plato's face bloomed with understanding. "Yes, of course," she said.

"Naturally," Ghoster seconded her. "I'm relieved that you agree. I was trying to explain it to Steel, but she wasn't convinced."

Cargo's eyes widened. He hadn't realized that to Ghoster, Steel was a she. He'd have to try to remember that. For a moment he wondered if she was attractive.

"Well, if that's settled, maybe we can go to dinner," Plato said. "I don't know about the rest of you, but I'm starved."

Cargo couldn't sleep. He was tired, worn actually, but his brain refused to shut off. He'd managed to obtain an extra blanket, and the cold wasn't as bad as it was last night, anyway, so he couldn't blame it on that. To be honest he would have to admit that he'd played mental reruns of the interview with Fourways until he was sick of them, but he couldn't find anything to support the idea that this was some divisive test.

He and Ghoster had been through tests like that before. They had always involved exposure to some nasty rumor about the other species in general. It had become second nature to discount anything anyone said about the Akhaid at this point. The tests were too common, too much a part of everyday life to even bother wasting time listening.

Fourways had been totally different. He hadn't mentioned the Akhaid once, didn't seem to care about anything Cargo thought concerning them or anything else. It had been a warning of some type, and if they had all received a warning then something was very wrong. Or very screwed up, which was more likely. He accepted that, was used to it. The problem was he couldn't dismiss it.

Somehow he couldn't resolve the images of his meeting with Fourways and Plato's and Stonewall's actions. From the first night there was something about Stonewall that Cargo found disquieting. It wasn't like Fourways. He actively disliked Fourways, but he trusted the commander implicitly. The man was sly and unpleasant and most likely even sadistic, but he was predictable.

Stonewall was a walking enigma. Last night when they met, he had managed to keep from introducing himself, and Cargo realized that he had never noticed till the end. Then Stonewall had known he was lying—or at least editing—the truth. The investigation of what had happened to Two Bits had been sealed and classified after he and Ghoster had been exonerated. Then, either Stonewall had been the only person in their class who hadn't been threatened in some way or there was some reason for his behavior in Stolie's. Otherwise, it didn't make sense.

Cargo tore it apart in his mind once more, reconstructed it yet again, and still found no answer. One thing that pleased him was that he had resisted telling Plato anything. Much as he wanted to compare notes with someone, get a reaction, he couldn't throw suspicion on Stonewall like that, and really for nothing. All he had to go on was some funny half of a feeling and a couple of facts even he could make up explanations to fit.

• • •

When the alarm blasted Cargo from bed come morning he wasn't sure he'd slept at all. He could remember thinking about Stonewall and Fourways, but it was dim and sticky like cobwebs. He washed and dressed by rote and was already on the way to the mess hall when he heard someone calling. Damn. He hadn't wanted to talk to anyone this morning, and especially not before his coffee.

"Where are you going?" Stonewall demanded.

Stonewall was the second-to-last person Cargo wanted to see that morning. "To get some coffee," he mumbled, not quite able to be rude but also unable to meet Stonewall's vibrant enthusiasm.

"But you are going the wrong way," Stonewall said cheerfully enough to deserve being shot. "Didn't you see the notice? We're supposed to head down to the hangars first thing."

Cargo blinked twice. "What notice? Where?"

Stonewall rolled his eyes heavenward. "The one that was flashing on your screen with an *urgent* on top," he said. "Like everybody else got."

Cargo shook his head, more to wake up than to disagree. "Didn't see it," he said. He couldn't have seen an elephant in his bed the way he was feeling. Vaguely, he remembered the constant buzzing. That must have been part of the signal. He had assumed that he hadn't managed to convince the alarm that he was awake, probably because it knew better.

He didn't really trust Stonewall. Not entirely, not after all the ruminations last night. But he let the other steer him away from the scent of breakfast and onto the path that led to a few rather flimsy sheds. If those sheds were the hangars, Cargo thought, then I'm going to transfer back to the *Torque* yesterday.

The shed Stonewall led him to was empty except for several cages Cargo recognized as construction lifts. Without a word he followed Stonewall while the other keyed in instructions. Cargo had never seen a lift that wasn't voice activated. It shocked him thoroughly enough that he barely noticed the levels they passed. The cage wasn't at all smooth during the ride and came to a halt with a heart-jerking lurch.

There was a small lounge where they were left, two sofas covered in a cheap cello print that had darkened and turned, so that what Cargo suspected had once been yellow flowers on a red background now looked like irregular brown clots in dried blood. The cello on the arms was shredded, and from the looks of things no one had made any attempt to patch it. The walls had been white a long time ago, and the pattern had faded from the tile floor, leaving it a mottled gray.

All in all it was quite familiar to Cargo. It contained the two most vital necessities, Ghoster and a coffee maker. Cargo ignored his Eyes, along with Plato, Glaze and Steel who were already assembled. He poured a double serving into a disposable mug and drank it all in three swallows. The stuff was bitter and viscous, exactly the way he liked it. He poured a second cup and joined the group.

"What about the other team?" Steel asked Stonewall. "Did you see them?"

Stonewall shook his head. "Scatter and Bugs, right? I haven't seen a sign of them."

Someone snorted. Cargo thought it was Steel. "What's going on?" he asked innocently enough.

Ghoster studied him for a moment and then came over. "I suppose you didn't read the notice. As usual. Schedule change, is all. We were supposed to take a look at the batwings this afternoon, and it got changed to the morning."

"Right," Cargo said. He felt awkward and a bit stupid, as if he still hadn't completely come to his senses. The only thing that saved him from utter humiliation was the fact that Scatter and Bugs hadn't shown yet.

Scatter and Bugs. Scatter had to be the Akhaid pilot. And with a sign like Bugs, the human Eyes was probably rated elite. He hadn't even spoken to them, Cargo realized, and he had already decided that they were sloppy. Late and sloppy, the two worst things they could be.

The lift came down again, and the noise of the cage rattling against the railings was unpleasant and decidedly too loud. The arrival had more of the hallmarks of a crash than a controlled entry. Scatter and Bugs had arrived, and neither of them looked good.

"So they got you last?" Stonewall asked.

The newcomers looked at each other and then studied the rest of the class. Stonewall laughed softly. "Yeah, every being here got it too. And don't bother to ask because we don't know."

"I thought it was a test," Steel insisted.

"Speculation is not encouraged." The door across from the

coffee maker opened before either Scatter or Bugs could get a cup. The being who had spoken was Akhaid with a Commander's stripes on his sleeve. Cargo figured this had to be Double. He could feel Ghoster's reserve even from this distance.

"I have already met some of you," Double said conversationally. "I am called Double, and I will be in charge of the engineering portion of your familiarization. Stealth technology is a little different from what you are used to. Today we shall inspect the ST-1115 disassembled. As there already was one down here for repair, it was more economical to use it this morning than to tear down another to fit our schedule."

"You know what bullshit means?" Stonewall whispered to no one in particular.

Cargo agreed but kept quiet. He didn't want to be distracted. It was hard enough to stay awake as it was with all kinds of suspicions and innuendos all over. How he was going to keep his mind on the session he had no idea.

The group left the lounge and ventured out into what Cargo was tempted to call the real batwing installation. Just as everything above ground was temporary, cheap and shoddy, everything down here was the best available. Beyond that, far below the bridgewalk, sat the batwing stealthcraft. Cargo fell in love again.

The black stealthfighters were different from the Kraits he was used to. Those gaudy little craft were all angles and bright lines. Batwings were nothing but curves, long and sleek and pretty, thin as a carbon blade without an edge on them. Cargo leaned on the railing and stared down, entranced.

"You'd better not stay here too long," Stonewall said sardonically.

Cargo glanced up. There was something that bothered him about Stonewall's deliberately easy posture on the bridgewalk. The loose limbs were ready for anything, including a fight. Anger didn't even occur to Cargo. He was too confused.

"They're beautiful, though," Cargo said, wondering if Stonewall was here for the same reason he was himself.

Stonewall's eyes narrowed and glittered in the harsh illumination. "Yes. But I wouldn't stay alone, all the same. It isn't friendly. It makes me worry, and I'd hate awfully to shoot you by mistake."

Cargo noticed the way Stonewall waited, prepared to fight,

but the significance didn't affect him. He felt totally removed from this place, this situation. If Stonewall attacked he would have to kill Stonewall. He didn't want to do that. He didn't want to do anything at all, only to understand what had caused the anger in Stonewall's eyes.

"Your first night on Vanity," Stonewall prompted.

Cargo didn't respond. It had been cold, and he had told Stonewall a story. Ghoster had gotten angry. That was all he knew, and he knew it wasn't what Stonewall wanted. Because he didn't know the answer the other was looking for, he simply waited, knowing nothing could hurt him. Invincible, like he was in a Krait.

They were locked together on the bridgewalk by their tension and their confusion. Stonewall probed and tested silently, Cargo felt, the question in his eyes changing slowly. Then there was understanding.

"What happened that night?" Cargo asked softly.

Stonewall glanced around and then smiled. "Nothing official. Only some rumint about a signal. I don't know much about it."

Cargo forced himself to smile in return. "Let's get back to the others. I don't know about you, but I don't want to miss any of this session. Can't know too much about equipment."

Stonewall muttered something that seemed to be agreement, and they crossed the bridgewalk together.

Chapter
3

There are all kinds of ints in the universe. There was ELint, short for electronic intelligence, which was the most important of all for the batwing. Enemy ELint was their primary target. Get rid of the constellations and the probability of surprise approaches one.

Then there was humint, which stood for human intelligence. There wasn't much of that except on viddie series that seemed to believe that sentient spies were more useful than mechanical devices and more expendable, at least according to Fourways. Cargo was unable to watch a spy story again. There weren't such beings anymore; people of either species weren't wasted gathering information. There were plenty of devices, toys, to do that, and the Third Directorate was coming up with more all the time. No one questioned what the Fourth Directorate, counterintelligence, did without spies to hunt down.

What the series producers didn't understand was that while there wasn't any humint anymore, there was covops. Or the Second Directorate, to be technical. But even Covert Operations weren't the stuff of hour entertainment shows. As far as Cargo had ascertained, there was no crack team of assassins who could hit anyone in the known manifold and make it look like an accident. One or two maybe, but it certainly wasn't standard procedure. Nor were there hundreds of sleepers in the Cardia systems, just waiting for orders to turn on their governments or sabotage the latest Cardia military designs. Beside the batwing, Covert Operations mostly dealt with placing

ELint devices and disseminating disinformation, almost entirely through open sources.

Then there was rumint for rumor intelligence, which served as the Club grapevine, and Godint for "Divine Guidance"—in other words, outrageous hunches and intuition that managed to work out against all expectations. Godint was rare indeed.

After a week on Vanity, Cargo felt like a member of the Club. He laughed at conspiracy theories which regularly appeared in the commercial flimpax. The bulletin board in the ready room was hung with pale green candidates for the "Worst of the Week" spot. Every Friday night the "Worst of the Week" was read aloud in Stolie's, and the evening's bar bill rested on who could or could not manage to get through it with a straight face. His favorite so far had been *Alien Shape-changers Sabotage School Children; Poison Lunches*, although yesterday Plato had found something called *Secret Cardia Group Mutant RNA Cache Hidden Under Trustee Palace Floor*. Stonewall and Double had money riding on that one to go all the way to "Worst of the Year."

Not that evenings at Stolie's were very long. Cargo had thought about going there but had decided against it for the second time that week. Between the amount of new engineering he had to absorb along with information about the Club, he'd spent more time studying than he'd expected. So after staring at the small screen in his room for hours, he stretched back in the hard chair and stared at the white ceiling. Stress numbers burned bright orange against his retinas and then floated away. He shivered slightly and pulled the blanket tighter around his shoulders.

Not cold this time, although his hope that the cold and wind would pass was gone. At least the cloth hangings he had used to cover two of the walls kept out the worst of the icy draft. No, he was tired. The bed looked very tempting and he tried to shake it off. Just a moment to close his eyes, that was all. Reading was still a strain and even guaranteed totally glare-proof shields didn't eliminate it completely.

A knock at the door brought him back to consciousness all in a heap as the chair skidded out from under him. Flinging the door open, he stood for a moment, frozen with shock.

Cargo had expected Ghoster and hoped for Plato. In his half-dozing state nothing else had occurred to him. Yet there stood Stonewall, slouching against the doorjamb with a disposable blue sack under his arm.

"Are you going to invite me in, or are we gonna drink this here in the hall?" Stonewall asked, a sheepish grin spreading across his features.

Cargo hesitated before moving aside so that Stonewall could enter. They hadn't spoken to each other since the confrontation on the bridgewalk, and Cargo couldn't think of a single reason in heaven or hell why Stonewall should want to drink with him now. Still, he couldn't refuse. The strain between them was bad for the group, bad for their morale as well as his own.

Stonewall stepped in and sat unself-consciously on the green carpet. He emptied the blue bag carefully, setting a sealed pitcher of dark beer and two glasses ceremoniously on the seat of the chair, and positioning a plate of dark red annies in the center.

Cargo sat down cross-legged in front of a glass. Stonewall unsealed the pitcher and plate. "I asked Ghoster," he said to break the miserable quiet. "He said you were particular about reds and dark beer."

Cargo merely nodded. He had wondered, although his tastes were common enough. Stonewall poured the beer and raised his glass. Cargo didn't move. To drink with Stonewall would mean that there was no trouble between them, and Cargo was still angry. The anger had come later and had fed on itself, so that Stonewall's every word and action took on subtle undertones of meaning. Beside which, it hadn't escaped Cargo that what had happened hadn't solely been between the two of them. There was more to support his theory that Stonewall wasn't all he appeared to be.

"About the bridgewalk." Cargo's tone was calm and quiet, insistent.

Stonewall lowered his glass slowly. "I am sorry about that. I'd heard things around, and then you went missing."

"No," Cargo said. "I want to know what you heard around, and where 'around' happened to be. And why did you say 'rumint?' I only found out what that meant after we started training."

Stonewall closed his eyes and draped his arm across the seat of the chair. When he spoke his voice sounded as if it had been forced from very far away. "You know that I prefer to be around people who know what's going on. So I started that Splash game the first night and it worked. I got in with a few batwings. I got the word from them. Both ways."

Cargo refused to smile, not that Stonewall would have noticed anyway. His eyes were still closed and his face tilted back at the ceiling. As if his neck was going to get cut, Cargo thought, or as if he was hiding.

"And I think I know why Fourways is being even more of an asshole to our class than usual," Stonewall offered carefully. Cargo held his breath.

The silence gained mass and grew. Cargo didn't move, didn't try to stop its advance. Finally Stonewall cleared his throat. "I hung on and went over to the duty office with them. Real real late. Maybe three hundred, maybe more. And when we got there people were running all over the place, frantic. They'd caught part of a signal from our base heading out band seven-seven-one Coombs wide. Narrow on Cycra."

Cargo ran that through again. He'd just begun getting familiar with Cardia ELint, but this was something he recognized. A micromitter made by the same kind of DNA adaptation as the chip he carried, on a very narrow beam, could make it as far as Cycra in Cardia territory. They worried about that, the Third Directorate did, but there was nothing anyone could do. Usually nothing operated long enough to get fixed. One good blast with datadensing might last one nanosecond, or less. The only solution was to go in and blast the constellations that carried the signals.

"You know what's wrong with that?" Cargo asked, his attention fixed on some theoretical point on the carpet. "Listen. Remember that the very first day even, Fourways makes this point that we don't use living spies. At least, hardly ever. It's not safe, it's not economical, and it isn't even very productive. So we use the Third's toys instead. Only, maybe you could tell me, and this would all make more sense, tell me why we're running around acting out some bad spy story. I mean, why in the name of hell do we act like they've got real live, warm, breathing sentient spies all over the place when we don't do it? Is there any reason to think they're more stupid than we are? Or was Fourways lying about that as well?"

Stonewall's eyes jerked open. "You are right, good buddy, you have seen the flaw in the reasoning. And I thank you for that as graciously as I can. Can't say it was ever so clear to me before. I knew something was wrong, just couldn't say what. 'Course, if you are a Cardia spy, you'd have got that all worked out a long time ago."

Cargo had to study his visitor's face for a few seconds before he realized Stonewall had been joking. "But I thought *you* were a spy," he said slowly, to say it out loud once and to give Stonewall as good as he got.

Stonewall looked shocked and panicked for a fraction of a second. Then both he and Cargo broke out into simultaneous laughter.

"Maybe I am," Stonewall agreed when he could speak again. "Maybe you are too. Maybe we both are. But if we both are, then what are you doing here? And if you are and I am, then at least we can trust everybody else, right?"

"You are drunk."

Stonewall looked shocked. "Of course I'm drunk. I'm naturally drunk. Do you think I'd come out to visit you in this miserable cold to make sure you drink yourself warm if I hadn't warmed myself up first. My mama didn't raise no fools."

Then Cargo began to laugh again, and this time the distrust between them was gone. He drank with Stonewall until the pitcher was dry and then took two of the dark red annies. It was good to drink, it was good to have a buddy, it was good to share the warmth of solidarity with a member of his own class. Morale had been so low lately that a little up felt like a whole lot more.

"And so there I was, in that clapboard church that my parents always went to," Stonewall was babbling drunkenly. "And they said that the light in front of the altar was the eternal presence of Jesus, who was there all the time to help and come to you. So I was about seven or eight, real curious, you know, and I got real bored with Tuesday Bible class. I mean, I still can't bear to think of all the Tuesday nights I spent down in the basement. Only they were holding class upstairs because there'd been some heavy rain, and the basement was flooded. So I was bored and slipped out to the coatroom and started playing with the light switches. And you know what? The eternal presence of Jesus left the church then and there. At first I figured that I was being punished for playing with the box when I should have been studying Timo-

thy. So I played some more, and damn if that eternal presence
of Jesus wasn't hooked up to the electric box just like every
other light I'd ever seen. I lost my faith then and there."

Cargo listened through a pleasant haze. Stonewall's story
brought him back to his mother's ofisa. The last one had been
up a flight of stairs over a cut-rate music shop when they lived
in Mawbry's Colony, the last place he remembered the family.
He had lived in the back room of that ofisa, sleeping on the
imitation-vinyl sofa behind the thick curtains that separated it
from the place where his mother told fortunes. He had brought
Sonfranka there for the time they were married, to live in
three rooms that had been built as an office without a kitchen
and the toilet down the hall. Then she had told fortunes in the
front room, too, and watched Sister Mary make the *bouzer*
more than once surrounded by the thick dark red curtains.

"My mother was a fortuneteller," Cargo started. "She was
called Sister Mary. Anyway, we all knew it wasn't for real,
but when I started learning how to make holotapes, I did a
whole series for her crystal ball. They were pretty good, too.
There was this one that started with white cloudy stuff turning
dark and then condensing down into a single ray of darkness.
Then the crystal filled with jewelry and credit slips and antiques, everything you can imagine, only vague and shadowy
under the 'evil light.' I had to be really careful to make sure
that everything was generic enough to pass, especially the
jewelry. That was for the *bouzer*."

"What?" Stonewall asked.

"The *bouzer*," Cargo replied. "When she had a client on
the hook, someone good and gullible. Then they did the
bouzer, all the fortunetellers did it when they could. Someone
who made the switch once, she was a real *boojo* woman.
Someone who did it twice, big, she was considered talented.
My mother did it at least five times that I remember. Anyway,
the fortuneteller tells the client that he or she has bad luck
because of something that's cursed. Usually jewelry, although
we did antiques too. Anyway, the tape goes very slowly from
one item to the next, only the client never sees the item
clearly. So the *boojo* woman tells the client that something is
cursed, and she will have to remove the curse, only it's very
dangerous, and maybe they'll have to get rid of the item, too.

"When a top *boojo* woman does it, the client doesn't ever
know. My mother once said this one being had a cursed neck-

lace. So in comes the client with the necklace in a handker-chief, and my mother breaks an egg over it to see if it's cursed. And there's blood in the egg, so it's cursed. They're always cursed, you understand, that's how the whole thing works.

"So, anyway, my mother instructs the client to wrap the necklace up in a blue silk handkerchief, and even gives out the right kind, and to take it to church and place it at, say, the statue of the Virgin and say a bunch of prayers every day. And then bring the necklace back next week to see if it's still cursed."

"And I bet it's still cursed," Stonewall grinned.

"Of course," Cargo agreed. "It's still cursed. So now my mother tells the client that they have to throw the necklace out of the airlock. And they do, all by themselves."

Stonewall gulped and sat upright. "You mean it just gets thrown out? Really?"

Cargo leaned back and laughed so hard his head hurt. "No. When my mother checked to see if it was cursed, she had a package made up from exactly the same silk with the same weight and feel to it. She switched the two. The client threw out painted nickel, and we kept the gold. Simple. Only you have to be very very good to make people believe you. When my mother got going I half believed her, and I made the holo-tapes for her crystal ball. Not to mention working out some great sound and light effect. Those drapes covered more than walls, I'll tell you."

Stonewall nodded solemnly. "So we are both people with-out faith."

"Except for the luck of pilots," Cargo added softly.

"Oh, yes, there's always that," Stonewall agreed drunk-enly. "Only no one guarantees that it's good luck we have. Sometimes we can get it real bad. But yeah, I don't believe in what the preacher told me, so it's a damned good thing he never preached on luck, or else I wouldn't have any of that either."

Cargo said nothing. When Stonewall left he clutched the Ste. Maries-de-la-Mer medal and wondered why he had told Stonewall too much about things that weren't his business.

In the hangars of Vanity base it was always night. The underground structure was brilliantly lit but there was no illusion of day. None of the colors of day existed down there, none of the brightness of the Kraits or even carriers. The only relief from endless black and grey, steel and concrete, was the readout on the big screen that dominated the near wall.

The red designating craft and the yellow for crews washed over the floor and the faces of those standing in front reading it. Underneath was a weather grid indicating the speed of Vanity's winds and storms in an economical data matrix.

Cargo stood under the board, translating the weather information without half trying. It was important, and while he wasn't particularly nervous, he was definitely more than ready. He'd already swallowed four Three-B's and couldn't be sure if the exhilaration he felt was simply the drug or real excitement. A check-flight always brought on the adrenaline rush, not like combat, but in some ways better. If they were going to be tested for competence and professionalism in this equipment, they would also be rewarded. Some people disliked check-flights, waiting for the board to evaluate the internal recordings and pass on their recommendation. Cargo reveled in the arena—the chance to flaunt his one great talent to those who valued it more highly than he ever had.

Ghoster stood beside him. "It is a day for becoming new," he said formally.

Cargo nodded. "Ready?"

"One is never ready for the next step," Ghoster replied, his ears up, and his eyes crinkled in what Cargo figured was his version of a grin. "But I'm sure it'll be soup."

Cargo shook his head and walked over to their assigned batwing. He did a brief walk around, checking the port cover latches before getting in and running instrumentation with Ghoster, who had a complete set of flight indicators along with his own controls.

Speaking through the chatterbox to the backseat never failed to disorient Cargo. Always in the last few moments before he put on his helmet and slipped into mode he felt strange distance from the moment. Talking to Ghoster was difficult when in the next few seconds they would be able to communicate effortlessly through the maze. Still, he didn't permit anything to interfere with these last checks. There had been cases of a computer maze getting out of tune, where the pilot hadn't realized it and had flown straight into the Wall. By tradition everyone had one worry, and that was Cargo's.

He had taken craft on manual for practice and pleasure before, but never from necessity. A crazy maze could put him in Ward Six for a long time.

"Ready," Ghoster's voice came through the box, and then it went dead and opaque as they met in the maze.

Once in mode, Cargo shifted his attention deeper into the system to the membrane where he and Ghoster communicated. Even with the precautions to keep them from experiencing direct touch, Cargo was almost painfully aware of Ghoster's differences. On the surface, concern about the craft and systems was cool and comfortable. Underneath, he could sense the jumble of images that he found meaningless, an essential alienness that he couldn't penetrate or even comprehend. Intellectually, he knew it had something to do with the way the Akhaid experienced the Other Six, the dimensions that existed only as mathematical proofs to humans. And yet, there was something comforting in that hideous difference, a familiarity that recognized his touch as equally distant and painful but bearable. The batwing's system didn't buffer them as much as the Krait's had, and even after thirty hours of flight time Cargo still found it raw and difficult. Then the recorders came on, both of them, as well as the cameras. He was used to that, although the second recorder, the internal, would be used only this once.

Cargo steadied himself. The straps that held his arms and legs firmly in place tightened, and he concentrated on resting his hands on the pads. Mentally he tuned the chatterbox to Vanity's Control, and relaxed as the maze responded instantaneously. He had barely completed the thought before the maze reported the function accomplished. Now that he had started the steps in mode, Cargo felt sure of himself. Here, at least, with the maze and Ghoster ready and responding, he was in complete control. Here all the choices were easy, pristine in their sharp dichotomy. There was us and them, right and wrong, good and bad, success and failure and no middle ground. With these choices he knew how to choose, in this situation he knew how to command.

The roll-out instructions didn't come over the box but through the maze. They were still close enough in range that mode worked real time, and as Cargo accepted and understood orders the system translated them into facts that were displayed on the four screens in front of him. Slowly the power built through the batwing's engines as the stealthcraft was towed to the taxiway.

A quiver passed through the chill of the maze as Control gave them the five-second call. At one second to null the clearance code came over the link as Cargo gave the order to go.

They hurtled down three kilometers of lightless tunnel before bursting through to the glittering violet sky. The wind assaulted them, buffeting the batwing's gently curled structure. Cargo didn't fight it. He banked toward the mountains and felt the turbulence flow under the craft, lifting and propelling it still faster rather than dragging it down.

His exhilaration flowed through the maze, touching Ghoster and making the link even more lucid. Ghoster's thoughts, filtered through the membrane, became crystalline, strange geometries that could still be admired and even used. As for mode itself, Cargo was perfectly in the center of a limpid glacial pool of mental activity. His slightest nudge of deliberation sent out ripples that smoothly completed a task as he imaged it.

Soaring above Vanity's plains, he could see the undulating grass submerged in the shadow of the mountains. The smaller moon was already high though it was barely twilight. They climbed over the ragged young mountain peaks, riding the high wind like a magic carpet over the range. In the distance he saw a thunderhead rolling over the foothills and urged the craft to meet it.

The wind was crazy here, switching back and creating low-pressure pockets. They fell suddenly through one, descending in a stomach-turning plunge until another gust caught them up again. Cargo didn't hear himself laugh. The physicality of endo was more primitive than vac, less civilized, as he himself was. Ahead, the storm was a boiling charcoal glory stretching up into the thinning layers of atmosphere, reaching for vac.

Cargo opened the craft to top go, plunging toward the ominous cloud at burn speed. He could feel Ghoster's efforts to keep them just below yield, to control maximum gees in the turn. And he smiled at Ghoster's efforts as he began to loop upward into vertical, belly to belly with the storm. They shot up the center as they had so many times before in a Krait, only this time they were pursued not by a sentient enemy but by a thunderhead that roared on, impervious to their presence.

"Isn't it time we got on target?" Cargo recognized that the thought had originally been Ghoster's, rendered and buffered through the maze into his own thought patterns. The taste of Ghoster's gentle sarcasm was less alien filtered through the system. The idea was one that existed in both universal contexts, and was therefore precise.

Besides, Ghoster was right. For the check-run they'd been assigned a target, a single satellite in orbit around Vanity. It was a mort, old style, but with more than enough sensing left to shoot them with a sear mark if they made a wrong move.

Cargo glanced at the fuel indicator, but the answer arrived through the maze before he bothered to change focus. He'd used nearly half of his reserve playing tag with a thundercloud and while he didn't have to be particularly careful he knew that playing with fuel was begging for the unexpected. Already on vertical, Cargo eased the craft over to an angle that would still bring them out exo but burn less fuel.

The high sky was dark and violent. Vapor whips flung themselves over hundreds of meters at hideous velocities and the battering atmosphere was no longer heavy enough to ride. Starlight cut through the thin air but Cargo didn't notice. He was too busy looking out ahead into the deep void where the target lay hidden.

Deep in mode, he didn't need to interpret the data, only visualize the relative positions of his craft and target to choose the course. He kept it conservative, slowing as he pierced the darkest violet and moved into vac. Suddenly it was silent. The buffeting, tearing wind had been cut off and Cargo knew that breaking exo was going home.

Target was below the horizon still, approach in seven minutes burn. The maze waited for instructions on a burn assume. Cargo fooled the computer and told it no go. The system didn't like that at all. Patiently and with controlled contempt, Cargo shut off each engine separately, specifying time so there would be minimum drift. Under the activity, he sensed Ghoster's confusion rubbing against his own train of thought. Only then did Cargo start to curse very softly in Romany.

The approach was slow but there was nothing to betray them. The soft curves of the batwing were invisible to the searching satellite, the night-dark hull indistinguishable to camera eyes. Even the infrared would have trouble finding them with the engines shut down behind the mask. In theory, the heat mask should take care of detection, but Cargo had listened very carefully when Double said that the greatest danger came from spectral seekers. The mask was effective when fully functional, but it was balky and delicate and even the faintest thinning on the outermost shell could invite destruction.

They crept up like thieves, Cargo thought. He could feel Ghoster in the maze, caught glimpses of data images of angled beams. His own link reported when the Eyes opened smoothly and the outside nodes rotated into position. Cargo couldn't hold down the pleasure he took in the knowledge that Ghoster was going to get the target just as it appeared over the horizon. Cargo rapidly did the calculations and felt the maze suck the coordinates from his mind. The burning horizon glare wasn't a problem, not with the silent approach that gave them both time to work out the exact position.

Alien anticipation flooded the maze. Ghoster was primed and ready, and Cargo was aware of a spring winding tighter and tighter and held. And then the barest fraction before the exact second the target could spot them the Eyes burst into life, their low-powered marker beam striking the target just as it came into range. The satellite was mort even as Cargo whispered, "Tallyho."

Passive sounders immediately went into action. Cargo indicated a long sweep to pass under the target to confirm their kill. Success was sure enough though, that the urgent adrenaline rush started to drain from his bloodstream. In mode consciousness Cargo was acutely aware of his autonomic systems. He could go deeper still and control them, feign coma if necessary. Now all he did was remove some of the most oppressive tension from his muscles. By the time they landed he would be in knots. That wasn't so different from the Krait after all.

"Watch the downside. Tallyho down." Ghoster's words were chilled by the maze. Cargo cursed and flung his awareness deeper into mode, demanding recognition and status of intruder as he imaged a corkscrew double twist to the maze. If the gomer was using Eye beams the twist would get them out, and Cargo didn't think they'd had time to arm spectrals.

The maze chilled down. The membrane that separated Cargo from Ghoster shimmered and went thin. Cargo could see through and understand exactly what his Eyes wanted and needed. The contact made his stomach lurch harder than coming out of the twist, but he held on.

"Sixes." The thought came from the maze.

Cargo could follow Ghoster's positioning of the Eyes while he whipped the stealthcraft in a one-eighty axis change. Ghoster fired as Cargo spurred the batwing to plunge endo. The maze confirmed their hit, and confirmed that their pursuer was still with them. The hit was only a marker, and they were starting to break into high sky.

No place to hide in vac, Cargo thought, automatically adjusting the angle of descent to minimize burn. He played switchback in top go, ignoring the velocity of the wind and the pressure eddies that hid in the air as he forced separation between himself and the pursuit. Two passes and he would be aggressive. It didn't usually last that long.

"Out of range," the maze entered his mind.

He searched the pale violet surrounding him, watching for what the other was doing, thinking. And he kept the batwing careening toward the dark peaks below, Ghoster giving him enough gees to keep their speed just below yield.

"Locate," Cargo shot to the maze and Ghoster both.

In less time than it took to think it he got the reply. "No joy."

That did not make Cargo feel any better. The fact that he couldn't see the enemy, couldn't detect any presence, didn't mean that they had gone. There were too many ways to hide. A maze couldn't see through anything solid and it could be tricked. Sure, it was fancy dancing but it could be done. Cargo had managed once or twice himself, enough to know not to trust safe data. The only way to stay alive was to always believe the worst and act on it.

The mountains were coming up fast and Cargo glanced at them with resolve. He didn't know where the enemy was, and he certainly was in no position to pull a trick. But there was no way anyone could track him through those mountains.

He waited until the rock was reaching for them, until he could see the scars torn deep into the mountainside, before he pulled the batwing to wings level. But only for a moment. The stealthcraft was nearly flat but broad, so much so that the first of the class had been called the Flimsheet. Cargo threw an image into the maze, the stealthcraft spread like a shadow hugging the mountains.

The craft turned around him. The wind shrieked through the gap between the wide body of the batwing and the jagged peaks, threatening to fling them from the pass one moment and to flatten them against the rock the next. His whole being screamed to get clear of the enveloping heights. Then the panic passed into the chill of the maze and was gone. Instead there was only pure, lucid thought and the challenge of control.

He adjusted the angle to cut the wind as much as possible, and the worst of the strain was gone. Then, with an image as light as a butterfly, Cargo instructed the maze to take them through at low go. Cargo concentrated on watching outside, scanning the cliffs for the unexpected. He brought the batwing lower to the floor of the pass, the low and slow drift it had been designed to make. His own observation and decision was foremost in his mind. He could feel the maze behind him, obeying, but not intruding with its own suggestions. He insisted on being the master of his craft, and the maze might not like it but it obeyed.

One thing Cargo had learned was never to listen to the maze. For all it might feel like an extension of himself into some supernatural realm, the thing was only a computer with the drawbacks of any computer. It had no imagination. What it might suggest as the optimal solution was often not the winning one. He could sense the maze didn't like being down so low in the mountains. No longer sensing a threat it wanted to ascend and throw on the burn to go home. So Cargo forced the link, instructing the maze that its primary objective was to operate the mechanical systems to achieve the effects Cargo imaged.

He could sense Ghoster faintly, and was pleased by the assurance and pride that rang through the membrane. Cargo knew what Ghoster was doing, reassuring and supporting him, reinforcing the messages he was giving the maze. He tossed a quick pulse of gratitude to Ghoster, but kept his mind on business.

He had flown these mountains only twice before. A wall of rock appeared before him and Cargo knew a moment of terror, sure that the passage was blocked, and he would have to expose the craft in pure sky. The maze firmly requested control, and he permitted it more input. A map showed the pass he was attempting, hard turns ahead but all charted and flown. Relieved, Cargo went into partner mode, letting the machine calculate from its data while he kept his eyes on the terrain.

Two switchbacks around the single cliff and they broke out over the plains, the foothills falling quickly below. They had left at twilight, and now it was fully dark. Cargo smiled without pleasure. If their pursuer had any knowledge of Vanity or the batwing, it could well be waiting for him to emerge.

He brought the batwing down, so close to the earth that the long whipping grass threatened the intakes. Black and skimming low, he was invisible to everything except maybe infrared. But this wasn't vac. Here the heat sensors would pick up other hot spots, small animals, one of the grass fires that plagued Vanity. If the mask held even part way, no one should be able to locate them through the hot reflection of the planet's surface.

"Tallyho," he heard through the maze. For a moment Cargo didn't know if it was Ghoster or the maze that made the sighting, or even if it was the same enemy. Not that it mattered. Cargo had a strange intuition about the intruder. Maybe there was such a thing as Godint after all.

"Engage?"—that was definitely Ghoster. Cargo knew he was already on the guns.

"No," Cargo replied. There was no reaction from Ghoster, but the maze rippled. "Our home tunnel's close. Let's see if we can get by without him seeing us."

All they had to do was stay way down, Cargo thought, urging the maze against its preferred strategy, keeping velocity barely above no go. He hadn't had the chance to appreciate it before, but the batwing had just been designed to float under nearly null power in just this kind of situation. He'd done it before in practice, but had never realized just how close to null he could get and still be well into the safety margin. In the absolute worst case, he supposed it was possible to ride it like a glider.

The maze tracked the intruder and fed the information to its living partners without question. Cargo recognized the search pattern overhead. Whoever was up there was instrument blind on the bat, fumbling in the dark. The tunnel was thirteen minutes ahead even at drift speed.

Their pursuer kept up the search pattern as Cargo nudged

the bat under the earth, leaving him lonely. As the tunnel swallowed them, Cargo felt himself become limp. It had always been like that in the Krait, too, the tension leaving its mark until afterwards.

The ground crew was there to steady them as he and Ghoster climbed out of the cockpit. His body felt like an overcooked noodle, and about as wet. The sterile zone at Level Two might have taken care of any bacteria, but it didn't give Cargo any comfort. It would be hours yet before their performance was analyzed and decisions made about who had checked out in the stealthcraft—about who had become a batwing.

Plato was sitting in the lounge on Level Two. She looked nearly as limp as Cargo felt. He didn't have the energy to do more than wink at her. She shook her head and pointed. Then he realized that she wasn't wearing her wings anymore.

"Take them off," she said, her voice heavy with exhaustion.

"What?"

Plato shrugged. "Peghead told me. Said we're not shiny anymore. Said there's some tradition tonight at Stolie's."

Cargo did as he was told, more because it was easier to go along than to protest. It struck him as wrong not to wear the one symbol he had left. It made him feel ordinary. But traditions were traditions, he thought. Besides, all he wanted in the entire universe was a hot shower and some clean, dry clothes.

Cargo had just pulled on a clean pair of pants and a fresh shirt when Ghoster knocked. Cargo groaned but headed for the door. He'd wanted to rest before doing a postmort, and had considered trying to get hold of Plato to head over to Stolie's before anyone else got there. Not, he told himself, that he wasn't pleased with what they'd done. He just didn't want to start in with details yet.

"You aren't in uniform," Ghoster announced as soon as he stepped in.

"I know. Tell me something new."

Ghoster sat in the straight chair without waiting for an invitation. "I intend to," he said carefully. "Have you spent this miserably long time thinking about who was chasing us today? Have you really considered the subject?"

Cargo sat on the bed. It wasn't postmort. In fact, Ghoster

was right. He hadn't been able to stop thinking about it at all. "You know what I figured," Cargo said. "Now, Vanity is a closed base on a closed world, right? And the Cardia wouldn't come one on one like that here, anyway. They'd go for the big targets. Why bother chasing us? So obviously it wasn't an enemy."

Ghoster grunted something that Cargo thought was an obscenity, but couldn't quite translate. "Obviously," Ghoster agreed. "So who was it?"

"Part of the test," Cargo replied.

"That is not a who. That is a what. I didn't ask what," Ghoster insisted.

Cargo sighed and rolled his eyes up. "I'm going to ask you two questions, Ghoster. One is, do you know who it is? I'm pretty sure you do, because otherwise you wouldn't be here baiting me. And the second is, who cares?"

The deep red pigmentation pattern on Ghoster's head went nearly purple. Cargo had seen that happen on the very few occasions when Ghoster was extremely displeased.

"I care," Ghoster said. "It is significant. Have you spoken to the others? Did the same thing happen to them?"

Cargo shook his head. He had a funny idea of where Ghoster was going, and he wasn't sure he wanted to be along for the ride. "I only saw Plato for a few seconds. She told me there was something on at Stolie's tonight and we're all supposed to be there. That's all."

The purple died down and Ghoster seemed almost pleased again. Cargo knew he enjoyed keeping secrets, knowing things and letting them out in small snatches. "I was talking to some of the Eyes. Glaze and Bugs. And they said they weren't pursued at all."

"What about Steel?" Cargo asked.

Suddenly Ghoster's expression changed again, in a way Cargo couldn't interpret. "I didn't see her," Ghoster said softly. "Stonewall and Steel weren't back in."

"You think Stonewall was after us?" Cargo demanded. That was more than he was prepared to accept. He'd been watching Stonewall warily, and there was something there he didn't trust. But Ghoster had been spending a lot of time with Steel. The whole thing didn't make sense.

"No," Ghoster said. "I'm certain. Stonewall might be strange, but I trust Steel. Besides, the maze would have identified another batwing. Anyway, what good would Stonewall get out of it? Even if he was a Cardia spy. That's what you think, isn't it?"

Cargo nodded. "So answer your question," he prodded Ghoster.

"We agree that Stonewall could get nothing useful by tracking us around. Obviously, even a spy wouldn't have engaged us, even if he'd wanted to. What would be the point? It would expose him. No. The person who chased us was Fourways."

That made perfect sense to Cargo. If it was part of the test, then Fourways was the obvious choice. The only question was, why them and not the other teams who'd come in? Or maybe it was just them and Stonewall and Steel who were picked out for special treatment. He couldn't figure it.

"Well," Cargo said after consideration, "I guess you're right. So it was Fourways. Thanks. You want to come over to Stolie's now before the crowd gets thick, or you want to get dinner here first?"

"Cargo, you have just proved that you are crazy. Crazy. I am crazy to fly with you. Do you know that? First of all, you haven't asked why Fourways singled us out for special treatment. That's important. And second, only a crazy person would consider eating on base when Stolie's has the half-price egg bar before nineteen hundred, including dessert."

Cargo had to concede on dinner. "But what about Fourways?" he finally had to ask. "How do you know, anyway? I mean, it was just part of the test. Drop it."

Ghoster shook his head in his most human gesture. "Fourways was trying to trip you up," he said softly. "Cargo, you've got an enemy and it isn't Stonewall. Fourways hates you."

"He's not the first," Cargo said, thinking of others who had envied his position with the Bishop and the honor of the Mirabeau name. The only answer was to stay very controlled and let it pass.

"I shall tell them all not to play cards with you," Ghoster said very seriously, and Cargo understood the compliment under the intention.

"You do that and you're mort," he responded playfully. Fourways wasn't going to go away tonight.

Ghoster hissed in an inaccurate and exaggerated sigh. "If

we don't leave now all the fresh choza will be gone."

"You, my buddy, are a true friend."

"I would rather be a true batwing."

Cargo laughed broadly. "That, my friend, makes two of us."

Chapter 4

As they walked toward the gate the wind tore into their flesh and the long grass grabbed their legs. Cargo was nearly used to it, but swore once again that he would go into the nearest town and get a windwagon as soon as he had time. Any windwagon. The personal kite he had found at an amazing bargain two years ago couldn't take Vanity's climate or the dust and grass-swept paths they called roads. Strictly colony transportation, that kite. So he cursed as he walked, and heard Ghoster curse in reply.

Even through the shriek of the building evening gale Cargo could hear the crowd already in Stolie's. At least there was no line outside for dinner. That was small consolation.

Stolie had planned the Thursday night egg bar well. Deliveries were made on Friday, so the base fare was generally mystery-meat stew. The egg bar didn't take a kitchen, just a couple of chafing dishes, and it was a good show as well as a decent meal.

Looking over the dishes of condiments spread out before the chef and the cookware, Cargo had to admit there was exactly one advantage to being stuck on Vanity. Along with the peppers, roast pork, herring, black olives and at least five Akhaid dishes he couldn't name, were heaping bowls of red and black caviar. It was Vanity's most famous trade product, and they produced more and better of that delicacy than anywhere else in the Collegium. The Cardia, too, for that matter. The rivers and seas of this planet were heaven for sturgeon and salmon, the pink gold of Vanity. Cargo had never thought of fish as a major economic resource before, but he'd never been in a place where smoked and broiled fish was available every morning for breakfast and caviar was set out next to the rolls on every table at dinner, either.

Waiting on line to order his omelet, Cargo decided to send the Bishop some of Vanity's number one export. It was cheap enough to buy here, and the Bishop had always loved good food. He had taught Cargo to eat luxuries like lobster and smoked salmon, pâté and raw figs. He'd introduced Cargo to good wines at his table, too, so that at sixteen Cargo talked about bouquet and color and legs and tannin content unselfconsciously.

The smell of the omelets was tantilizing, but Cargo didn't have much of an appetite. He was too busy thinking about Fourways, about Ghoster's allegation.

Ghoster, in Cargo's experience, always told the truth. The whole, unvarnished truth. So if Ghoster said Fourways hated him, there was a pretty good probability that it was true. Cargo had never figured out where Ghoster got his information. He assumed there was some special Akhaid rumint mill and that Ghoster was plugged in to the center of it. Still, he hoped that Ghoster was wrong. Cargo had had enough of being trouble on sight.

Half the reason he'd joined the navy, he thought sourly, was that the Bishop said there was no prejudice, especially against his people. But then Cargo knew even then that the Bishop was essentially unworldly, a good and sincere being, without guile. The problem was, he generally credited others as being as guileless as himself, which even when he was young Cargo knew was somewhere between charity and stupidity.

"Yes, I'm nervous," Scatter was saying ahead of him. "It was too easy. When something's that easy you know there has to be a trick somewhere. That wasn't the whole thing, right? Just for fun."

A laugh responded. He was sure it was Plato, but he couldn't see her. In front of Scatter, probably. The Akhaid pilot was tall enough to hide her.

"It sounds like you missed all the fun," Cargo said. "We had a great time, getting chased through the mountains by some unidentified craft."

Scatter looked at him. "Are we all here now?"

"Stonewall," Cargo said softly. "I haven't seen Stonewall since we left."

Cargo noticed that Scatter scanned the crowd before returning his attention to their group. "There's something different about that one," he said mildly. "Perhaps because he's from your homeworld? *We* generally think they're, well, bloodless. Decadent, maybe."

"Self-defense," Ghoster whispered to Cargo. He knew his Akhaid partner had come from the home planet of his species, but Cargo had never noticed that there was any strain between him and anyone else. Or perhaps Scatter was one of those colonials with an inferiority complex. Cargo had seen that frequently enough.

Not that he understood it. Maybe it was different for new colonies with their cylinders still shiny and even the public parks still smelling of the factory. Or newly opened planets that were seriously underpopulated and couldn't support a resident stadiat or a soccer team and didn't even want to, where fashions were always a generation out of date and the "simple values" included a fair dose of xenophobia and intolerance. At least he imagined it that way from what he'd seen on the entertainment channels. The gypsies usually avoided those places in their travels. There wasn't enough money to be made, his mother had told him over and over again. Homesteaders didn't have much and were tight with what they got. Sister Mary didn't get enough business from them to bother.

Only Cargo suspected that there was more to it than that. He wouldn't be surprised to find witchburners among the homesteaders. And as for the new habitats, the residents there could be just as narrow-minded. Old Piluka of his mother's parents' kumpania had been tried for stealing a Gaje child on Azar when it was new. Almost unbelievable that that old story could gain currency in an environment designed to be one of the new industrial centers. As if the Rom didn't have enough children of their own to raise.

He was still pondering the difference, and the fact that it seemed to affect the Akhaid as well as the humans, when it was his turn to be served. He pointed at the black caviar, green onions and hens' eggs. Butter sizzling on the grill made his mouth water. If only there was a really fine chablis, he thought, or better yet a champagne. The Bishop would be horrified at the cheap vinegar that passed as wine at Stolie's.

Cargo got a carafe anyway. No matter what the circumstances he couldn't force himself to drink beer with caviar.

Vic Stolie, grease stains on the belly of his freshly laundered white apron, handed over the plate. Cargo took mustard, his carafe and a glass and started to look for a table. Plato waved him over. As he settled down across from her, he noticed that Ghoster had joined Scatter and Glaze. Cargo only hoped there wasn't going to be a fight before he finished dinner.

Plato had noticed it, too. "It seems to be a normal schism in every culture," she observed quietly. "Have you ever noticed that there aren't too many colonials in the military?"

Cargo stopped chewing midbite. He hadn't thought of that. He swallowed rapidly, his mind turning. "Are you saying there's something besides splice-life and economics between us and the Cardia? Not counting their earlier attacks, I mean."

Plato looked at him and then ate a morsel of her omelet elegantly, with the delicacy Cargo had learned at the Bishop's table and had never seen anywhere else. Without thinking he refilled her glass.

"I didn't realize you were a determinist," she said. "Yes, of course I think there's more than simple economics. Not that the Cardia couldn't use the Veil resources, but I didn't think you were the type to just believe the flimpax. They make it easy because people want it that way. Nice and black and white and everything in a neat little box. We're defending ourselves against the evil, greedy terrorist faction that is forcing large numbers of people to live in poverty so the corrupt Cardia splice-life can live in luxury. And if God had wanted gene splicing and viral DNA mixtures between species, He wouldn't have created two separate species in the first place. Just because one individual is in power and insane isn't reason to condemn everyone. Damn—I hate the party line. How are we ever going to reincorporate after this is over? If it's ever over."

"And what's your opinion?" he asked caustically.

Plato regarded him steadily. "The real issue is a difference in philosophy," she said quietly. "The Cardia is basically ideologically isolationist. And there's the Dekmejian factor. Cardia worlds and habitats, human and Akhaid both, all date from the third wave of emigration. The cultures that grew up there were deeply influenced by the Dekmejians, who preached that the more one suffers, the better one is intrinsically. They were pretty widespread at the time. Anyway, the colonies of that period did have the bad luck that their early years coincided with the Cycra disease pandemic. By the time the pandemic was brought under control they had suffered, and according to Dekmejian philosophy, were now the righteous. So they honestly believed that they were completely entitled to whatever they asked for. They had also begun the experiments before the outbreak without Collegium approval. Personally, I think that Shodar is the result of contamination. And it just took the whole thing coming together, the Dekmejian philosophy and the pandemic and Ki Shodar all intersected at one unfortunate point in history. You know, sometimes I wonder if just one of those factors hadn't existed whether there would be any problem today."

"Aren't you forgetting something? Like Luxor?" Cargo couldn't believe that she had not been frozen with horror over the eighty days when the terrorists held the pleasure planet hostage. And the seventy-two days of murders, broadcast live. It wasn't simply that they killed their victims. The terrorists of Luxor had become insane enough to make it a fine art.

Cargo remembered one in particular, an image so overpowering that it still kept him awake nights. The victim had been a young girl, about ten years old. They had painted over her mouth and nose with liquid superdrying cello. Cargo had watched, sick and fascinated both, as she suffocated on live news.

"No," Plato said patiently. "But I would have hoped we were beyond fighting wars of revenge. I guess not."

"Then what are you doing here?" Cargo demanded bitterly. Her brittle cynicism cut through him like the wind of Vanity. It was one thing for him, he had nowhere else to go. But Plato, someone like Plato—Cargo knew that she hadn't joined up to avoid being drafted, or even because the military offered one of the few real chances for success to someone from the lower classes. No, Plato's family was rich.

She hadn't ever spoken about them, but Cargo wasn't Sister Mary's son for nothing. The clues were subtle but unmistakable, the clean accent and choices of words, the complete lack of conscious thought about manners, the perfect appropriateness of small behaviors. Like the way she ate the omelet, no different at Stolie's than at the Captain's table. And an underlying confidence that he suddenly realized had been camouflaged all along by traditional fighter jock arrogance. He had known by pure instinct that she was rich. In that moment he understood why. In fact, she probably could have bought out entirely. It made him angry that she was there, flaunting her cynicism as one more privilege of her class. But her presence also demanded Cargo's respect. He, at least, had something to gain along with something to lose. Plato did not.

"I Walked," Plato said simply. "I'm still Walking."

Something inside Cargo wanted to explode. "I saw two Walkers once, human ones," he said, and his tone was ice cold. "One was dead. Starvation I guess. The other was sitting on the ground and I figured he didn't have a whole lot longer, either. They were so filthy and thin that I couldn't even tell what sex they were."

Plato laughed incongruously. "They failed," she explained. "It's not something to laugh at, really, but you really shouldn't judge what it's all about by people who failed."

Cargo just shook his head. The anger had left him as suddenly as it had come. Plato was a human, a flier. He'd worked with her and knew her worth. Besides, since she had brought it up he could ask now without being rude. "Why? I mean, the Walk is an Akhaid thing. The way I understand it, the Akhaid have a very slow physical maturation process, and they need different types of stimulus to release certain enzymes. That's what the Walk is about, at least that's what I understood. It doesn't have anything to do with us at all."

Ghoster had told him that, one late night after a long and boring routine patrol before they had joined the *Torque*. They'd been on the light ship *Grath* then, with a short complement on escort duty. There had only been ten Krait teams to cover the whole convoy. Merchies felt safer behind light ships and cruisers with their full array of armaments.

The rec facilities on the *Grath* didn't include drink or annies because the Captain and most of the crew were from Biet Salaam. There wasn't any pork aboard, either, but that didn't bother Cargo so much. The Captain had earned the *Grath* the title "the Good Ship Lollipop," and what was more, wore it proudly, but Cargo and Ghoster had paid dearly for his conviction.

It was their second crossing, and Cargo had brought a bottle of arak aboard and secured it in a vent line. He must have been pretty gone to have done that, he thought now. He should have chosen something that tasted better. He hated arak. Perhaps it was all that was available, he couldn't remember now.

Still, he'd had the bottle and he and Ghoster had been very dry for a long time. So he'd shared it in secret, never thinking that the Akhaid would react differently to one kind of alcohol than another.

Cargo had seen Ghoster all kinds of drunk before and since, and all kinds of gone on annies, but he'd never seen his tongue as loose as it was with the arak. Maybe it was just a mix of the drink and the *Grath* and the patrol and boredom. Maybe it was exhaustion. With only ten crews to cover, they were on watch-alternate shifts, which meant only four hours of sleep at a time.

Or maybe it had something to do with the merchies who'd come aboard that evening, who had had the bad grace to be touring the flight deck just as he was powering down. Cargo hadn't thought anything of it at first. He had been more interested in uncramping his legs and getting to the head than with any official visitors. They weren't his concern. Besides, it had been a long patrol and a boring one, the kind where he was jumping at every dust mote and asteroid, trying to stay alert while Ghoster repeated over and over again that there was nothing out there at all. The Krait's maze kept Ghoster's reactions out of his touch. He couldn't even feel how strongly Ghoster thought any of the things he said. They were using the hot line to communicate, not the maze itself. One of those things that could make a Krait slow, Cargo thought, unless the team flying it developed some additional sense for each other's moves. The batwing's maze avoided all that, but Cargo wasn't sure he liked it. Ghoster could predict him well enough as it was, and even the minor contact with an alien mind was disturbing.

Still, it had to be the kind of patrol that anyone forgot as soon as possible, only those visitors on deck had to stick their oversized ears into everything.

"Did you see anything out there?" one of them asked.

"No, sir," Cargo answered, making a concerted effort to be polite. A trip to the head was more necessary every second. Kraits weren't equipped that way.

"Why do you do it?" another one, an Akhaid, asked.

Before Cargo could answer, a fat human woman wearing a

fortune in rings interrupted. "They do it because they like it. There's a waiting line a mile long to get in. All kinds of glamour and perks, I hear." Her voice grated at three-hundred decibels.

Cargo tried to slip away again, only this time he was confronted by a short bald man in a creased jacket that Cargo judged none too clean. "Don't you run off when we're trying to talk to you," the merchie said. "You're gallivanting around in high powered Kraits for the fun of it. We saw where you were out to, nowhere near the rest of us. If there'd been an attack do you have any idea what would have happened? Our ships would have been wiped out, that's what, and carrying munitions and food and ground troops too. That the government makes us carry, dirty things, when my best ships specialize in fancy fruits and electronics and luxury transport vehicles. I'm losing money on you, so you can stop shifting around and stand there like I'm paying you."

At that point Cargo had turned his back and left. He had tried very hard to be polite, but it seemed they didn't appreciate that. They didn't seem to appreciate the fact that he was the one facing the Wall in case of an attack, either. He stalked off to take care of the business at hand, knowing that if he stayed even a moment longer he would put his fist through the bald man's face. Unless he strangled the woman first. No, he thought, the woman would be second. Strangulation takes long enough that even the bald man might have a chance to run away.

That was what had prompted opening the bottle of arak on the Good Ship Lollipop in Cargo's quarters. The man who had the overhead rack was on patrol and would be gone for the entire watch. There had been enough time.

"Those walking eyeless spawn of turtle dung," Ghoster had said when half the bottle was gone. "Those slime-mold beings who desire sex with diseased fish. Those merchies."

Cargo had drunkenly agreed.

"Now I ask you," Ghoster said, his diction becoming slow and careful. "I ask you, isn't this necessary? For what reason would any sane being do this if it wasn't necessary?"

Cargo managed some sort of affirmative.

"But I mean for your species," Ghoster insisted on continuing. "I mean, for us, you know."

"No," Cargo had said. "I don't know. I never did figure out why you're here."

Ghoster had looked at him in astonishment. It was strange, Cargo later recalled, that he had understood the Akhaid so well at the time. Perhaps their mutual drunkenness was responsible.

Ghoster finished looking and leaned back against the lower rack, his head lolling on the mattress. "I don't know a whole lot about you. Always figured you were people, you know, like us. So you're people. And people have to have experiences to grow up. Physically. Something to do with emotions and hormonal release. Selective advantage there, that only the most experienced survivors live to reproduce. You have selective advantages, I assume?"

Cargo gravely assured Ghoster they had selective advantages, too.

It hadn't taken much longer for them to pass out. The next morning, feeling like someone had taken a sledge hammer to the inside of his skull, Cargo remembered what Ghoster had told him and figured he had been too drunk to hear right. A few days later, piously sober, he had queried the maze.

The whole tradition of Walking, he discovered, as well as the major Akhaid presence in the military, was directly linked to their biology. He was astounded when he realized that Ghoster, his buddy, and all the other Akhaid he worked with and depended on, were there solely to achieve certain emotional pressure states which eventually would lead to their ability to reproduce. Ghoster was immature. What was more, he'd called Cargo the same. Cargo didn't know whether to laugh or explain it or let well enough alone. He decided that discretion was the better part of survival.

He blinked twice, almost shocked to realize that he'd been so lost in the reverie that he'd forgotten where he was. Stolie's. And his omelet was getting cold. He cursed himself soundly. Memories were one thing, but those that interfered with dinner were strictly something else.

"Why do we Walk?" Plato repeated. "It's not like the Akhaid, I guess. I never talked to one of them about it. No. More like, well, a place to find answers. To know yourself to be of value. To meet a challenge and answer it back and be aware of your power and weakness."

"You sound like you had that rehearsed," Cargo accused with a smile.

Plato blushed deeply enough that Cargo noticed even in the dim light. "I've been asked enough," she said.

Cargo didn't say anything at all. He wanted her to talk, he realized. The Walking had always bothered him and fascinated him at the same time, and Plato was the first person he had ever met who was from that world. He admitted that he found her strange. No, he corrected himself, not precisely strange. Exotic, and very attractive.

"I waited and waited and it took me forever to figure out that you were already here," Stonewall's voice boomed from the door. Plato and Cargo looked over at him and stiffened involuntarily, as if trying to ward off some clinging evil. His eyes grazed the room and located them. Cargo didn't even dare hope. Stonewall was on them, dragging over a chair and pushing in between them, before Cargo even had time to curse his luck.

"We were wondering where you were," Plato said blandly.

"Let me tell you, I have had a most interesting and informative afternoon. But as to where I was, I was eating exactly where I eat every night, and I could not for the life of me figure out why you had run off and left me alone. It took all of dinner hour to remember that it is Thursday and infernal egg night."

"You mean you ate on base?" Cargo asked, not quite certain of what that indicated about Stonewall's sanity.

"I hate eggs," Stonewall said simply. "The smell of them across a room makes me want to puke. I do not know how you all stand this. Well. It's just as good that I stayed because I've got some rumint that you would just give your brand new black-as-night wings for."

"You mean you know who passed check-flight?" Plato asked, unimpressed.

Stonewall shook his head. "Where's Scatter?" he demanded. Then he stood on his chair and yelled, "Scatter, get your ass over here yesterday, buddy. The old rumint mill is turning them out by the gross, and you don't want to be left in the cold."

Every being in the tightly packed bar was staring at them as Scatter made his way over.

"This had better be worth something," the Akhaid pilot

said. Cargo thought he was disgruntled, but couldn't tell for sure. It wasn't like he was Ghoster and familiar.

Stonewall smiled like an angel. "Oh, my buddies, oh it is. Stonewall has something to tell you all that's going to make your skin so creepy crawly. Now, there's all four of us here, right? And our Eyes are all over there, right? Well, take a good look at these two tables because someone sitting here is a spy."

"We're all spies," Cargo said, disgusted.

Plato laughed. Stonewall slammed the tabletop with his flat hand. "That is not what I mean and you know it. I would suspect you, Cargo, only I would suspect everyone. You know I mean a Cardia spy. You know what I mean."

Cargo stood up abruptly, angry. It was too much. He'd had it with Fourways and with all the damned suspicion around him. "You're the most likely candidate," he said to Stonewall, his whole body threatening a fight.

"I agree," Stonewall said lazily. "I would most certainly agree and oblige you if I could. However, so far from what I heard at dinner, you do understand that there were a few people indiscreet enough to make this all table conversation, was that yesterday's mission team went out to find that the Cardia constellation had been maneuvered to defend against certain capabilities that were documented in our orientation."

"So? Anyone could have had that information. It's standard," Cargo replied.

Stonewall leaned back in his chair and started whistling.

"Are you going to kill him or am I?" Plato asked Cargo and Scatter.

Cargo's remaining eggs were cold and rubbery. Even filled with caviar they were unappetizing. Somehow they found an appropriate home on Stonewall's head, just as Plato got him in an armlock and Scatter wet down a table.

"You do like to play Splash, don't you?" Plato asked as the three of them heaved Stonewall up and threw him on the beer-slicked table as if they'd rehearsed it.

"Stonewall was joking," Scatter announced. "He is always joking like this, and someday he will learn that it isn't always funny. I do not always understand this form of humor."

Stonewall looked up from where he had skidded at the edge of the table. "You're always just a laugh a minute, Scatter. For real, just a barrel of fun."

"Let's get out of here," Cargo said to Plato. She said nothing but made her way out of the bar. Cargo looked around once more before he left. Something was strange, wrong. He concentrated. Then he knew what it was. Ghoster. Ghoster was gone. He had been over at the table with the other Eyes, Cargo was sure of it, but now he couldn't locate the Akhaid anywhere.

It would be like Ghoster to leave when things got edgy with Stonewall, Cargo told himself. Ghoster hated any fracas, especially when he wasn't in the middle of it. But no matter what rational explanation he came up with, Cargo was uneasy. He hadn't seen Ghoster leave, and he didn't like that. He didn't like it at all.

Bishop Andre Michel Mirabeau ran his fingers over the glasslike polished surface of the antique wood of his desk, following the rich red graining. He wasn't aware of his hands moving over the austere and bare wood, didn't notice the spicy fragrance that came out of the ventilating system, didn't even hear the gentle chime of the ornate eighteenth century French clock that sat on the mantle.

Usually he found the chimes soothing, a sound that had marked events in his family for nearly five hundred years, or six. He always forgot. It troubled him that the thing was worth so much, like the desk and the faded pastel rugs. He enjoyed them, and was perfectly aware of the fact that their very richness sometimes stood in his way. Greed was not even of Bishop Mirabeau's minor sins. Only two things had ever motivated him in his life—compassion and power. It was an uncomfortable mixture.

Right now the two came together. Only one of his boys was still alive. He had received word that Yojo, who had become Two Bits for reasons the Bishop didn't even want to contemplate, had been killed in action. It was something that angered him, but the anger was irrelevant. Today had marked the tenth Mass the Bishop was offering for the Rom. It was the most important thing he could do, he told himself, but it wasn't all. Especially not now. Only one of his boys was still alive, of the three he had taken in more than ten years ago. He didn't want to be alone again.

He held the heavy formal paper in his hands, caressing the thick texture of it. The black words had been printed in one of the more ornate styles. He exhaled softly. Maybe, just maybe now his last boy wouldn't die. No one's would.

He'd been working for fifteen years for this one piece of paper. An invitation to Marcanter, to talk to leaders of the Cardia opposition party, their peace faction, to explore the possibility of opening negotiations. It was only the first hint, he told himself firmly. And there had been two other missions earlier that had ended in failure.

Still, he couldn't hold back the hope, the yearning pain he felt. A treaty in a year, perhaps. Maybe he could even work out an agreement for a truce, a trial period. He tried to keep his optimism firmly in check. It had always been his weak point.

He pressed a discrete button under his desk. The heavy carved door opened and his secretary came in silently, his feet muffled by the deep Aubusson carpets. Bishop Mirabeau studied the young cleric thoughtfully. If he had had sense he would have made someone like this his protegé, someone in Orders who would appreciate all the Bishop could do for his career and who wouldn't have to be taught how to use a fork correctly. It wouldn't hurt to consolidate the legacy of power he would leave to another generation.

But he was also compassionate. As a young man, Andre Mirabeau had wanted to travel to strange places and meet strange people, to learn different customs and have a life full of adventure. He had wanted to be a missionary. His family, too rich, too cultured and too proud of their heritage, had forbidden it. Instead, he had become a diplomat.

And once, in perfect compassion, he had started a war. Those who knew refused to credit him, but Bishop Mirabeau knew better. In all his life there had been one act of charity that he could not regret although he was agonized by the consequences.

He gave instructions to the secretary who said nothing as the recorder took notes. Reservations, travel arrangements, times and dates as well as messages to various people at the Collegium. The secretary nodded with the solemnity of a bow and departed.

The Bishop went over to the window and leaned against the old-fashioned sill. Out there the colony bustled. Kites swooped by, and he could hear the screech of wing struts scraping against the Cathedral's projections and winced. He'd have to get the building supervisor to put up the screens again, much as he hated that. The Cathedral was the largest building in this quadrant of the habitat, and teenagers with their first kites seemed unable to resist attaching gaudy plastic rings to various bits of the structure. Every year one or more of them would get caught and have to be taken down, or would fall.

At least his boys had never played on the Cathedral roof. They hadn't had kites. They'd been too young and too poor. And now there was only Rafael left—Rafael who had insisted on being called Cargo ever since he'd had the right to it. The Bishop had never gotten used to that.

He'd never gotten used to the way the boys thought he was innocent, either, the Bishop thought. All of them tried so very hard to protect him, maybe because they were in need of protection themselves. Maybe because young people, with the first blush of innocence gone, seem to believe that they are the first who have seen the soft and rotted core.

It brought back memories of the first successor he had trained and lost. More than these boys, Aliadro had always thought him far too unworldly.

He turned away and forced himself to sit at the desk again. He was wasting time, and right now he didn't have much to spare. According to the report he had received this morning, the Cardia peace faction was willing to talk. Finally.

The message had come to him and not the Ministry of Security, although by all rights and channels it belonged there. He was no longer a Trustee of the Collegium, but only the Bishop of this colony habitat. He no longer had any official say in policy; his statements didn't even get into the fine print of the flimpax anymore.

It had been carefully planned that way, and now that the plan was going to bear fruit, Andre Michel Mirabeau was excited enough to forget his ninety-seven years. The radical peace faction had grown rapidly in the past several years. By the time the secret negotiations were ready to go public there would be general support. All he had to do was to get to Marcanter as a show of faith.

The Bishop had no doubts that certain people traveled to Cardia planets. Unofficially of course. He had to figure out how to be one of them. To get there, to make contact with the Cardia peace faction that he suspected was making inroads as fast as his own party in the Collegium. A thought struck him and he smiled.

He had resigned as a Trustee of the Collegium in anticipation of this day. The Cardia wasn't ready to approach the Collegium officially as yet. But some feelers to people who had retired from public office, a hint or two about possible rapprochement, and the groundwork would be laid. Besides, the Bishop suspected that there was more behind the early stages of secession than anyone knew. Privately, he suspected that some third party, not precisely Collegium or Cardia, had staged the Luxor incident for their own benefit and had forced Shodar's hand. The Bishop was certain of that because he knew Shodar and, more important, knew where he was when the Luxor Incident had taken place. He had spent the past fifteen years trying to figure out exactly who the Luxor terrorists were and what they stood to gain. So far he had been unsuccessful, and it was the first time in his life if he counted. He didn't. He simply decided that the job wasn't finished and had no doubts as to his ultimate victory. It only took time.

This time he didn't ask his secretary to put through the connection to Sebastian Agular. The secretary couldn't be trusted to keep his mouth shut about the Bishop of a smallish and not terribly central Colony having a direct access line to the UnderMinister of Security.

"Agular. Your business?" the line opened. It wasn't polite, but the UnderMinister of Security was always busy, and he no longer had to be polite. At least, not to those who called on this line.

"Mirabeau," the Bishop identified himself. "I have some information that could be useful. About Cardia equipment on Marcanter."

Agular groaned audibly. "Damnit, Andre. You aren't cleared for that information and you're talking on an unsecured line."

The Bishop chuckled. He felt guilty about enjoying the UnderMinister's discomfort, but he couldn't resist the opportunity to play the game just a little. Besides, there was no way Agular would react reasonably to a simple request for military transport under truce to Marcanter.

"Calm down, Sebastian," he said after a reasonable pause. "I just wanted to make sure you could see me. The day after tomorrow, perhaps?"

"If you're going to give me any of your hypotheses you can forget it," the UnderMinister retorted immediately. "I'm sick up to my eyeballs with your conspiracy theories, you know that? An intruder is an intruder, and Luxor was fifteen years ago. You aren't even supposed to know anything about that. No."

The Bishop was glad he had insisted on leaving the screen off. Agular would be insulted to see his smile. Instead, he adopted the smooth tones of the professional diplomat that he had honed over nearly half a century of active service to his Church, the Collegium, and the general populations of both species. "I had no intention of mentioning anything of the kind. I believe that I might have information valuable to the investigation that I'm sure the Fourth Directorate is conducting. It might save them time. You know I wouldn't ask you lightly."

He let Agular ponder that for a moment. "What kind of information?" the UnderMinister asked suspiciously.

"You, yourself, pointed out that this is an open line," Mirabeau said, sliding back into his old habits easily enough.

Finally the UnderMinister relented. "But if this is one of your tricks, Andre, it won't be funny. I'm canceling an important meeting for you."

"Thank you, my friend," Mirabeau changed back to the Bishop persona again. "I look forward to seeing you again. The last time was not the most pleasant circumstance."

The receiver went opaque as the Bishop grinned. Agular was one of his favorite opponents. Now, he just had to dig up something worth telling the man.

Conspiracy theories indeed, Mirabeau thought as he closed the compartment and stared at the empty desk again. Agular knew next to nothing about the big picture. Certainly the man was good enough at Security, the Bishop admitted. He was much more capable than most, and that was a blessing. It meant that he was also more efficient and more powerful. In fact, he was far more powerful than the rank of UnderMinister indicated. The Bishop knew how it was done, why Agular avoided the final leap into the spotlight. With no one looking his way, he had amassed a vast empire inside the bureaucracy. He'd built a dedicated and talented team who made things work. The last thing a person like Agular wanted was the glare of a Collegium appointment and investigation, all the attendant media coverage and the prying into his personal life and professional history. Maybe his personal life could take it, the Bishop decided, but his professional conduct couldn't. There was too much authority in that one office for anyone else in that department to feel safe.

Agular was a functionary, Mirabeau decided, a little person with too much power. Theories, indeed. What Agular lacked was imagination, the Bishop decided. He couldn't make the leap that both faith and genius demanded. Anyone who really knew anything about history wouldn't toss off his concerns so lightly. And Mirabeau knew that he knew more about the Dekmejians than most. He'd spent five years as a liaison on three major Cardia planets, albeit before Cargo had been born. But he'd gotten to know them, to know what they thought and believed more than any other diplomat who had ever held the post. No other liaison in those days had cared much about intangible twists of philosophy. That was a real pity, since it was central to understanding an alien culture. Central to understanding our own, too, he added for good measure, just that no one ever quite saw it that way from the inside. No, his superior knowledge of the Dekmejian philosophy was not a matter of pride with him. It was a matter of sorrow.

It was because of functionaries like Agular that good people, boys like Yojo, were getting killed. And there was Raphael, Cargo, still in the middle of it all. Now that Cargo was a batwing he had passed from the jurisdiction of the Ministry of Security to the Independent Trusteeship. A batwing. Covert action.

Wheels started in the Bishop's head. Covert action was exactly what he wanted. He had to get in to Marcanter unseen. And under that guise so much was classified that Agular wouldn't really have access to whatever data he dredged up. He could invent something just as well, but lying went against his background, his self image and his honor as a Mirabeau. Still, the fact alone that he knew where he wanted to go was useful. He'd see what his niece in the Fifth Directorate had to give him. She was stationed down on the Collegium, only a six-hour shuttle jaunt away.

Covert action. He wondered if he could see Cargo, too. It would be natural to have a Second Directorate escort into Marcanter, wouldn't it? And it could as easily be Rafael as anyone else.

He was proud of the boy, he couldn't deny it. Rafael, more than any of the Romany boys he had adopted from juvie, had the potential to do honor to the Mirabeau name. Not simply clever and venal like his cousin, Angel, or simplistic in his thinking like Yojo, Raphael had the ability to go the full course. Maybe as high as the Collegium itself.

He was not Aliadro with Aliadro's special talents, but in the long run that was probably for the better. Aliadro had not survived, not simply because of bad luck but because of some fatal flaw in himself.

Mirabeau let himself smile. He had picked a worthy successor after all, and better that he had adopted instead of married. Like the Roman emperors. That was Marcus Aurelis' one fault, that he had chosen a natural son over an heir adopted with proven abilities. No, he thought, Rafael had the capability, and Mirabeau had given him the training and the connections. Now all he needed was some luck, and with additional training at the peace table as well as at war, Raphael Mirabeau would emerge as one of the young, up-and-coming leaders of the postwar period. The Bishop could see it very clearly.

Then he sighed. Already he was guilty of a few minor sins, enjoying Agular's discomfort, pride in Cargo and not incidently being perfectly pleased at entering the arena again. And it wasn't even lunchtime yet. He decided to skip dessert at dinner as penance, which was particularly severe since his cook was making peach charlotte. In fact, he decided that he had been harsh enough to permit one or two more venal sins. He would need them. Since the entire next day would be spent in transit, he had only this afternoon to gather the data he had promised the UnderMinister.

Chapter
5

"I told you you shouldn't buy it," Ghoster said.

Cargo muttered under his breath. Ghoster was probably right, but the bargain had been too good to be true. He decided that he deserved to be shot. If anyone should know about too good bargains it was a Rom.

The windwagon looked as though it would collapse before it reached the gate, let alone make the four hundred kilometers into town. One of the elevation planes was crumpled and had never been repaired. Cargo reached a finger forward and stroked it gently, afraid it would fall off with any pressure. The tracks that had been specially designed for Vanity's grass looked worn and thin and ready for replacement. Inside, the panel had been cannibalized, and there was more than one blind hole where a redscreen used to be.

"Well, let's see how she runs," Cargo said tentatively.

"No," Ghoster replied firmly. "Let's see if it runs at all. I think we might consider telling our friends that our trip to town has been postponed."

Cargo got in the driver's side and opened the other door without a word. The hinges screamed and Cargo winced, certain that the door would fall off. That it didn't was no relief.

Ghoster recoiled fastidiously, and then gathered his wits and entered. It amused Cargo to see the Akhaid so obviously distressed by mere dust. It was engine trouble he was worried about.

"Did you at least test-drive it before you paid?" Ghoster asked.

"Yeah, of course I test-drove it," Cargo retorted. "What do

you think I am, some kind of wipe head? I test-drove it, and it was fine. Not real fast, but stable and in the legal limit."

"You're sure it wasn't jury rigged?" Ghoster continued.

Cargo threw up his hands. "I don't know," he breathed, exasperated. "It went fine, full go, before. So it looks like dead slime mold. It's only got to last to the end of the month, and then we're out of here. And I won't miss Vanity, that's for sure."

There was something about Ghoster's face that Cargo didn't trust. His Eyes looked all too innocent. "I suppose you're planning to sell it when we leave," he stated. There was no reason to make it a question.

Cargo snorted. "Naturally. And I intend to make a profit, too. A little paint, a good shine, a couple of cheap boards. It'll come out of the beer money, that's all. And I'll make it back more than double."

Ghoster appeared to relax. "That's what I thought. I get worried sometimes that you might try to be like the other humans. I keep thinking that Plato's going to convert you to morality."

Cargo pretended not to hear. He concentrated on the ignition code instead, and after the most perfunctory cough the windwagon began to glide forward on its heavy tracks. Heartened, Cargo punched up full speed. The wagon heaved, shuddered, and threatened to die. Then, as if aware of making a great effort, it began to accelerate. The process became easier, and finally they were making the perimeter at just under top go.

"You see," Cargo crowed triumphantly. "It wasn't such a bad buy."

They had come nearly the full circuit and slowed before they pulled up in front of quarters. Plato was waiting outside, watching. "How is it?" she asked, screaming over the wind, as they got out.

"It is sentient," Ghoster replied.

Cargo shook his head and went straight inside. He didn't say anything until they had all collapsed in the lounge. "It'll make it to town tonight. If we're still on."

Plato's eyebrows shot straight up. "What do you mean, if we're still on? Why shouldn't we be on? Oh, no, not Stonewall's crap again. Nobody's listening to that."

Cargo didn't say anything. He didn't have to. Stonewall

wasn't his favorite person, although he did acknowledge he had reason to be grateful. If it hadn't been for his paranoid colleague, Cargo figured that if there really was something behind all the rumint, he would take it to the Wall. Fourways wanted him gone, and Cargo disliked Fourways almost enough to satisfy him. Stonewall had managed to get suspicion spread around a little more evenly. Much as it was easy to like the flier, it was easier to edit his obsessive concentration on possible spies of all shades. Which meant that Cargo figured no one noticed him at all.

Cargo was going to make some smart reply when Steel appeared in the doorway. He—no, she—Cargo corrected himself, seemed more agitated than he had ever seen Stonewall's phlegmatic partner.

"Assignments are due out in seven minutes," she said, staring first at Ghoster, then at Cargo and Plato. "Do you plan to sit here the whole time?"

A loose, lazy smile spread across Cargo's face. "Sure," he said. "Someone'll tell us, so what's the hurry?"

Steel regarded him as some specimen lying on a disection table.

"He is trying to be amusing," Ghoster said. "If you ignore him it goes away. Like a beta-feedback doorknob."

Steel made a low growl in the back of her throat, the Akhaid public display of pleasure, and Ghoster got up to join her. "I suppose we can both check this out together," he said in their own language. Cargo didn't know whether to be pleased at having understood, or to be discreet and pretend he hadn't. He hadn't made his mind up by the time Ghoster and Steel left.

"The curiosity is killing me," Plato admitted as they entered the lower lounge.

Cargo was surprised. They knew well enough that the assignment would come today, that they would leave by the end of the month, and that they would most likely all be assigned together. Or they would be split into two teams with two different objectives. The senior batwings between assignments on Vanity had told them that much since they'd gotten their black wings. One way or another it didn't make much difference, and Cargo said as much.

Plato ran her fingers down a tear in the cellosoft cover of the easy chair. "Of course it makes a difference," she said after awhile. "Once we know the target, we have some idea of where the next incursion will be."

Cargo nodded abruptly and stood. Plato had never told him where she was from, but suddenly he understood that while she might be rich she was also from one of the Disputed Territories near the Veil. Two or three hadn't been attacked yet, but they had been under constant threat, and no wonder. It was the Veil that the Cardia wanted and the Disputed Territories where the losses were heaviest. "Which one?" he asked.

"Paragon," she answered softly.

A wave of pity came over him. He'd heard of Paragon. The Bishop had been there and told him about it, although Cargo would be hard pressed to find a place where the Bishop hadn't been. But Paragon had sounded special, a utopian experiment that hadn't exactly worked but hadn't exactly failed after four generations. Mostly, he remembered what the Bishop had said about their cities, with high ceramic towers glazed in every shade of pastel rising between blue-green trees against a turquoise sky. Public parks wound around the towers, the footpaths lead past bits of statuary or chimes hung from high branches, or over arching bridges over tiled ponds filled with purple and pink lilies, and fat red-gold carp. It had sounded too much like a story to be real, and Cargo had wanted to go there. Only Paragon, like most experimental communities, had laws against transients.

"I don't think you'd be happy there," the Bishop had said gently after they had finished viewing the screens. "There are two philosophies of perfection, among humans and outside the Church, that is. One is that perfection is found in absolute freedom, that left to itself the individual will find useful forms of fulfillment. The other is that the individual is a social animal and must conform to an increasing series of expectations. Paragon is like this. It is very beautiful, but choices are very limited. You might like to live in a ceramic tower, but if you decided to live in what they thought was an ugly wooden structure you would be banished from the community and your home torn down."

It didn't sound so different from *marhime* at the time. Suddenly Cargo looked at Plato again. Only this time he could see her, could see her past and her choices, why she had Walked. Of course. It was the one choice of freedom a person could make on Paragon. And, like himself, she couldn't go back.

She was as much an outcast as he, and yet she was still concerned about the fate of the people who had shut her out. Only because she was braver, more complete, more herself than they.

He stood up and went over to the chair where Plato sat. He held out a hand to her. She looked up at him, and Cargo could read it in her face that she understood the change in his perception. She touched her palm to his, letting him pull her up. Her hand was smaller than he had expected, the bones narrow.

"Well, what are you waiting for?" he asked to break the tension. It didn't quite work. He was still too aware of her as an individual, as a woman, as they left the lounge. He felt vaguely uncomfortable following her into the room, which was closer than his own, to call up the assignment board.

The flickering "Waiting" message intruded into his awareness. Much as he couldn't pretend that Plato was just another colleague anymore, couldn't ignore the warm spicy smell of her hair as they bent near the screen, neither could he pretend disinterest in what the assignment would reveal.

One assignment was like another, another carrier, another target, he had always thought. Being a batwing didn't change that. But this time it mattered, this time his curiosity was aroused, although ten minutes before it hadn't mattered. As Plato had emerged as unique to him, with a history of her own, suddenly the various places along the front also came to have their own distinct identities to him.

He could feel Plato breathing softly on the screen, small white teeth biting into a full lower lip, drawing a single glistening drop of blood in anticipation. It hung there, a single brilliant speck on her pale, expectant face until she flicked it away with the tip of her tongue.

Then the "Waiting" dissolved from the screen. Instead a stream of color-coded information flickered by so quickly that Cargo couldn't make out any of the letters. Then the display froze. Eight names glowed in amber light against the dull gray, and next to each of them the *CSS Horn* written in pink, complete with several sets of coordinates following.

The *Horn*. Cargo muttered something about the *mule* of his ancestors and his hand went unconsciously to the Ste. Maries-de-la-Mer medal. The *Horn* was an unlucky ship, had been unlucky from before she was launched, from the vacyard accident that had blown a fusion lock and killed seven workers inside.

"So that's what all the rumint was about," Plato whispered.

"We should have waited," Cargo said, not realizing quite that he had spoken aloud. Everyone knew when assignments were posted; the thick formal packages would be handed over tomorrow, with all the particulars they would need to know. He wondered where the *Horn* would be going, and thought briefly about just waiting until the final word to know the worst. Maybe he could pretend for the rest of the night that the luck was better than it should be.

Only Plato hadn't heard his thoughts and was already keying for as much information as the system cleared her to receive. There was a flicker of hesitation before a series of coordinates appeared, remained for three seconds and were gone. There was no vocal. Cargo, leaning over Plato's right shoulder, saw only part of the display before it disappeared according to security regulations.

Plato recited a long chain of foul language in a monotone.

"What's that about?" Cargo asked.

She looked up at him and then shook her head. "You don't want to see that. It's probably grounds for justifiable suicide. We're going to the Collegium to pick up some VIP and pretend that we're worried about surveillance. As if they could get a constellation through the safes. And then on to Zhai Bo, another hot spot on the front lines just bristling with covert targets. And after Zhai Bo, we join up with the Seventh Fleet convoy at Mudra." Plato hunched over the key ledge, keeping out of Cargo's line of sight. "You know," she said in a very small voice. "You know, I really thought I was doing something, coming here. I thought it would matter, to Paragon too. I guess I was stupid."

Cargo understood the despair in her, shared it. From the first he had been convinced that the batwing had the best, the hardest tasks, enough of a challenge to keep him focused most of the time. To keep him Cargo, to forget that other person. He had looked forward to it, to slipping in and destroying the Cardia's snoops.

Uninhabited constellations were one thing, but snooper-craft flown by real live beings were another. The First Directorate had a few superexpensive snoopers, and they'd even met a couple of the pilots the week they began evaluating countermeasures when confronted by a forward intelligence team. That's what the snoopers called themselves. Only they were about as likely to find snoopers around the Collegium as they were to find tequila at Stolie's, and they both knew it. Still, Cargo couldn't resist trying to be reassuring. "No way they've got a constellation in, but a really ace snoop might be able to sneak by," he said lamely.

Plato laughed. "Nice try. Nice of you to try, too. Oh, dammit, Cargo, this is as bad as it gets. It doesn't get any worse!"

Cargo smiled incongruously. "Well, if this is the worst possible case, then it must get better, right?"

"Optimist," Plato charged.

Cargo shook his head. "Maybe we should pick up the others. It's more fun to bitch together. Besides, the wind-wagon's waiting, and maybe you'd rather spend tonight at Stolie's, but I had my heart set on getting to Matta. Or at least on getting out of here."

"Just give me ten minutes to change, all right?" Plato asked.

Cargo nodded. "If you'll give me fifteen," he replied, and then left. It was a long way to his own quarters, and he wasn't going to show up in Matta in uniform.

Deciding what to wear off base actually was more difficult than Cargo had foreseen. He wondered which persona to choose, wondered who the others would show up as. Except for Ghoster and the one evening with Plato very long ago, they had never seen each other out of uniform.

Cargo stood motionless, going through the list of possibilities, weighing each and wondering how the others would respond to him. He considered wearing a diklo and immediately discarded that. With Two Bits it might have been different, but the Rom weren't always appreciated. The group knew his ethnic origin, of course, but the uniform hid any real recognition. Cargo knew he looked like a terribly average human, his skin the exact median shade of light brown, height and build somewhere around the mean, features that could easily have come from the common Eurasian/AmerAfrican mix. Only once he put on the soft cap and ragged neckscarf that was common among the Tshurara he no longer looked the part of a respectable human. The other choices were a resident of Mawbry's colony and the Bishop's nephew.

The habitant was his usual persona. Mawbry's was large,

considered sophisticated, in orbit in the Collegium system. It's A-grav hospital had served most of the top politicians of the past seventeen governments, its stadiat had a canopied section down front reserved for the Trustees, and had been used for some of their broadcasts when the government wanted to demonstrate popular support. The persona was Cargo's favorite because no one could claim that he was either really a colonial or a decadent, and he could be expected to be cosmopolitan without being pretentious. Most people generally thought of habitants as the stereotypical "good citizen", the type who paid their taxes and sent their children to school and enjoyed all the legal recreations while flirting with one or two of those not quite approved. Salt of the earth and all that, Cargo thought. It had almost always served well.

Only this time when he pulled the neat habitant suit out and looked at it, he thought of Plato. Plato had been raised on Paragon, a utopian society just out of its first flush. And while it was generating a strata system, it seemed obvious that Plato had been thrown up on the top. No, Plato would ignore a habitant if she met one, her prejudices would insist that he was most likely dull. That was the general disadvantage.

The third option was the Bishop's nephew. Not that there was any blood relationship between them, but the Bishop had always said that he thought of the boys as more his nephews than those who shared his genetic heritage. Cargo had always hesitated to use the word protegé in public, with its politely understated sexual connotations. To the best of his knowledge, the Bishop had taken his vows and never broken them, and while for himself it would be simply a misstatement of his preferences and one easily remediable, to the Bishop such an assumption cut at the foundations of his honor. So he had always been the Bishop's nephew in public, which created less essential misunderstanding while it created rather more useful assumptions.

It also answered all questions about his use of the Mirabeau name. Only once had he made the mistake of saying he was the Bishop's son. Those who knew the Bishop's career knew he had never married nor publicly claimed paternity of a child. What he had done since he had retired from the Palace of Trustees and become the Bishop of Mawbry's was not published anymore, but the one time he had tried to explain, the party in question had accused him of lying. He had been thrown out of a very expensive hotel banquet hall in an all too humiliating fashion. And all for nothing.

In the right circumstances, of course, Cargo had found the reaction to a relative of the Bishop Mirabeau to be very favorable. Not that he enjoyed people fawning over him, trying tastelessly to get his support and preparing to drop his name the next time they met with less exalted company. Andre Michel Mirabeau, Bishop of Mawbry's Habitat, was known well outside of his Church as a canny politician and diplomat to be approached cautiously. The Mirabeau matriarch had been one of the founders of the Pax Societas, and all generations of Mirabeaus thereafter had retained power in what was now the majority opposition in the Collegium. Except the radical, Andre Michel, who had gone off and formed his own party shortly before the Luxor incident.

That was not the way Cargo viewed the Bishop. There had never been any hint of why he was no longer the Trustee with Diplomatic Portfolio of the Collegium, Ambassador to Zhai Bo and later Nto Igrad, and Legate to the Cardia Group. Indeed, it was hard for Cargo to imagine the Bishop as any of these things. So far as he was concerned, Mirabeau was the Bishop of Mawbry's Habitat, a man old enough to be his grandfather and innocent of anything evil. Still, the persona of Bishop's nephew while necessarily political was necessarily discreet. And, as Cargo considered the matter, he knew that it was the role Plato would respond most favorably to.

That certain, he took out what he privately called his Mirabeau clothes. He'd come by them honestly enough; the Bishop had given him credit at a famous Collegium store to outfit himself suitably for a Cathedral reception. Given the Bishop's stance and the Church's position, wearing uniform would have been imprudent. A human clerk had been on hand with prior instructions from the Bishop, and Cargo had been given a selection of only the most classic colors and styles. The soft, gray silk pants and white shirt were notable only by the richness of the fabric. The short draped suede jacket was also a good conservative dove gray and lacked the fringe, tooled design or flashes Cargo liked but immediately recognized as either cheap or Gypsy. The clerk had permitted him a certain freedom in choosing a cravat and armband in a wine and turquoise abstract pattern, which was admittedly a touch daring when the men Cargo had seen dealing with the Bishop had invariably worn solid blues. In the end it had been quite a revelation to see himself as the perfect aristo. Even the Gitano arrogance appeared as a perfectly appropriate Mirabeau sneer.

He was used to it now, and was oblivious to the shock he generated when he appeared for the group rendezvous in the lounge. Not that he was so different from any of the rest, he thought. They had all seen each other and formed impressions based on mutual experiences. Now, they were looking at each other's private identities, and it was interesting to say the least.

Cargo noticed Ghoster sitting talking to Steel, who was dressed in some Akhaid fashion he didn't recognize. It was impossible for a human to follow all the ins and outs of Akhaid society, anyway. They would exchange information the next time they were alone and could clue in each other on various aspects of personality people had chosen to reveal.

"Are you sure that old junk pile will move with all of us in it?" Stonewall asked casually.

"The more mass the greater the stability," Cargo responded gravely.

"I know," Stonewall said. "I'm just a touch concerned about the problem of inertia. It does look like that object is going to stay at rest until the end of its natural life."

Cargo shrugged elegantly, feeling the careful pleats of his jacket rearrange themselves around his shoulders. "If you prefer other transportation, I won't be offended."

There was a moment that was uncomfortable, when Cargo wondered if he and Stonewall had gone too far. And then Plato swept into the room and laughed, breaking the tension. She led them out to the windwagon and Cargo followed gratefully. It was the first time he had left the immediate environs of Vanity Base in six weeks and he was restless. They all were. That was all it was, he told himself. A change of scene would clear the air that had gotten too thick and full of suspicion. All Stonewall's doing, Cargo thought as they climbed into the windwagon. All Stonewall's fault that they were an uneasy team. And all too soon they would report to an unlucky ship.

· · ·

Matta wasn't really a city by Mawbry standards, Cargo
decided as they closed in. The last time he had been here,
transferring to the Base jumpcoach, he had spent all of
twenty minutes picking up his bag and kicking a coffee
machine that refused to deliver. He hadn't been concerned
with Matta at all.

Now approaching the town on a traffic route, he was
mildly irritated that they didn't begin with directionals until he
was less than a kilometer from Midcenter. The cellofab housing units that lined the road were dull and sturdy looking but
without any decoration, prosperous enough, the people bragging both about their long-standing building and their lack of
finery. Cargo thought the lack of color, let alone relief accents
and trim, made the place look like the Puritan camp the authorities had considered sending him to.

He concentrated on driving. The town maze was interfaced
with the windwagon, and they were being directed to parking
accommodations next to the Midcenter Tower. Cargo wondered just how much the parking charge was. He'd been taken
before on one of the automatic interface setups. The town
maze always insisted on filling municipal coffers. Especially
from the base. Somehow, locals were always guided to public
spots. He cursed very softly in Romany.

"Let it go auto," someone yelled from the back. "No use
worrying now."

Cargo hated to agree, but it wasn't worth it. Too many
general high spirits filled the windwagon, and it was impossible for him to ignore them. Deliberately, he twisted the interface dial to full control and swiveled his seat so he was facing
the rest of the group.

"And you know, when I heard about it, I thought, that's
impossible. I mean, I've heard about paranoid but this is mix-
ing annies. Only my uncle claims he was there and heard it all
firsthand. So, I went and checked his personnel file, and damn
straight. He was the Admiral's aide and he was at the Collegium," Bugs was saying.

"And how did you happen to get into those files, do tell,"
Stonewall retorted with an unpleasant edge. "I assume they
are classified. And if they aren't they most certainly are under
personal code, I should think."

Bugs giggled. "They are classified. You want to know
how I did it? Buy me a drink and maybe I'll tell you. And

maybe I won't." She tittered again and fluttered her hands around her.

Cargo had never really noticed her before. Species aside, she hung with the Eyes and never sought out his company, or Plato's or Stonewall's either. Now, he decided that he didn't like her. Not that he didn't admire her ability to break into classified data like that, even if they were cleared for it. But anyone who could do that ought to know better than to talk. Either she was a total moron or lying. Either way she was dead dangerous, and Cargo didn't like that at all.

For just a second he had a flash that maybe Stonewall had seemed too interested. And then, like a blazing explosion in the void, Cargo knew. Everyone else did, too. There was absolute silence in the wagon.

He hadn't even noticed that the vehicle had stopped moving, that the red parking light was flashing. Cargo's whole being was intent on Bugs. If she was the one they were looking for, then it all made sense. She had slid into the background perfectly, and his own assumption about Stonewall had blinded him from seeing anything else.

Only one thing hit Cargo wrong. He wasn't precisely sure what it was, only that he was uneasy.

Bugs looked around, her eyes flashing from one to the other, her skin a sickly shade of gray. Cargo couldn't decide if it was fear or just the light.

"What's going on?" she asked, and her throat closed halfway through so it sounded like she was choking.

"You admit to freely accessing classified information," Stonewall demanded coldly.

Bugs closed her eyes. "No," she whispered. "I was lying. Honestly, I was just putting you on."

"I think you ought to tell us how you did it," Stonewall went on as if he hadn't heard the denial. "Maybe if you volunteer the information now, it'll be a little easier for you. There's got to be a public link somewhere around here."

Bugs swallowed hard. Her hands hung limply on her thighs. She shook her head back and forth as if she knew the denial was useless, but she had no choice but to make it anyway.

Stonewall was already climbing out of the wagon. "You all keep her covered till someone comes to get her. I shouldn't be too long. Anyone know if there's a public link around here?"

"If we're in stack lot two, there's a link on the top floor next to the lift," Glaze said.

There was nothing to do. The wagon was hot with all of them packed so closely. Cargo tried not to watch the numbers change on his chrono. No one said a word. They all waited, and to him it seemed like they waited forever. Bugs was trembling slightly and breathing in short, jagged gasps. Cargo couldn't tell if she was trying not to cry or was in shock. Maybe both.

Stonewall had logic on his side, and Cargo had heard her admit to a very serious breech in security if not downright treason. Admit to it freely, at that. The fact she denied it all meant nothing.

Only Cargo sensed something wrong. He had a hunch that she had not been honest with them either time, but that she hadn't tampered with classified data either. He was sure enough to swear to it on the old oath. *Te merau*, may I die if she is the one Fourways is looking for. *Te merau*, may I die if she is from the Cardia.

Then he closed his eyes and could see the face of old Pulika grinning. "So you swear by the old way, may you die if what you say is not true," the old *chal* had said when they had questioned him and he had sworn before the *kris*. The memory of the trial still stung deeply, Sonfranka's brothers looking at him as if perhaps they would kill him no matter what the *kris* decided. So he had sworn but they still had not believed him, had declared him *marhime*.

Now he swore may he die if what he said was not true. As if that mattered. As if the Wall wasn't staring him in the face every day, as if he had time after tomorrow. "You've got to want to live forever," an instructor had once said when he was in the middle of flight training. "You have to want to live forever to be willing to do whatever it takes. The point is to do your job and get out alive. You didn't hit the Wall because you were a hero. You hit the Wall because you fucked up."

Cargo heard it in his head like he had heard it a thousand times before. Only this time, he didn't believe it. This time he knew it was out of his hands, caprice. The Universe was joke in Brownian motion, a drunk lurching through sentience. His oath meant nothing.

All the same he knew he was right. Bugs was innocent of

the big one. He remembered that he was the son of Sister Mary, the greatest *boojo* woman of the Tshurara. Even before he could walk he remembered hearing his mother talking about her art with other women. About how to read the subtle line of a client's walk or tension in the face, how to listen to strain and confidence in voices and bodies. Cargo didn't know exactly how he did it, only that he had been trained by the best. He spared a thought for the Fourth Directorate. Counter-intelligence was missing a knowledge more useful and pure than truth fields, of that he was certain.

The more he was sure, the longer the time seemed. He wondered when they would come, and who the they would be to take Bugs away. He wondered what Scatter would do. He wondered how long the investigation and trial would take and if Bugs would be acquitted.

It seemed like he had all night to ponder these things before the backdoor screamed on its hinges and two MP's tried to get in. There wasn't enough room. One had to move aside, and the other took Bugs by the wrists alone. He didn't need any help. Bugs was beyond resistance. Her head rolled on her neck and her breathing was shallow. Cargo was sure she was hardly conscious. It was probably better that way.

"Well, are we going into town?" Stonewall asked when Bugs was gone.

Scatter's ears came down abruptly, and the darker golden skin on his head colored deeply. Plato looked at him and said nothing.

"I'm not heartless," Stonewall protested. "Just that we're already here. And it'll be worse if we go back. At least this way we can try and distract Scatter here."

Plato looked at Stonewall as if he had suggested mass sui-cide. Cargo understood. He might have to agree with Stone-wall, but he had to admit the other was right. It was bad enough. Going back would only make things worse.

"Stonewall's right," he said gently. "And we wouldn't have to face anyone down at Stolie's."

He knew it would get them in the end. One by one, Akhaid and human exited the wagon as if resigned to some terrible fate, not a night on the town.

"Just remember, Matta Mid isn't Spin Street," Glaze re-minded them.

"Don't worry, we're housebroken," Stonewall said caustically.

Cargo winced. He wanted to get away from Stonewall, his dislike of Stonewall, and into someplace dark where they served things that cost too much and required nothing else. He took Plato by the elbow and steered her away from the wagon down the lit MidCenter.

"Where are we going?" she demanded.

"Sorry," Cargo said. "I'll buy. I just had to get away from him, and I didn't want to go alone."

The Matta Mid was about as appealing as anything else on Vanity. The paved central plaza had no trees, no benches, nothing that attracted a visitor to linger and pay attention to the various bars, annie and alkie, the assortment of food places and even a few shops. All the doors were the same colored celo each with the name and type of business written in one of three contrasting shades.

"Annie or alkie?" Cargo asked.

Plato shrugged. "Start with annies if we're going to do the whole thing, I guess. Or dinner. But I'm not hungry."

They chose the first door that advertised annies, the orange swirl of celo aged and faded. There was just enough light to see the flight of stairs that ended somewhere below in the muddied dark. Cargo didn't really care. If he'd hoped the MidCenter would be better than it appeared, Bugs's arrest had destroyed all hope of a pleasant evening.

Beneath they were greeted with a scene Cargo thought had been taken from one of the Bishop's more macabre paintings of hell. While above things were unkempt and tawdry, down here they glowed. The bar opened onto an underground street that was lined with trees and lit with old-fashioned yellow lights. The ceiling was low, and there were no separation of any kind between the various establishments listed upstairs. Instead, people drifted from one to another, flitting down the central plaza from shadow to pale light. The square had been based on some skewed conception of an ancient Earth town, the paving stones rounded cobbles with a fountain in the center. The builders hadn't understood that there had been various styles, or perhaps hadn't chosen one, but the red brick-faced hotel across the plaza clashed badly with cut stone of several eateries which warred with elegant arabesques and tile work at what seemed to be a game house with shops on either side.

Plato chose a table close to the plaza, where they had a good view of passersby. The serving cart rolled up to them and Cargo chose a dish of blues that had been hand-rolled and formed into seashell shapes. Plato's greens looked like dragons laid out on a porcelain plate with a similar theme. The first round cost nearly three day's pay, and they were barely starting. Cargo hoped he hadn't gone too pale, or that if he had Plato would think it was Bugs.

The blues tasted good before they took effect, and Cargo decided that the price wasn't too ridiculous. It took great skill to make blues taste better than bitter paste. If he didn't need the slowing effect he wouldn't have ordered them at all.

Across the plaza he saw Ghoster and Steel take a seat at the restaurant. He wondered how Matta could cater to their dietary needs, and then the blues hit. He could feel the tension released in his back and shoulders, the tension also of the past hour fade away. He was enclosed in a private cocoon of cotton batting, shielded from the manifold.

Plato sat across, smiling and humming to herself. Cargo looked at her seriously for the first time and decided she was beautiful. Not in the classical sense, of course, her skin was too bleached out and her mouth too large. Sitting in the soft yellow light and smiling faintly as the greens touched her mood, she reminded Cargo of Vatican holos the Bishop had shown him so many times. The persona she wore only accentuated the resemblance, a pale blue diaphanous tunic with a hood over a patterned unisuit. The hood framed her hair like a halo in the Bishop's pictures.

There were no more annies on the plate. That made sense. He was getting silly, staring at Plato like at a millenium old painting.

"It sort of reminds me of a Walker's nest," she was saying happily. "They weren't very official, but we could find them anywhere. Any Walker would tell you enough about a city, if the nest was on the top of an abandoned building or under an old bridge. Those were the favorite places. There were foam rolls tied up there that anyone could use for a bed, and often a can fire or two. Going to the nest was the best part of it."

Cargo blinked. Even deep in the blue haze he tried to grasp

what she was saying, what he had wondered and could not comprehend.

"Sometimes in a nest you would talk to people," she went on. "Other Walkers, of course, no one else would be in a nest. But some of them were further along and some were going down the low road. Those you could tell because they were so thin it looked like the bones in their elbows would cut through the skin. They stank, too. Not that a nest has any facilities, but there are rivers and public baths in most places. Begging in front of a public bath you'll always get money to go in, too, unless the management decided to let you come in free, so there wasn't ever a reason not to bathe. Except on the low road it doesn't matter any more."

"Why?" Cargo asked, not sure it was appropriate in the conversation. He hoped he'd remember. Better, he hoped she'd remember and tell it to him sometime when he could really make sense of things.

"Oh," she responded. "The low road is choosing failure, so it isn't failure. It's actually the highest success, to say that one thing is no different than another, that being clean is no different than being dirty, and that being alive isn't any different than being dead. They were the best of us philosophically. Because we all die in the end, nothing else matters. At least, that's what I understood of the low road. The ones on it don't talk much, either, so I never got much more. I never accepted it totally, not emotionally, not physically. I couldn't stand being dirty, and I didn't like being hungry."

"I don't like it either," Cargo said. "Are you hungry? Do you want to go over there and get something to eat?" He pointed at the tables where Ghoster and Steel sat, where the smell of food came from.

He wasn't hungry at all, blues did that for some reason. No, he'd thought about when he was little and living in the back of the ofisa on Clay, two stops before Mawbry's. The citizens of Clay were stolid farmers, the kind who got agronomy degrees and didn't like Sister Mary's business at all. There was enough time there to be hungry before they were run off.

"No, I'm not hungry," Plato said. She leaned over the table toward him, and he could see the pink flush up her breast and throat under the thin blue scarf. She lowered her voice and began to whisper as if she were telling the most classified secret on Vanity. "I want to tell you about it. I never told anyone before. It isn't something you talk about, you know?"

He nodded. "It's the greens."

She shook her head violently, dislodging the hood. "No. It's not the greens. That just makes it easier." The pink deepened and reached her face. "It's that I want to tell you, Cargo. I don't know why I think you'd understand, or even if I do. Maybe I think it's a bargain, and you'll tell me something."

Cargo's eyes widened suddenly. "What do you want me to tell you about?"

Plato laughed. "You know, I know all about me. I've even given you plenty of information about me. And Stonewall, who doesn't know all about Stonewall and the family home on Earth and his how many times great granddaddy who fought with some general named Stonewall or something like that. And about how nobody outside of Charleston knows how to make a mint julep or barbecue."

She rolled her eyes, and Cargo broke out laughing. He laughed so hard that he nearly fell face first into the empty dish painted with red chrysanthemums and green dragons. They'd all heard Stonewall tell the stories so many times that Cargo thought even the Akhaid could tell them with exactly the right intonation and fervor. "He said once," Cargo said, wiping the tears from his eyes, "he said he was Chinese."

Plato nodded. "Yes, when he's nearly albino and even more colorless than me. Yes, I heard him."

They began to chant it together, just as they had heard Stonewall tell it before. "The citizens of Charleston are purely Chinese. They live behind high walls, they eat rice, and they worship their ancestors."

"So I know Stonewall and me," Plato continued. "And I knew something about Bugs, even. Scatter told me. She was from Clay, ran off and signed on a merchanter before she was of age. She learned something about Eyes when her ship was in a convoy and the escorts were shorthanded. Everybody had to learn. It turned out she had talent, so there she was. She was a good enough shot to get a field rec off the convoy ship, else she'd never be cleared for flight. And all that stuff about her uncle and all the rest of it is, as Stonewall would say, purely bullshit."

Cargo nodded with respect. He wondered how Plato had found out about Bugs. "Why did she lie anyway?" he asked. It was the kind of question he could ask, and it would be taken one way. The fact was, he was more interested from a professional angle. Any Gaje could lie, but most of them get caught. They weren't properly trained in the art.

Plato waved over the serving cart and picked up a second plate of greens. Cargo smiled and chose the pinks, which were arranged like flowers. Pinks and blues were good together, one of the mixes that didn't go wrong no matter how the analogues were compounded. Plato began to punch her id into the box but Cargo pushed her hand away lightly. "I said I'm buying," he reminded her.

She looked at him quizzically. "Why? You know, with anyone else we'd share rounds. You don't do that much, do you? That's what I mean. You're strange in some ways that I can't get a hold on."

Cargo smiled. "Among my people, in our tradition, a being is not wealthy because this person possesses anything. It's how much you spend that makes you rich, not how much you keep. I once met a millionaire. He didn't have anything at all, only one jacket with a torn lapel and no kite. But he'd spent a million in one year. He was a real big man, a Rom Baro. Everyone respected him. That's why."

Plato studied him while they ate the delicately shaped annies slowly.

"I don't know for a fact why Bugs lied," Plato said. "But I'll tell you what I guess, and I'm pretty sure I'm right. I think Bugs is uncomfortable with the fact that she doesn't have any degree to hang on her wall, and because she comes from borderline poverty."

"Clay's respectable," Cargo countered. The pinks mingled delicately with the blues in his system, and he enjoyed the heightened senses that went with the drug. "Besides, who cares? She's good at what she does. No one's going to hold it over her that she didn't study five years of quantum engineering."

Plato sighed. "I didn't study five years of quantum engineering, either."

With his enhanced perceptions, he realized that Plato smelled warm and tempting, like a hot spiced drink. He didn't want to talk about Bugs anymore. The words were just there to fill up empty space and there wasn't enough distance to matter. "Do you want dinner now?" he asked again.

"I'd rather go there." Plato gestured with her eyes to the red brick hotel.

"Before dinner? I was going to ask you after dinner. Isn't one supposed to indulge in the art of conversation first?"

Plato shook her head in disbelief. "What have we been doing here? What have we been doing for six weeks? I've been waiting for you to say something. I thought that was part of the reason we were coming here tonight in the first place. If I waited any longer I'd be dead asleep, and it would be time to report to the *Horn*."

"You mean you knew exactly what my plans were? Or not exactly. They did include a decent dinner."

Plato made a face. "I can see into the future and into the hearts of men. Cross my palm with silver, and I will tell all."

Cargo started. "That's my line."

Chapter

6

He awoke in the dark, and the first thing he noticed was the silence. The constant wind, howling and seeking out the smallest seal cracks in the celofab walls, was gone. He remembered where he was, and that Plato was with him, but it took longer to remember that because the complex was underground it was shielded from the ceaseless shrieking gale that had become the constant backdrop to his life.

Dim yellow light filtered through the sheer curtains, casting a warmer glow than Vanity's natural violets. His eyes adjusted to the gentle shadings. Plato's hair fell in sepia tendrils over her face. He brushed them aside carefully, pretending that he didn't want to wake her, but he was glad when her eyelids fluttered and she smiled slightly.

"What's your name?" he asked softly.

Her eyes opened slowly, and she stretched languidly against the warm sheets before she answered. "Beatrice," she said. "Beatrice Sunday."

"Yes," he said. "Appropriate.. Eyes to lead the damned from hell."

"I thought you'd studied engineering."

"Don't worry," Cargo replied. "Dante is one of my few major aberrations." He was inexplicably irritated. Talk was annoying—it only got in the way, only tangled things up more. Instead he leaned over and tasted her nipples again. Nicer without the annies, he decided. Definitely much nicer.

The plaza was still drenched in night when they left the hotel. Now the darkness was disconcerting in its insistence;

the yellow lights flickered feebly against the violet brilliance on the surface. The bars were still doing business, not quite as briskly, and the arcade occasionally erupted with game-generated squeaks and bangs.

At least there wasn't a wait for a table. After missing dinner last night, Cargo was ravenous. The menu glittered silver in the deep, translucent black of the tabletop. Time must be truly meaningless here, he thought. The selection ranged from dinner entrees to scrambled eggs and toast. He touched the coffee selector twice before ordering chicken. He hoped it wouldn't bother Plato until the serving cart appeared. Cargo tried not to gag as Plato nonchalantly took her plate of steak topped with Jalapeños.

"Good morning. Or should I say good afternoon? I thought you two would get hungry sometime, I just didn't know it would take so long." Stonewall had come up to their table and dragged over a chair.

"Excuse me," Cargo began, when Stonewall cut him off.

"We've got to get back to the Base as soon as possible. I mean a couple of hours ago would have been fine if I could have found the two of you at all." He stood up and seemed irritated that they didn't follow. "What are you waiting for?" he demanded.

"We're hungry," Plato said. "I'm not moving until I finish breakfast, if that's fine with you? I thought we had the whole day, anyway. What's the problem?"

Stonewall sat back down, exasperated. "I've got Glaze waiting over at the expensive annie bar, the one where they charge three times as much for the pretty shapes, and Steel and Ghoster are in the arcade. I rounded them all up nearly two hours ago and we're all ready."

"And Scatter?" Cargo asked.

Stonewall shook his head. "That's what I've been trying to tell you. That's how I know. Scatter went back to the Base last night, because of Bugs. You know that. I called him this morning to see how he was. You see, I figured you would be out of it for a while, so I could just borrow that old heap of a wagon you bought and run him back here. I truly thought you'd be pleased, since it would save you a nice mess on the parking price."

"You are not being informative," Plato said firmly. "You are not giving us any data. You are interrupting my breakfast."

"Well, I am sorry, Miss Plato." Stonewall's voice dripped with false sympathy. "I thought the background would be important. Given the circumstances, my Daddy would have been quite sure that the topic under consideration was not fit for the table. I think you ought to trust me and do likewise."

Chicken curry and rice were disappearing from Cargo's plate at a furious rate. Curiosity didn't quite overcome appetite at the moment, but it was a very close second. Not that Cargo trusted Stonewall. Stonewall had some reason of his own for pushing them no matter what had gone on. Only he did have to know.

Still, he felt a grudging admiration for the way Plato acted as if she weren't at all anxious for the news. Whatever news.

For a moment Cargo wondered if they'd been transferred and wouldn't be reporting to the *Horn* at all. He pushed the hope out of his mind. That kind of information was more than fit for the table, and the only thing Cargo did trust about Stonewall was the Charlestonian's impeccable manners. If Stonewall insisted that the only reason he did not tell them more was because it would violate the propriety of the meal, Cargo was certain that that was precisely the reason.

"You were a tad late," Stonewall said. "Don't you believe in joining the rest of the universe at a civilized hour?"

Plato raised an eyebrow along with her coffee cup. "It's not my problem if you didn't have a good time." The slight smile was provocative. "And if it had been a real emergency, you knew perfectly well how to reach us. Not that it mattered, since you have already told us you were prepared to—borrow—the wagon. Only in a case of necessity, I suppose."

"Naturally," Stonewall replied.

Cargo put his empty dish on the serving cart. Stonewall stood and reached over to take Plato's.

"Wait, wait," Plato said. "I'm not done yet. I'm getting dessert. I love pecan pie."

Stonewall glared down at her. "I can tell you now, I had that pecan pie last night and it is not worth a dead, rusty pie tin. My Aunty Hilda in Charleston would have died and turned over in her grave once more knowing that such a thing had been done in the name of authentic Earth Regional cuisine. On my honor, my authentic knowledge and my great Aunt Hilda's sacred rest, I ask you not to take that poor excuse for a fine old tradition."

Plato shook her head. "How can I resist that argument? How can I possibly say no to that?"

"You can't," Cargo said. "He won that one. True or not, he's got us beat."

Stonewall had already keyed his id into the serving unit and had begun to edge away. Cargo noticed Glaze already waiting on a bench near the fountain and Ghoster watching from the door of the arcade. He felt surrounded, as if they were all waiting to pounce on him. He and Plato followed doubletime until he stopped short by the bench.

"All right. What is it?" Cargo demanded.

Stonewall shook his head. "This is not the right place. This is not proper."

"Dammit, Stonewall, you can't drag us out and not tell us anything," Cargo exploded. Then he turned to Glaze, who had risen from the bench and was watching. "What is going on here?"

Glaze's ears flattened against his skull. "It is a shameful thing."

Ghoster and Steel had arrived and were waiting a little distance away, as if they didn't want to be associated with any of the goings-on.

"We're not going anywhere until you explain," Cargo said softly.

"Bugs committed suicide," Stonewall said at last. "I'm not sorry, I still think I did right, and I'm not sorry."

"Wait a minute," Plato interrupted. "If Bugs is dead, our hurrying back is pretty useless. A couple of hours one way or another doesn't matter anymore."

Stonewall glared at her. "It's not Bugs that I'm talking about. It's Scatter."

Plato looked confused. Cargo was. He wanted to ask Ghoster but wasn't sure it was proper. Glaze had seemed very upset, and Ghoster didn't look as though he was going to start talking in front of everyone. Not that Cargo could blame him, if they saw it so differently.

"I admit that I don't know anything about this," Cargo said. "Just one thing—yes or no. Does Scatter need us?"

There was a long hesitation. Finally it was Ghoster who spoke, which made sense. He was generally more verbal than Steel, and Glaze was downright taciturn. Scatter had always been the most extroverted Akhaid in their class.

"It could be important," Ghoster said carefully. "Maybe he will listen to someone. I can't be sure."

Cargo turned and led the way back to the lot without saying anything. He wanted the quiet to think. He didn't understand what the problem could be for Scatter; he thrust that from his mind. Right now he was just the driver. Probably one of the Akhaid, most likely Ghoster, would be the one who could help him if he needed it. And Cargo was sure that once the crisis had passed, whatever it was, Ghoster would tell him—privately and carefully, making sure to fill in all the background, the way Cargo always tried to explain things to him. That was the only way it worked, or else they could forget trying to communicate outside the maze at all. Some people chose that. But Cargo thought that trusting Ghoster was worth learning something about the Akhaid, even if he wasn't curious.

He thought about Bugs again. That was what had started this anyway, and it hadn't ever felt right. From what Plato had said, Bugs was no spy. A liar, perhaps, but not even particularly good at that.

Any Cardia agent who had gotten this far, who had managed to stay undetected in the batwing base for six weeks, wouldn't have blown it all on a stupid lie on the way into town, Cargo reasoned. What Bugs really had done was not exactly smart, but it would have been a billion times more idiotic for someone really under cover. There was no way in the known universe that she could have been responsible for sending out the code on the SN–1109. Add to that everything Plato had said, and there was a perfectly reasonable explanation—an elegant one, even. And one thing Cargo believed in fiercely was that the elegant answer was usually the right one. Nature is ultimately simple, human and Akhaid as well as otherwise.

He'd seen enough of it in the ofisa, in the clients who came in and begged to be told that they would become rich or fall happily in love. Usually both. They would pay huge amounts for worthless reassurances. So she had needed to make herself sound more competent, more educated than she was. He knew all about that. How many times as Rafael Mirabeau in school had he denied the Romany *chal* who hadn't even learned to read until he was fourteen? Bugs was another one like him, another little fraud. And they weren't looking for the little fraud but for the big one.

The wind whipped around them when they emerged from the Mid. The rich afternoon light stained the cheap slab pavement red lilac under their boots. The fresh air cutting through the grass smelled good, alive and wholesome, and the jutting boulders sparkled like jewels. Low on the horizon a shadow flickered and was gone, another batwing riding the high trails to dancing vac. Vanity was hard and bare and windy, but it was beautiful. It was alive.

Cargo didn't even look at the parking charge when he finally got the windwagon, convinced that if it didn't move it would be turned over to a salvager only after torture and mutilation. The thing rattled in protest. Cargo tried the code for a third time. His face gave away nothing, but he slammed his open palm against the control panel. The wagon jumped to command and its treads dug smoothly into the loam.

They rode to the Base in silence. When they arrived the parking court was deserted. The Akhaid left, most likely to find Scatter, Cargo figured. That, and to leave the humans to react to the death as they would. Grief was something both species shared, but suicide was something different. He didn't know what the Akhaid thought, or even if they had several different ideas. Right now that wasn't important. Scatter's own attitude was the only one that mattered.

He turned to Stonewall and asked how Bugs had done it.

"Jumped," Stonewall said.

"Wasn't she in custody?" Plato asked as they walked aimlessly back toward quarters, or maybe the lounge.

Stonewall nodded. "The bridgewalk."

Cargo said nothing at all. He listened to them and realized that they had become accustomed to talking over the ever-present wind. Part of him was blank, empty; another part filled with rage that he fought to suppress.

Jumped. Why did she have to jump? Why couldn't she have hung herself in her cell, the way they were supposed to? Or maybe the guard would have left a pencil and she could have pierced the cartoid. Easy enough.

"Stolie's?" Plato asked. "I think I want to get very old-fashioned drunk."

Stonewall shook his head. "Everyone'll be down there,

asking questions. I've got some hootch. You're both welcome to join me."

Plato stepped over to him. "Cargo?"

He shook his head. He didn't want to talk. "I want to walk. I'll see you later."

Cargo refused to look at the two of them. He was frightened in a way that he hadn't known how to be frightened before. He didn't know what Plato had meant; it had been a long time since he had made love to an equal. And he knew he was going to want to see her again tonight.

But now he needed to be alone. If Plato went off and chose Stonewall there was nothing he could do to stop her. He only hoped she wouldn't.

He was glad the base was wide and undeveloped, that the wind was hard in his face and the grass tangled around his ankles, so he had to fight at every step. He needed something to fight, something for the fury. And the whine of the gale drowned out his words when he screamed himself hoarse.

He'd gotten the news from the Bishop that day and the transport couldn't move fast enough. School had been good enough already. Angel had passed a test for the first time that semester, Rafael himself had made the honor society, and best of all Yojo hadn't seen that bastard Tol Farland and thus hadn't had to make good on his threat to cut his right hand into ribbons. Yojo had a big mouth, but Farland deserved it. He had actually kicked Yojo in the schoolyard the day before, which was the final action none of them could tolerate. Some things were sacred. So Rafael believed.

Still, it was Gaje who fought and hurt and killed, not Rom. The Rom loved dancing and drinking and loving and stealing and lying, but not killing. That was a Gaje vice.

They had not told the Bishop about Farland, which was as well because he would have forbidden Yojo to defend his honor. And not one of them would dare defy the Bishop, who was more like an angel to them than a man. After all, if it hadn't been for the Bishop, Rafael knew he would never have learned to read, to make the holotapes that had brought so much business, and even given him hopes of a university career.

The others hoped too, he knew; the Bishop had encouraged all of them. But it was Rafael who was permitted to use the

Mirabeau family name, Rafael that the Bishop wanted to see every Thursday afternoon. And so, this being a Thursday, Rafael had left the others and taken a public chute out to the Cathedral. It only took half an hour, and there were always good things to eat at the end of the journey.

That day, that very wonderful day, he arrived on time. Usually he let himself into the back study and waited until the Bishop was ready. There were books in the back study, real paper ones bound with cloth and leather and glue. They smelled of richness, of greatness, and Rafael loved to touch and hold and smell them. He read them, too, but very carefully, always using the velvet-lined stand to preserve the decaying pages. Much as he loved the books, he felt more comfortable reading in front of a screen. He couldn't destroy something of immense value that way.

This Thursday the Bishop was already waiting in the back study. The polished tulipwood reading table held a tray heavy with glasses, a bottle, thick slices of cheese and sausage and a whole loaf of bread, and a smaller tray filled with the Bishop's favorite cream puffs. Rafael knew something special had happened. While he didn't love cream puffs, the Bishop did and always served them when there was something to celebrate. The last time had been Rafael's Church marriage to Sonfranka, which had happened in this study.

Not that Sonfranka had wanted the ceremony or the sacrament. A Romany wedding was the only one she believed counted, and that had happened months before. Rafael had agreed with her, but he also knew the Bishop thought it was important. The Bishop hadn't liked the idea very much anyway. He didn't think children should get married, he said. Rafael and Sonfranka had been shocked. They were fifteen and according to Romany tradition that was exactly the right age. So he had relented and the thing had been done.

Rafael had no idea of what it could be this time. He knelt and kissed the Bishop's ring, and then stood straight and silent until the Bishop invited him to eat some of the cheese and sausage.

"How is your mother?" the Bishop always asked. "And how are the others, Angel and Yojo, how are they getting along? And Sonfranka, how is she?"

The Bishop had always asked these questions, but this Thursday he did not. Nor did he invite Rafael to help himself

to the food. Instead he poured two glasses of champagne—
excellent champagne, very dry, out of his private stock. It was
the same as they had drunk at the wedding, and Rafael liked it
better than the cheap whiskey Yojo's father had given them
once.

The Bishop handed over the glass and held his own in the
air. His face shone like polished obsidian, brilliantly alive
with pleasure. "To you," he toasted Rafael. "To the first of my
boys assured of the university." Then he hung his head.
"Maybe the only one. Well, we can only pray for each of you
one at a time, and accept whatever the Lord delivers."

Rafael started and then froze. He wasn't sure he understood exactly what the Bishop meant. Did he mean that the
school had recommended him for the Faculty of Mathematics
at the Delhi-Cygna Institute? Or that he had passed the bac in
probability? He dared not hope that the deferment had already
been approved.

"But what about the war?" he asked hesitantly.

The Bishop looked almost disappointed. "Rafael," he
began softly. "That is exactly what we are celebrating. The
Division on Probability in the Faculty of Mathematics has already accepted you and your deferment has been issued. I
received the papers yesterday."

"Why?" he asked. He must have been thinking aloud.

The Bishop ignored the good, hearty food in front of them.
Instead he poured more champagne into Rafael's glass and
served him two cream puffs. Then the old man sat down in an
overstuffed chair upholstered in real leather before Rafael took
his usual chair near the table.

"Because," the Bishop said, wiping his fingers after his
first pastry, "you have a gift. I have told you this many times,
and you don't listen. Maybe we should take you and get your
hearing tested, do you think? You have a gift that is very
useful to the service of God and of knowledge, but that
doesn't mean that it isn't also very useful to the Ministry of
Security as well. Reliability testing is important defense work,
too. What I understand from the papers is that you are only
deferred, not exempted, and you will go in as an officer-spe-
cialist. That is to be preferred."

Suddenly Rafael felt very light-headed, and he didn't think
it was all the champagne. "I'm very lucky," he had said.

"Have another cream puff. They won't keep very well. The

pastry gets dry or soggy, depending on where it is. Then we'll go to the chapel and say our thank-you's and then you can tell me about school and your family and the other boys."

Rafael tried to talk to the Bishop, but they were both too excited. They finished the bottle of champagne instead. Then Rafael asked to use the Bishop's link and he called Sonfranka.

He told her about the deferment and his acceptance with so much enthusiasm that he didn't wonder about her lack of conversation. That was to be expected. She was as thrilled, as astounded, as he was. His words to her were the first coherent thing he had said since the Bishop had told him, and he believed that the champagne had made it much easier. It relaxed him so that he could handle the excitement.

He didn't ask to speak to his mother. She was with a client and couldn't be disturbed. His younger brother and sister were out, Sonfranka told him, his brother giving out flyers that read *Sister Mary, a holy woman with knowledge of the Spiritual Angels, reads and advises on all questions. Ask about Love, Business, Family Relationships. Sister Mary can help You.* He had written the flyer a few months ago—it was better than the one they had had before, the one the Gaje Chang Hua had written. Now he was working on one for Sonfranka, whose professional name was Little Anne, Daughter of the Oracle. His sister was out selling flowers "to help the refugee children from Pierson's End" in front of Mawbry's best hotel.

Sonfranka congratulated him. He assumed the lack of enthusiasm in her face was that it hadn't hit her yet, not really. It hadn't quite hit him yet, either, and he'd talked to the Bishop about nothing else for an hour. He promised to bring a cream puff home for her and shut down the link. Then he returned to the back study and said his goodbyes.

The Bishop didn't want him to leave just yet, wanted to enjoy their triumph together as long as possible. So Rafael sat and they opened another bottle of champagne. He ate all of the cheese and most of the sausage. The Bishop wanted him to stay for dinner and he was tempted, but he had promised Angel and Yojo that he would meet them later and tell them what happened, the way they met every Thursday night. The Bishop didn't know about that part.

Not that the others were jealous. They didn't like school quite as much as Rafael, and Angel thought going to school was close to doing time in the detention center. Only this way at least they were free at night and the parole office didn't keep them locked in. That had been the worst for Angel: the locks on the doors, with bars like cages. Years before when they were in juvie, all three thought they were going to die behind the locks, because of the locks. And Angel didn't know about the cling net at night and the terror that was in him. Raphael prayed Angel would never know, or his cousin would tell the *kris*. He would be disgraced and never married and maybe not even permitted to travel. Anything was worth the price to remain free.

The Bishop said he didn't mind Rafael leaving. He would be back next Thursday at the very latest, and maybe they would decide on a night to go to Ambrouisine's, Rafael's favorite restaurant. So, happy, and very very drunk, Rafael got on the chute in the direction of Column Toomie.

Underneath and overhead were lost in a gray-green mottled blur. The chute rode near the center, and above him Rafael could see other chutes from other hemis, all of them keeping their own orientation. Almost directly to his right he could see the stadiat rising on the gentle curve of the inner structure. The stadiat was the one landmark he could recognize from anyplace in Mawbry's, even from the far diaphragm docks. The stadiat glistened white and faintly rose in the shadows, its overarched pennants stretched on stiffened mesh just a play of color from this distance. Then his car dipped slightly and began the descent for the Column Toomie station, swerving down and slipping smoothly into the platform lock.

The platform itself was an open mesh cage. None of the carefully tiled and layer-stained design walls that decorated the Place de Roland and Cathedral stations. Here the decorations were all the work of amateurs using illegal burn boxes. It was hard to read any writing or pattern in the loose metal weave, so the patterns were abstract series of shadings, a good bit of it deep purple and midrange violet. The gangs used the cages to practice their burn technique, and some had overdone it long since. Not that that mattered. It didn't damage the usefulness of the platform, and that was all the authorities cared about. So every year the Column Toomie station got darker and darker. Some day Rafael was sure it would look like Spin Street, every centimeter of strut and support burned a deep glowing black-purple. Maybe by then they would leave. They'd been on Mawbry's a long time anyway, and he would be leaving for Dehli-Cygna in another year. Maybe they would pack up the ofisa and set up again planetside, a good distance from the university. University districts were notably bad places for business.

The thought of moving excited him. They had stayed here too long already. If it hadn't been for the Bishop and his parole, they would have left long ago, gone perhaps to the Collegium itself, or maybe out toward Mindanar or Nwenge. There were several kumpanias out that way, Tshurara and Lowara as well. Not that Rafael or any of the Tshurara particularly liked the rather too gentle and traditional Lowara, but they were famous for good musicians and parties, and it had been a long time.

He missed the Gitanos. Since his father's death, his mother had stayed clear of them. Dangerous, she had said, and she was right. But Rafael loved their music, the flamenco that was pure and raw and without the Gaje restraints. He had his father's guitar, remembered the man playing it when he wasn't drunk or angry. Rafael kept the guitar but had never learned to play. His mother wouldn't permit that music in the house, and it was her house. It was her money and her business as well, just as it would be Sonfranka's one day. And Rafael knew that Sonfranka disliked the Gitano music even more than his mother did, distrusting the Gitano strain in him, fearing that he had his father's violence.

There was no way he could make her understand that it wasn't violence at all, but undirected rage. And there was no rage in Rafael. Learning had channeled his energy, something forbidden that was addictive and finally necessary beyond the family and love and living. It was something that horrified Sonfranka. Gaje learning was not for the Rom. This she had been taught, and this she believed with her full heart. Rafael could not make her see why he had to follow this thing like the love of God Himself.

These were the things Rafael thought about as he walked the seven blocks from the station. He did not think about the kite he wanted to buy so he wouldn't have to walk. He could see it wheeling above him now, the iridescent colors of the kite wings. Soon he would be at Delhi-Cygna, which was a real planet, and a kit would be useless there.

When he arrived at the block there was a crowd on the downway under the pedforms—right in front of his building, he saw, right under the windows. He looked up, wondering where his mother was, if she was watching from above. The window was open and the long fringe of the heavy red curtain in the front room hung over the sill as if it had been pulled or torn.

The crowd let him pass. They were people he knew, merchants and neighbors as well as shoppers that frequented this street. The fact that they said nothing to him and looked the other way, moving aside to give him room, chilled him. Just as the police sirens blared their arrival, he saw.

Sonfranka lay splattered and broken on the downway. Her thick hair had fallen forward and decently shrouded her face from view.

"Sonfranka?" Rafael said gently, wondering why she wasn't breathing, wasn't trying to get up from the cluttered pavement. It wasn't so far, only two stories. No one died if they fell two stories, he had heard. He didn't know why she wasn't moving. He reached out and touched her arm and the flesh was warm.

The police came over and took her away. "Are you next of kin?" an officer asked him.

Rafael nodded. "Brother," he said, although it was a lie. The police wouldn't like the idea that she was his wife. They were too young, that was a thing only the Rom would understand now. When they were older, his mother had promised. Only Sonfranka would never get any older.

The police took him along in a separate carry. He felt strangely abstract, as if it hadn't happened, as if this whole farce would be over and then Sonfranka would get up from the morgue and laugh and tell him it was a good way to fool the Gaje. He had seen her and touched her, and he still didn't believe that she was dead.

The police questioned him. They questioned other people on the block, in the building. Rafael insisted to himself that she had been pushed and was angry. He told himself she might have fallen. The way the drapes were hanging, dragged out the window—she had tried to hold on, he thought. It was no good. Everyone else knew that she had killed herself. Even the Bishop had a hard time deciding on how he could bury her, although it was common practice in these cases to acknowledge that a suicide was by definition insane and therefore not responsible for their actions. The Bishop was realist enough to know it wasn't always true, but compassionate enough to admit that he could never be sure in any one case exactly what happened. So he ruled that Sonfranka had been insane and could be buried from the Church.

The night before the funeral was the only time Rafael ever cried. Sonfranka's brothers would arrive the next morning and that would start a whole new phase of existence. He was no longer free. No, Rafael thought, he wasn't sure he could ever say he really loved Sonfranka. He had never met her before they married, although his mother had paid out over ten-thousand marqurad along with the dress and the party and all. Everyone said they would learn to love each other, and maybe that would have happened. Rafael could not make himself believe that there had even been a beginning.

He had never loved her, and later on when her brothers came and brought him before the *kris*, he began to hate her. But on that one night sitting alone with her as she lay in the fancy coffin, Rafael had truly and passionately mourned her death and the manner of it. And until he met Beatrice Sunday he had never taken the chance of loving an equal again.

When Cargo returned after his walk, it had grown dark. He had missed whatever dinner had been served on Base, and as it was not Thursday there was nothing at all available at Stolie's. Which meant that he could go hungry or eat some excuse for food at the snack bar. He chose the snack bar, managed to swallow the sandwich before noticing much of the taste, and returned to quarters. He was pleased he could eat. Usually, after remembering Sonfranka's death, he couldn't. Maybe some of the hate was wearing away; maybe someday he would be able to recall events with only a tinge of sorrow.

Now, though, the wind and the grass, the hard walking and the cold had leeched feeling from him. The corridor was dark. He hadn't thought it was late. Or maybe the generator had gone out again. That didn't make sense. For a planet whose highest evolved form of life was grass, there were a lot of bugs in the system.

He opened the door to his room, which was less dark than the hallway. Natural light filtered in through the unclosed shade. It didn't look exactly the way he had left it, but he was uncertain how it was different.

There was movement in the corner that caught his eye.

Slowly the shadows resolved into shapes, and one became a two-legged being, though he couldn't tell if it was human or Akhaid. The visitor said nothing but came closer, stocking feet curving gently against the floor. The only sound was the relentless wind.

He could not make out her face, but the warm spicy scent of her filled the space between them. "You're here," he whispered, not quite sure of his luck, wondering if it could be someone else with her perfume and shape.

Plato stepped out in front of him, arms open and inviting. He folded her to him and, for this night again at least, laid the *mule* of Sonfranka to rest.

Chapter

7

The *Horn* looked like any ship of her class. The bulkheads had been blasted electric blue and the doors were a combination of pinks and yellows. The hangar decks were clustered around the hull, and the smallest was the private property of the batwing battle group aboard. This was not discrimination; they were informed. The batwing group carried fewer craft and could fit comfortably in the smaller space. Unless they preferred to be mixed in with the regular squadrons?

They demurred. Cargo thought back to when he was part of one of those squadrons—they would have been displeased with a black interloper in the Krait cradle. Now he was just as glad to be out of it, to have the space. Besides, security would throw tantrums if the heavily classified and shielded Black Beauties were on public display in an X-hangar on a Spica class carrier.

"We say yes to that and the Fourth Directorate's gonna have us all on truth and water," Stonewall observed casually.

Their quarters were assigned the same way, all in the same section on the same corridor. With four doubles to the six, assignments were very comfortable.

"Although I do think," Stonewall said, "that instead of me taking the single, we should let Plato have it."

"Jealous?" Cargo asked.

Stonewall shrugged. "Can't blame me for trying."

"Think of it this way," Plato interrupted. "This is a very big carrier. You meet anyone you like, no roommate problems. Right?"

"Or you could room with Glaze and then we'd have two empties," Steel said.

"Are you out of your mind? You let the quartermaster get wind of that and the next thing you know they decide that we don't need any four rooms at all ever for the rest of the existence of the manifold. It doesn't matter if you need it or not, if you let someone know you're not using it right now you can't ever get it back again. And we might get another team," Stonewall argued vehemently.

They all fell silent. Scatter had left. Cargo didn't know where, and Ghoster hadn't come and told him. He wanted to ask, but it wasn't the kind of thing they could discuss in front of the whole group. Even if everyone else was as involved as they were. There just hadn't been a chance, not since they had reported to the shuttle up before there was more than last night's coffee in the cafeteria. At least there was always coffee.

After Vanity, the narrow corridors on the ship were confining; the tinier rooms were more cramped than hours in a Krait. Cargo had barely finished stowing his gear when the signal chime on the message unit buzzed. Plato cursed and got it. After a few moments Cargo heard a curious humming in the corner.

"Briefing in Security Command, ten minutes, classified code Mirror," Plato said softly. "I thought we had our briefing before we left," she added with curiosity.

"That's what I thought," Cargo agreed. "Do you think we might have a new teammate? There were four batwings in the hangar bay."

Plato shrugged. "There's only one way to find out."

"Ask Stonewall," Cargo said, grinning. Plato joined him with a brief laugh before they lapsed into silence again. Speculation was profitless. In ten minutes they would know exactly what they needed anyway. There was something to be said for the way the Second Directorate handled matters, Cargo reflected. They were fast. They didn't keep anyone waiting longer than necessary—not for an assignment, not for a briefing, not for anything. That at least was an improvement.

"Your stuff is all secured?" Cargo asked. From Plato's look he knew he shouldn't have.

They left the cubicle that was properly referred to as a stateroom and made their way through more than half the

length of the *Horn* before reaching the Security office. Spica
class was old, Cargo reflected, and the *Horn* was one of the
originals. It showed. The Security office was just forward of
the tracking lasers, an old-style layout that used the constant
hum from EW as noise masking. The layers of black filament
had been added over the original structure, not built into a
deadspace between the bulkheads. The effect was that the
small, crowded area appeared even smaller and more tightly
packed. The viewtable wasn't mazed, so no necklaces dangled
from hooks around the steel edge, which was the only missing
clutter. Otherwise the place was heaped with yellow and green
flim. Pages of it spilled over the entire table so that the plasma
screen was completely covered, and even the seats of several
chairs had been used to catch heaps of documents.

Cargo reached over and looked at the pile on a blue molded
chair. The first sheet dealt with Cardia fighter craft; the page
after that was yellow and contained weeks-old specs on the
weather on Noda. The next three in the pile were half-finished
crossword puzzles torn out of an ethnic-language newsflim
run. Greek or Russian, Cargo decided, but he wasn't sure
which.

He deposited the stack of flimsies on the floor before he sat
down. Plato had already cleared the pile hiding her section of
the viewscreen and was starting on another when Ghoster arrived. By the time they were all present and seated, the floor
was ankle-deep in several varieties of printout, but at least the
seats and table had emerged.

"This is disagreeable," Steel said to no one in particular. "I
don't see why they couldn't wait until we were out manifold."

"Couldn't agree more," Stonewall said.

Cargo agreed privately, but kept quiet. Interesting that it
came from Steel. He'd never thought that Bugs had delivered
those specs, anyway. But someone had, and he'd always
thought Stonewall wasn't exactly what he appeared. It would
make sense to put together a team to accomplish the task, and
that Steel was Stonewall's confederate in whatever job of
work they were about. Cargo wouldn't have put money on it
being completely innocent.

Without preamble, Fourways arrived and looked them
over. "This briefing was called early because I wanted you to
know exactly why you're here. This looks like a gum run
from the outside and we speculated whether to send a bunch

of novos out on this at all. You might have had some faith that
we weren't about to waste our investment, if nothing else."

Cargo blinked. It was going too fast. And there was something wrong, something that didn't fit at all, but he couldn't
place it.

A snort came from some undefined part of the table. Even
the species of the scorner was in question; it was exactly the
sound either would make given the right circumstances. Fourways froze, looked each of them full in the face as if measur-
ing, and then dismissed the lot.

"As I said," he began again, "there is more here than General Rumint could report outside the classified dining room.
Our task here is not simply keeping a lookout for possible
constellations. Two new factors have entered the picture. The
first is our VIP. I don't even have data on that yet. Second,
there's a batwing out here, reported snooping near the Collegium and in the inner worlds. We found out about it when
Collegium Base called to confirm it friendly."

"Excuse me, sir," Glaze said, "but didn't you tell us four
weeks ago that Cardia snoopers don't work independently,
that they are invariably part of a battle group and are involved
in active direction?"

Fourways' expression did not change. "Yes. I did say that.
I might have been wrong. Or the Cardia might be up to something a little dirtier and more audacious than we'd expected.
Or maybe not. The point is, the past four inner world convoys
have all reported seeing something they classified as a batwing
and it wasn't ours. It's been catalogued as a mirage. No readings off it, just a shadow passing by for the ones who've seen
it at all."

Cargo smiled slowly and tried not to lick his lips. He could
almost taste the mirage, a thing that might only be fantasy like
the monsters that hid under the bed when he was four or the
muggers breaking in down the airshaft when he was eleven.
Or it might be real, the leading edge of the enemy batwing, a
prototype that was in third-stage testing realtime, passing
through the minefields and sentries that cordoned off the inner
worlds from the battle zones. So far the inner worlds, including Mawbry's in its orbit around the Collegium, had been
safe.

Might be, or might not be. This was something intriguing,
something tempting. Cargo knew he was being pulled in—

that Fourways was playing some kind of game and he was in the middle of it. Maybe because Fourways had played it before. Still, there were anomolies that echoed strangely through his inner logic, things he didn't consciously notice that made him uneasy all the same.

If he had believed at all in luck or gambling, Cargo would have walked. All his intuition and his half-ignored, submerged reactions were screaming at him to hit the deck, duck, check the down and sixes. Only reason held him, and he sat and turned the logic on and sat hard on the fight-or-flight that threatened to dominate him. Keeping the lid on felt good. He hadn't lost the clean, iced edge that made his reactions so accurate that even he was startled at times. But he hadn't lost the control, either, the rational process that was almost too acute outside the functions of the maze.

His skill, his gift, came from the tension between the two. Cargo knew it and ignored it, because to examine a gift too closely was to offend the giver and risk having it taken back. The balance between reason and terror was so delicate that even a glimpse of it might weigh one end or the other.

That was why people hit the Wall, he knew. The knowledge chilled him slightly in the temperature-controlled environment. One end won. The balance got worn in all of them, and eventually it slipped one way or the other, and then it was time to live on the Wall.

In front of him, the table had awakened from its dull gray. Now the Collegium and seven of the inner systems followed their placid orbits in its depths. Points had been marked in brilliant green forming a trail from the MM109 octant in the general direction of the Collegium.

"Sighting data on the mirage," Fourways said in monotone.

"So that's why we're playing ferry to wonderland," Stonewall said, unpleasant humor crinkling his eyes. "Doing a little sight-seeing on the way, I guess."

Fourways cleared his throat, and Stonewall had the good sense to shut up. "The Sixth Directorate has been working on descriptions given in the sighting data we have so far, which may or may not be accurate. The mirage is masked with interns as well as absorbs, so all data are under serious distort. Still, the Sixth Directorate believe that it masses under fifty tonnes at zero velocity, runs blue-blue near max and may carry up to eight Eyes."

"Sounds like the batwing's mirror twin," Plato muttered under her breath.

Cargo nodded almost imperceptibly. He had had to resist the urge to comment on that fact as well. "Can it go out manifold?" he asked casually.

Fourways shook his head. "We don't know. It masses a little on the small end, especially if they're carrying all the listening devices that we're carrying, but we just don't know."

Cargo blinked. He'd taken a look at the carrier's manifold drive exactly once, and it didn't look as though a craft the size of a batwing could carry it—but he didn't know exactly what was essential and what wasn't to hook into the oscillation through the Other Six dimensions. The math didn't bother him, and he never cared much as long as it worked. Now he wished he'd paid more attention.

Out manifold runs had been done in fifty-tonne craft twice, before there was any thought of a war, first by Amalie St. Juste in Kiss to collect the prize purse offered jointly by the Nakamura family and the Lodz industrial group. Kiss was a Lodz original racer, the only one of its class, and the ploy had been successful. Lodz stock had risen—sales were up fifteen percent—and the Nakamura Fumiko was appointed to chair the Industrial Development Commission. Commander St. Juste had invested heavily in speculative heavy mineral rights and died broke. No one remembered the second time at all, which was why there was no third. The Akhaid, who had been the ones to work out the principals of the linked-drive piercing through the out manifold dimensions by connecting with string wave as they oscillated through the ten, ignored the whole affair.

"So to sum up, we have anything between a full-fledged interstellar batwing to a ghost," Fourways said in a final tone. "Our job is to find it and neutralize it. Are there any questions?" The look on his face said that there had better not be.

"Excuse me, sir," Stonewall began after a decent silence. "But we're short a team. I'd guess this was a job for at least a full working unit."

Cargo was glad Stonewall asked. He wouldn't have wanted to call down the silence and icy look Stonewall received from his superior. Fourways didn't answer, and in the hush that followed, Cargo understood what his presence meant.

He'd known there was something wrong with Fourways being aboard outbound. Now he wished for almost anything else. Fourways had been bad enough on Vanity. To accept him as a member of their team was nearly unthinkable. From the lightly veiled shock and horror reflected around the table, Cargo knew he was not alone.

"I will see you when we reconvene for orientation and patrol coordination," Fourways said, then turned and left as if they were still in training on Vanity.

"Damn," Stonewall breathed into the sound-absorbing black filament.

"Well, at least he didn't take our singles," Glaze said. Steel and Ghoster laughed. Plato rolled her eyes.

"We've got half an hour till we leave the manifold and I don't want to spend it sitting around bitching," she said.

"Anyone for a game of khandinar?" Cargo asked personably.

"Why didn't they wait until we were out?" Plato asked for the third time.

Cargo closed his eyes and tried not to feel the soft restraint webbing that clung to his skin like warm, sticky velvet, ready to fasten itself rigid to any surface in case the skin resisted. *Skin of timespace*, Cargo thought, and the image made no sense to him. He rather thought of it as slipping through a net, like the restraint around him; finding the right aperture and aiming down its tunneled throat.

The webbing that made him feel like spider chow was almost never necessary. He'd never been on a cruise that hit one of the "dimples." He'd always gone through easy as water and had not worn the hated safety restraint the last three times. He hadn't intended to wear it this time either, only Plato had insisted. It had been easier to go along than get put on report at the time, but now he had a few doubts. The very softness of the clinging web made him breathe deeper, as if the breathing was going to get very difficult, as if the web itself would pull tighter and tighter and cut off all the air. He could feel it pressing in on him about his nose and throat. Waves of panic secured him in the lightly padded depression that served as a bed but now made him think of a coffin. The panic was no less real because it was irrational. He was more terrified of the clinging net than he had ever been of combat.

"That was the first thing we ever heard on Vanity, remember?" she went on. "Out manifold is secure. Nice tight blackout. So why didn't he wait? That seems very suspicious to me. And then, how come Fourways is here at all? Honestly. Do you think he'd pick a unit this green? On his own? Just to do it? Cargo? Are you all right? What do you think?"

"Sure. No problem," Cargo managed to say. He was aware of Plato shooting a quizzical glance before he turned toward the bulkhead. *Concentrate on the colors*, he told himself sternly. *Try to find the line where the green becomes yellow. Stand up straight, stand up straight*, he chanted to himself like a mantra.

He heard his own voice, and then the voice of the Bishop echoing his own. *The animal has reason to panic*, the Bishop had said firmly the last time he was so scared he couldn't breathe. *You are not an animal. You are a being of light and thought and in the image of God. The image of God should stand up straight.* He couldn't deny the Bishop. He had tried to stand up while the old man tugged at the sleeve of his jacket and adjusted his armband. It wasn't until they faced the court—together, as the Bishop had promised—that he could feel the clingweb creeping over his face, holding him down, and then the soft and persistent pressure of a hand, a sheet, the smell of flesh.

When the all-clear rang after another uneventful pass into the honeycomb configuration of the universe, Cargo was sweating. He tore the restraint from his face so sharply that it went rigid and pulled a thin strip of flesh with it. Cargo wiped blood away with the back of his hand. The rest of it, diluted with perspiration, stained the white lining of his collar pale rust.

"You want to tell me about it?" Plato asked kindly.

"No." He knew he'd been too brusque, but some things were sacred. Only the Bishop and Ghoster knew about his fear of the nets. Ghoster had seen him like this before, and at the moment Cargo missed the way his partner always pretended that there was nothing wrong. Perhaps to Ghoster there wasn't.

"How long?" he asked absently. It was something he should have known before they'd gone in, and probably had.

"Fifteen days subjective."

Cargo groaned. Now all there was was the paperwork. Funny how they prepared you for everything else, for all the emergencies and contingencies, for all the various contortions of victory or defeat or the thing that was neither. All those things he knew, had studied and then lived over and over again until they settled down and did their job like family. Until then there were all the little administrative duties he secretly believed had been invented to fill up the waiting time.

This time out he had the unenvied position of sortie officer, which was a fancy way of saying head clerk in the group sortie office. The four enlisted ratings did most of the day-to-day filing of forms, but he'd have to sign off on everything that applied to the batwing group. At least it beat Plato's paper job. She'd pulled the schedule board, which meant keeping all listings up to date and tracking down anyone who didn't catch changes on their own.

He hated manifold time. Mostly, Cargo told himself, because he hated the unrelenting forms and flims that had to be filled out in fifteen copies and zoxed and sent twenty-million places. It bored him to distraction. But it was better than sitting around with too much time on his hands to think about the people who were running the *Horn*. He could never figure out why anyone would want to fly a carrier, and he had to trust that they knew what they were doing.

Cargo didn't like trusting, didn't like someone else being in control. It was unnatural. So the waiting was a disease that was to be avoided, and once contracted to be lived through, endured. There was always khandinar.

On their second day in manifold, Cargo signed off in the sortie clerks' office and found Plato working at the tiny terminal in the stateroom. He'd thought about trying to get up a game of khandinar in the ready room, and decided to flop on the bed and wait for Plato to finish her current update.

"You know," he said lazily, "if we didn't do any of this, it wouldn't matter. Once we get back into our universe we won't see a form or a flim for months. So a couple of hours now won't matter."

"Omygod," Plato gasped. Cargo wheeled around to see her grasping both sides of the board with white knuckles, her jaw open and tendons standing out on the sides of her neck. It only took one step to get to her, to put a hand on her shoulder and try to reassure her. When she turned to him there was a strange mix of anticipation and comprehension in her face.

"I've got it," she said slowly. "Pure Godint. Only sit down and let me tell it a little at a time."

Cargo obeyed and sat in the sleeping depression in the middle of the floor.

Plato took a deep breath. "When I was in school on Paragon, they always said that you had to line up all your facts. If you didn't have enough facts then you couldn't say anything at all. Once you had data, you had to remain open to the simplest analysis. The universe is essentially elegant. The simplest explanation, the most elegant equation is most often going to be right. The problem is we aren't very good at seeing what's simple. At least I'm not. It's easier to make up a long and convoluted explanation of something than to see the obvious."

"So what's so obvious we're not seeing it?" Cargo asked lightly. He wasn't so much interested in her interpretation of recent events as he was involved in the logic puzzle. If khandinar got dull, which was unlikely, they could spend forever analyzing Fourways.

Plato smiled triumphantly. "Fourways is looking for a spy. We knew that. We thought it was Bugs. With Bugs and Scatter gone, well, it's a whole lot easier for us to trust each other. Now, let's surmise that Bugs and Scatter were both totally innocent. The spy he's trying to catch is here. It's one of us. So along comes Fourways, not to join our unit but to watch us. So he briefs us on something that may or may not exist before we go out, to give the spy time to get off a message. So he can trace it."

Cargo whistled through his teeth. "You're right. It is obvious. The only problem is, who don't we trust? I mean, I trust you and I trust Ghoster and I trust me."

"Add Glaze to that," Plato said automatically.

"So it's got to be Stonewall and Steel, either together or separately," Cargo finished off quickly.

Plato closed her eyes and leaned back against the wall. "Not so fast. What about Fourways? Besides, why should we even trust each other?"

Cargo threw up his hands in frustration. "I guess we can trust each other because if a transmission was sent between the briefing and when we went out, it wasn't either of us who did it. I didn't see you get near any communications devices at all. Not one. Never. Look, why don't we forget all about this stuff and play cards? It's all Fourth Directorate anyway. How about a couple of hands of khandinar?"

Plato groaned.

They were playing four-deck khandinar, which wasn't too challenging but could be put down any time. Cargo held four three of spades, which according to his system meant or two rounds. Even if it was only four-deck.

They were playing a humans-only game. Cargo didn t have any preferences, but it bothered him that the first thing Ghoster did at any new post was to warn all his species about Cargo's particular abilities. Some beings would play with him a second time to make sure the first hadn't just been luck. Often a third was not forthcoming and a fourth unthinkable. The only way he'd gotten his current opponents was the pledge to play for points. Already he was well enough known on the *Horn* that no one would sit down with him for money.

Plato and Stonewall were in the game, Plato because she was trying to uncover Cargo's system and Stonewall because, as he had said, he had never been beaten so consistently by anyone. It was a point of honor. Cargo had tried to rope Ghoster in, but he had demurred on the grounds that it was boring to always lose, so instead they had one of the engineering officers. She had already lost more than once to Cargo's ceaseless gaming during the fifteen days out manifold and the two uneventful days since, and the only things that persuaded her to join them were the fact that no money need be risked and the chance to see the inside of the batwing hangar. As usual, the Krait drivers on the *Horn* had been less interested in the batwing than the engineers, who found the parameters of stealth more fascinating than the actual working capabilities of the small craft themselves.

"Seven-seven, seven-nine, up by double, calling spades," Stonewall droned.

Cargo's face remained impassive. It could go either way for him, even with his quad. "Open second round," he said quietly. "Seven-nine, nine-three, up by five, spades is called."

Stonewall's eyebrows went up and Cargo tried not to laugh. So Stonewall hadn't expected him to call another round, let alone bring the betting up two levels. He couldn't have more than two black aces, either. The others had been played. Cargo had been counting.

Plato and the engineer both gave their "in" call. Now there was a moment of silence: the delicate decisions as to how to play out the hand to match up the called point spreads. Cargo decided to pass the third exchange. He held good cards, he told himself. There were no bad cards, only stupid plays. Each card could be used to advantage.

As others took the third exchange, he shifted the position of the cards in his hand, rearranging them and fanning them out again singlehanded. The screen of the viewtable was obscured by various throws and casts, as well as a couple of unofficial running tallies in the small windows at each place. The graphite colored antiglare shield that made up most of the surface of the table had been badly scratched at least once, and the deep ridge that ran through the opaque crystal was useful for leaning up discards. Four batwings rested on twin tracks less than two meters away and the air smelled of a mixture of lubricants, stale water and the roast beef that had made up most of the lunch menu.

Fourways was behind a translucent blue celo screen coding what Cargo assumed was paperwork into the Commander's terminal. Steel and Ghoster were crouched in a corner playing toonie, which Cargo had learned and then managed to lose every time he tried it for eight months. The problem was he kept thinking it was chess, he decided, when the real object was not to capture the opponent's pieces at all, but to flow through them to reach the objective on the other side. No matter how many times Ghoster had explained the technique of "flowing through," Cargo never quite understood it; finally he had given up. It wasn't the big differences between the species that made him uneasy, it was all the very tiny ones.

"Stop it. I'm trying to think!" the engineer said.

Cargo blinked. So did the depths of the table, the gray flickering and gathering in on itself. With startling speed the display cleared and resolved into a multicolored distort of the octant.

"We got a sighting, you think?" Plato asked.

Fourways emerged from behind his screen, quickly but not as urgently as Cargo thought proper. "A merchie reports something on vis," he said, jamming a thick finger against the sickly green marker under the glare shield. "Out here. EW's got nothing. So we've got to go on sneak and peak."

Cargo placed his cards face down on the bright display and was halfway to his craft before a vocal explosion froze him. "Damn!" Stonewall said, staring at a hand of cards. "I could have won. For once I could have won and we get a call. I swear I am going to convert because God has got to be on his side."

Cargo couldn't resist laughing as the canopy locked. He didn't need to hear Ghoster's hiss over the chatterbox to know where the Akhaid's sympathy lay. He tossed down four Three-B's dry and went through his final phase check. The basic checklist was done twice a day for the batwings, but now he waited impatiently for the passive receivers to shed their safety casings before committing the bat to a roll down the track. They were already starting to move, the double magnetic fields pushing the craft out the open airlock, before the Three-B's hit and the maze opened just before they left the protection of the *Horn and Hardart*, the ungainly beach ball of a mother ship that had been home long enough.

"To sighting one-three-one-one," Cargo told the maze. It set the course with a hint of disapproval. *"Traffic?"*

One-three-one-seven, Lodz Soganbaltz, registered merchant, Collegium. Two-two-nine-four, Kraits spectral, twenty-seventh. Nine-three-nine-six, carrier Horn. Other batwings as follows.

"Enough," he told it, and then demanded data on any unidentified or enemy craft.

Negative data, the maze told him with an edge he would have called smugness in a living being.

He went into the maze instead of just commanding it, manipulating it from the inside until he was close enough to Ghoster that the alien thought processes chilled the back of his neck. He was deep enough in the maze now that words, civilized cohesive thought that served as well to separate beings as to bind them together, no longer served. The deep maze linked in to a more basic part of the brain, a more immediate response—not one devoid of reason, or there would be no point in coming to the maze at all. It was more the place of knowing before forming the word to fit them. And at that level, touching Ghoster was dangerous.

Shielded with language, they could both pretend that the differences in their perception were minimal, that they were in

fact closer than physiognomy suggested. In fact, they were
further apart. This deep in the maze there was no hiding the
fact that Ghoster was alien, essentially unknowable.

The thin membrane between them cleared and brightened.
Images appeared on it like a mirror or a storybook, or the
holotapes he had made for his mother's business. Only this
time the images were of Scatter packing and handing over his
wings. Scatter staring at a picture of Bugs and then leaving. A
band of colors, a chord descending and then the membrane
clouded chalky gray. He still didn't understand, and on some
basic level his need to know became something else, became
one of the nonspectral specific rainbows that permeated the
barrier between them.

Emotions came to him, confused when they could be understood at all, as if the sorting mechanism had gotten twisted
between species. Stubborn, he stayed. He had to know, not for
himself but for Ghoster, who understood these things—
Ghoster, who he'd gotten drunk and stoned with, flown with,
nearly hit the Wall with on more than one occasion.

The bands separated. Cargo understood that there had been
shame, not for anything Bugs had done or not done but because Scatter should have been aware of his partner's proba-
ble-possible not discrete to cannibalistic behavior. Twisted
again, and there was another angle, this time fury at command. Not Command, not the people who sat with stars on
their shoulders in the snug red brick admin offices. Instead
Cargo caught a fleeting impression of something less struc-
tured, more intimate, far more compelling, something Akhaid
in every detail. As if there was a separate Akhaid command,
as if Ghoster's species was not split Cardia-Collegium like his
own. But they were. He knew they were. He had hard data.

His mind rebelled and argued, screaming out for Ghoster to
acknowledge and make it clear, make it fit into the universe he
had always known.

All he got from Ghoster was frustration edged with golden
violet shading into butter-scented scales. Cargo had touched
those scales before, and Ghoster had only been pleased and
called them "The Walk." Now there was no pleasure in the
contact. Cargo withdrew from connection with the membrane
and watched it reshape itself so that it seemed a bloody web in
a limestone sediment, pulsing ugly somewhere between matter
and birth.

Still shaken, he came up to the second level of the maze. He couldn't go any deeper if he wanted to get the mirage on visual, and vis was the only way this sucker showed. The maze, programmed to believe both his efficiency and safety lay in its deepest levels, protested. He threw a strong negative at it and continued upward until he was back to the level of words. He didn't need to react faster than he could think, this wasn't combat. This was only a gentle look-see at something that might not even be there.

For a moment Cargo tried to justify himself to the maze. There was always that temptation, to forget it was just the functioning that he and Ghoster created together with the computer and the craft itself when they were in full mode. And after four Three-B's he was in good and hard. The maze was much more tempting than to force himself to look out with no more equipment than the eyes he was born with. But that was the only way to catch the thing. Vis.

He hadn't been vis with a gomer since before the *Torque*. Not counting that last ambush over the horizon, which was more a cat fight than a certified battle. He'd seen them that time, but had been so deep in the maze that visual impressions hardly registered. This time he was on organs only, and it was rather depressing that the best stealth technology could make something massing fifty tonnes just about invisible to every sensor he carried except his own inborn eyes. He didn't like trusting that.

In training he had learned to trust his instruments before his own senses. The senses distorted, especially with all the scale of space to work in. Instruments were more reliable. All along he had gone by the book on that, always sure that the readings the maze implanted before he could bother to look at the display in front of him were more accurate than his own physical judgement.

Besides, cold logic told him that Plato was right. The whole purpose of the mission to the Collegium was to flush out a traitor. It had nothing to do with any enemy mirage at all. Probably Fourways had invented the sightings as a way of keeping them all in line, of giving them some trace data to catch a spy. That was all.

Still, it was good to be back in the manifold, to feel the fine responses in mode. He'd missed it. The batwing was in its element, a ghost dancing vac in the silence. Without re-

striction or drag, without the rise and fall of the winds of
Vanity, the batwing wheeled and turned, spun and leaped,
free.

As they approached the perimeter of the sighting the maze
flashed a warning into his mind. Having already swept the
area with instruments, the maze calculated they were simply
wasting fuel and suggested recall. Cargo only smiled. The
maze was his tool not his master. It was too easy to follow the
maze's suggestions, assuming that it was more competent than
the being who controlled it. Bad pilots were those who had
too much respect for the maze and not enough for their own
skill.

Cargo pressed on. He held the mode link firmly at the
fringes of his consciousness. The best of cybernetics wasn't
going to help him now. Instead he shut down the infrared and
began to scan the star fields with his unaided vision.

The surrounding depths were deceptively still. Without the
infrared schematic he couldn't see the great floes of electrons
cast off by the stars, couldn't perceive the differences in brilliance one from another. Instead of the hot red-yellows of the
usual display it was nearly as cool to the eye as the tempera-
ture indicated. Even the red giants, two of them full ahead in
his sight, were a cold and forbidding color. Everything else
was very slightly overcast with a bluish pallor, result of his
own speed that wasn't quite enough to make them appear like
the gleaming sapphires in the shift that he had seen from the
Krait. That wasn't his job. He had to look, and for that he
needed to be a little slow, searching for motion. The human
eye sees movement before anything else. His father taught
him that when he was first learning to steal.

Under the full canopy he could see almost half the sky. The
beauty of it held him as it always had. He noticed the creeping
darkness subconsciously at first, knowing it was there without
really focusing. It took nearly a full minute for it to register.
Immediately Cargo recognized his mistake. He had been
scanning for an image, not the negative of one.

It was three o'clock and above. He turned slightly to watch
further, the belts of his harness biting into his shoulders and
rib cage, trying to restrain the move. He didn't care.

He watched it glide across the starfield, tried to see the
shape of it against the depth of the void. What he could make
out, with everything he could see, was the exact image of a

batwing. It could be Plato or Stonewall in that craft, but Cargo doubted it. His maze was locked in to the other batwings in his group, and this wasn't registering as one of them. This wasn't registering at all.

The mirage was no story after all. Cargo watched as it glided overhead and, one at a time, blotted out the stars.

Chapter
8

The Collegium central had always calmed him in the past. The great white and green tiled plazas of the Ministry of Diplomacy were set with trees from nearly every world in the Collegium and banks of flowers carefully tended in boxes. Mirabeau knew the boxes and pots for the trees, the carefully arranged benches and fountains and sculpture had all been strategically placed to trap or slow down possible saboteurs. That had been done in the days before he had moved to the Trustee Palace, when his office had been on the third floor of the main building with three picture windows overlooking the Diana and her Chariot fountain, when they worried about Cardia terrorists who had yet to try to secede. Still, he was pleased that the planters were no less decorative for being practical.

In those days everyone who had worked in the three buildings at Diplomacy Plaza believed that it was just a few extremists causing trouble, the SNDIP and the LFPN in particular. There had even been some talk of a possible alliance between the two of them. Mirabeau had been one of the few dissenters. Surely everyone knew that the extreme right and left couldn't come to any compromise, or so the Deputy Minister for Security had said. Mirabeau thought she was a fool, and had said so. The fact he had been proven right, that the two groups had more supporters than originally suspected and in fact had begun to coordinate their activities, had only made his enemies angrier.

Enough enemies had made him an old man sitting in the sun on one of the ornate benches under a fragrant fruit tree. In

a collarless blue shirt and well-worn pants he looked like one
of the retirees on a package tour. Except there weren't too
many tour groups any more. The Luxor Incident was fifteen
years in the past, but most people still preferred not to travel.
Most intersystem traffic these days was military convoys and
merchanters carrying war material. The bishop sighed and in-
haled the fragrance that surrounded the tree.

The luxury liners of his own youth were gone now, refitted
for outpost work. He had taken the Cunard *Prince of Wales* on
his first outbound journey when he was eighteen, leaving the
Mirabeau homestead for the Gregorian College and Earth. The
Prince of Wales had had seven dining rooms, not counting the
grill and the ice cream parlor. Five boasted an assortment of
Waterford chandeliers. The sixth, the Princesse Marie Claire
room, had Limoges service and Belgian lace table cloths. The
apple-green and cream room had been his favorite. If it was a
little too ornate and perhaps a bit fussy, it was also cheerful
and homey, and best of all served the familiar cassoulets and
ratatouille and chicken crepes he had eaten at home. Eating
the six usual cruise-line meals there every day, he had used
table assignments to meet fellow travelers who held important
positions.

His name had helped. So did the fact that he had already
been very well versed in Collegium affairs. At least, that had
been his opinion at the time. Now he realized that at least two
of his most helpful traveling companions had seen only a boy
who ate in the same dining room at the same seatings, obviously more at home speaking French than Indopean. Perhaps the then Vice Minister for Mining and Mineral Rights
had originally felt only pity, or perhaps he had wanted to improve his French with a native speaker, Mirabeau never knew
which had brought him to the older man's attention. But by
the end of the cruise he had an offer of an internship in the
Ministry.

Not only that, but the Vice Minister had drafted letters, the
old-fashioned, formal kind handwritten in black on heavy
cream-colored paper, to certain contacts at the Vatican. Mirabeau was marked for the Diplomatic service and served his
internship when the Vice Minister was opening negotiations
on Veil rights with what was then the centralized Akhaid government.

The Vice Minister, it turned out, had far higher ambitions

than Mining and Mineral Rights. So did Mirabeau. It was a good combination. His first mentor had already become expert on Akhaid culture and government, had positioned himself through the mining contacts to move into Diplomacy. There he stayed a Vice Minister and taught Andre Mirabeau a very important lesson. He taught young Andre that power held behind the back of someone else was more valuable than a high-sounding position. Eventually, his mentor held far more power than the Minister of Diplomacy, more than the Minister of Security too. Power was knowledge, the immediate information on what precisely was happening and information on who could use that data best. Who would remember the favor, would be able to pay it back when you needed it. Most of all, how to know when to call in your debts. Those were the important things Andre Mirabeau learned during his internship.

The other thing he learned was about the Akhaid.

Most people didn't know much about the only aliens humanity had ever met. Most humans had never seen one, although there were at least three comedies current in the entertainment selections about species misunderstandings. Mirabeau had watched two and immediately recognized a French farce and a Restoration comedy. There was nothing really alien there at all, not anything like what he had experienced in the negotiations, and later, as Legate.

It was not that he didn't trust the Akhaid as individuals. What he didn't trust were the sets of assumptions that neither side questioned. The Bishop, being a man of the Church as well as the State, had rather more motivation than some. He had asked some well-meaning questions about death and faith, carefully phrased to fit into the mining-rights format. Things like, if a miner is killed in an accident, what procedures should each side follow? Very cautious, not at all rude curiosity.

The answers had been strange; denials and referrals and asking what the humans would want done in similar circumstances. And that was what the Akhaid had asked for, exactly what the Bishop said his own people would want. As if the people became a one-way mirror that was reflecting back at him.

On the whole, he had found them pleasant and good people. It was only their paradigm he didn't trust, and that only because they kept it so perfectly secret that it seemed as if they didn't have one. On the whole he was not pleased.

It was the paradigm problem that had created the conspiracy theory. Only a few of the older Akhaid hands went along with it, those who had dealt with the aliens long enough to know that there was something essential they were not seeing. And only among those who had been around the Collegium long enough to know that the Cardia independent terrorist organizations seemed too well funded and too well trained for amateurs.

The Bishop's theory was simple, elegant and explained everything. He believed that there was something in the basic Akhaid paradigm that led them to fund, train and organize the Cardia rebellion—which everyone outside his own coterie pointed out was sheer stupidity. After all, even the Bishop couldn't argue that well over half the Akhaid holdings, including their mother planet, were well within the Collegium boundaries. They were well behaved, with no history of supporting terrorism, and besides that, there was no reason why they should. Originally, the Cardia-Collegium split had been a human-only argument. The Akhaid had come in on both sides according to geography. And they fought on both sides too.

His detractors had argued that long-haul economics between the colonies and the inner systems were irrelevant to the Akhaid—the basis of the split in the first place. Mirabeau did not belittle economics, but he was rather more of the opinion that isolation and home rule, along with a real hatred for the interstructured dependency of the major worlds and habitats, had a lot more to do with the current situation. The colonists were essentially survivors and integrators, fiercely independent. Historically they despised their more dependent and developed brethren, and held them in contempt.

The prevalence of the Dekmejian heresy among them had strengthened the split. And it was a heresy, something the Bishop saw as a theological as well as a political problem. The Dekmejians believed in salvation through suffering, that pain itself insured the Kingdom of Heaven, denying both grace and good works. This had been reinforced in the Cardia Group during the pandemic, when they had most needed support from their established sponsors—and got nothing.

Not even all of this would have been impossible if it hadn't been for Ki Shodar, the Bishop reflected. He had met Shodar only twice, and both times had been disasters. Outwardly no one thought of the Cardia's rebel-in-chief to be either fully human or Akhaid. There were good reasons the Church was adamantly opposed to splice-life experiments. Creating sentient beings from viral-construct DNA altered to cross human and Akhaid traits was not simply immoral, the Bishop had argued more than once. It was evil. There had been ten individuals created with this technique, and now the only one who survived was Shodar.

And it was the Akhaid who had created them, who had started the experiments in the first place. Mirabeau had always wondered why, wondered also if they had ever considered the consequences or had foreseen them and had gone ahead in spite of that. Or maybe because of it.

The Akhaid on Cardia worlds didn't subscribe to the Dekmejian outlook, at least so far as the Bishop could see. They seemed more sympathetic on strictly topological grounds. They, too, had a cultural split between residents of the younger colony worlds and those who chose to live in the relative comfort of civilization.

The Bishop had argued for giving the Cardia their freedom the first time they asked. It was expedient. The new colonies would need to trade, and their grandchildren would have either moved on or lost the wild streak that had brought the current crop. In the end, relations would have normalized, and no one would have been troubled. That was when the Cardia were asking nicely, through representatives in the Collegium, before the radical hotheads had gotten together and begun the seventy-two-day killing spree on the pleasure planet Luxor.

The Bishop knew better than to try and hold back a tidal wave. Revenge was the credo of the day. It saddened him that his people were still so savage, that despite their technology and their scope, despite Mozart and Shakespeare and Dante and Pelton, it was wild, insane emotionalism that committed them to war.

He had tried to salvage something from it, create a sane haven in the Cathedral. He had saved three Gypsy boys. Now all but one was dead, and that one, his favorite, was part of it.

One thought had given him pleasure since he had gotten the call. Perhaps someone thought that Cargo was a Cardia agent. The Bishop was sure it wasn't true, but if it was he knew in his heart it wasn't treachery. It was that he had done something right. He hoped desperately that Cargo was still the Rafael he had known before, had trained and set off on the Collegium military. He had tried to temper Rafael, to teach him to weigh and think and not strike blindly for revenge and visceral satisfaction. He hoped that the man who was called Cargo remembered those things.

The Bishop felt the warmth of the sun shift and the tile under his left hand cooled just slightly. He felt very old, and it wasn't years. It was knowing how long he would have to wait, how far the future was that beckoned. And it reinforced his resolve.

In Aguilar's leather-and-brass office, less grand than the one he had occupied in the Trustee Palace, the Bishop had delicately fenced around the subject of Marcanter. Aguilar was not in his party.

"It would be quite a coup," he'd said with perfect confidence. "You know the movement is growing. The Cardia isn't seen as the same kind of enemy they were fifteen years ago. If we can reach an early accord, there's going to be some re-shuffling in these offices. And you know that."

Aguilar had tried to stare the Bishop down, and finally had to avert his eyes. They both knew why. Twenty-nine years ago, when the Bishop had been Legate, he had taken on a youngster named Sebastian Aguilar as an intern. He hadn't been particularly impressed with the youth's intelligence or his outlook, but had noted that the boy was clever. That, and the fact that Sebastian Aguilar was his brother's son by a household mannequin, had secured the position. Mirabeau had not so much felt sorry for Sebastian as he remembered the youngster's mother, who had been gentle and kind as well as a beauty. And Sebastian could have been his son as easily as his nephew, except for the intervention of fate.

That, however, was no reason to love the man he had become. Whatever venality had been lacking in the mother found full expression in the son. But Sebastian was clever, the Bishop had made no mistake there. And while Sebastian hated him, he would also do what the Bishop asked, partly because he hated the debt he owed and partly because, much as he hated his uncle, he hated his father more.

So when the Bishop asked for secure transport to Marcanter, Aguilar cleared his throat and glanced at his appointment calendar more than once before he agreed.

From a military standpoint, the only decision was how to get through Cardia early warning, and deliver the goods; namely, the Bishop. Security had assigned that to the Second Directorate. The batwing could take care of it. Infiltration and dirty tricks were exactly what they were commissioned to do.

The Bishop had already thought that through and came to a similar conclusion. "We can't afford to endanger this by even a breath," the Bishop had said softly. "No fanfare, complete secrecy."

"I could lose my position," Agular said, twisting his pocket-cord in his fingers.

The Bishop smiled unpleasantly. "You could lose a lot more. On the other hand, you stand to gain a good bit as well. You've never learned to play khandinar, have you?"

Agular snorted. "That hasn't got anything to do with it. I can divert the *Horn*. They're passing to Vanity now to pick up a complement of batwings. I'll divert them and figure out some convincing lie to cover up."

He sighed heavily, hopelessly overburdened by the Bishop's demands. Even Mirabeau knew it wasn't easy to recut orders for a carrier the size of the *Horn*. For a moment, he wondered idly if using a ship of that mass was intended to tip off the Cardia outright and sabotage the talks before they even started.

"One more thing," the Bishop added brightly. "There is a batwing pilot. His call sign is Cargo. I want him in that complement."

Agular's face turned cherry red. "I can't guarantee that," he protested. "Isn't the *Horn* enough for you? Why should you bother with some damned batwing pilot anyway?"

"Why should I bother with the illegitimate son of a household mannequin?" the Bishop asked mildly. There was no cruelty in his gaze, only sadness. Agular sucked in his breath sharply.

The Bishop's only choice was Cargo. Rafael, he thought, I would rather put my own nephews and nieces in danger. You are my son. To choose between my son and my enemies, between Rafael and Sebastian Agular, that choice was one he did not want to make. No one, he felt, had ever had to make that choice before. No one except God.

The Bishop had never wanted to compete with God. He tried to tell himself that it wasn't demanded. He could let

Cargo go on. But he knew in his heart he was first a priest, and as a priest he had given up a family so that the whole universe could be his family. It was his own fault that he had found a child for his old age.

But that was why he had chosen the boy, educated and molded him. To serve a cause, not a person, a cause that the Bishop knew deserved more than one life. It was his own immortality, the continuity of policy. Cargo had had some life of his own. He'd spent four years flying Kraits, four years when the Bishop was certain every time that he opened the maze he would be officially notified of Rafael's death. He had let Cargo go that far alone. Now it was time that the boy proved his worth. He'd been playing. Now it was time for him to grow up.

The warmth of the late spring light lingered on the tiles of the courtyard, staining them pink and deep gold. The shadows crept up behind him and a pink-white petal drifted from the cluster above his head to rest on the bench next to his hand. He and the petal had much in common. Both were finishing the course of their lives, and both were dying to nourish their people. The man crushed the flower against his thumb, and the scent nearly overwhelmed him with sweetness.

It was a message, he decided. He was sad, but he would live with himself. And that wouldn't be much longer. He pushed himself up and stood stooped over, his legs trembling and the light chill of evening tearing through his thin clothes. Truly, he thought, he was getting old, and he shuffled out of the plaza back to his hotel. There he made the call that would bring Cargo to him, and himself again to the decision he had already made.

Cargo was certain the mirage hadn't seen them. He'd mirrored the enemy pattern like an echo, and stayed well down and out of vis. And it didn't look like the mirage was turning, trying to get a bearing on him at all. He smiled. The batwing was invisible to the mirage's systems.

In the maze, Ghoster made him aware of broadband seekers in uv and radio frequencies bathing their craft. Cargo did nothing. The outer hull of the batwing was coated in absorbant ferroporcelain. The iron molecules, all lined up the same way, were supposed to channel any seeker beams down into the honeycomb substructure of the second hull. By the time energy had finished bouncing around from ring to ring of the hexagonal microchambers there shouldn't be enough left to read higher than background. From a sensor's point of view, the beam had been sent out and, not having reflected back off anything, was still going out. Good trick when it worked.

What Cargo couldn't understand was why the gomer had let him in so close in the first place—unless he was so deep in the maze that he wasn't watching vis, or wasn't trusting it. Stupid. Cardia pilots knew about the batwings.

Then Cargo realized that the batwing always operated out at the front lines or as close in to Cardia worlds as they could get. A batwing in the Collegium system was between rare and impossible. If he were a Cardia flier, he wouldn't believe that the enemy would waste expensive stealth this close to home.

"Engage now?" he signaled Ghoster through the maze. The chatterbox might have been easier, but Cargo didn't want to chance even sound waves through a mike.

He could feel Ghoster hesitate. "Rather capture," came back to him, half words and half deep-maze images.

Cargo wondered if Ghoster was insane. It wasn't possible to capture the mirage with their small batwing and no tractor facility at all. The only way would be to force the mirage into the *Horn and Hardart*, and that would require calling Plato who was flying wing.

Cargo sank a little deeper into the maze, careful not to go so deep that he couldn't keep the mirage visual and aware. He'd never had to engage at this level before, using only half-full mode. The maze was not reading his images, but taking them from his mind half complete and doing what he ordered before he was finished. He shot a rainbow through the maze, getting Ghoster ready to target the Eyes on the mirage's drive spectrum.

The image that came back was turtle dung, Ghoster's favorite expression. The fact he got it wrong annoyed Cargo, only he was more annoyed about the failure to get a good lock. He didn't want to close in. Moving up would take them out of the mirage's blind spot and put them on his vis. That was not smart.

The maze showed it to him, and he didn't need much. Of course. The mirage's heat mask was keeping the spectral info out of flow. Cargo snorted while the maze suggested politely that there was nothing there to shoot at anyway. He could sense Ghoster thinking through the parameters of the Eyes. Only with the maze refusing to believe there was anything out there, it was impossible to take aim.

Cargo thought inside the maze, layered thought that was faster than even the half-formed battle images that he had always used to control the Krait. He knew where Plato should be, in loose formation well to his nine and high. She could be vis to the mirage, but he didn't seem to be acting like she was there. So he didn't see her.

He threw a quick bolt through the maze to Ghoster. Get ready. He didn't wait for Ghoster's response when he pushed the batwing into a flaring high-go climb. Pouring on speed, his drive shielding foundered and exhaust trailed like a cometary flare.

As the mirage swung to catch him, he cut the engines and drew the trim so that momentum alone would take him off on a different course where the mirage couldn't follow The mirage went up a notch of go and started a search-and-patrol pattern.

Cargo sucked in his breath and prayed. Plato, if Plato knew what he was doing, if she could follow his reasoning and intuit what he meant. Two Bits would have, but he had known Two Bits all his life. Plato didn't know his moves that well, hadn't played enough chess and hockey and khandinar with him to know how he thought.

The mirage was opening up, no longer keeping the mask profile. At least he wasn't masked at more than low go, no more than the batwings. Thank God their engineers hadn't figured a way to do that too.

Cargo sat frozen and waited. The batwing drifted, propelled by her own momentum on a trajectory just thirty degrees arc off of what the mirage seemed to expect. *Overshoot us, let's see some speed*, Cargo prayed.

Through the maze he could feel Ghoster's frustration, trying to get a fix on the mirage's exhaust spectrum. Only the mirage wouldn't turn to them long enough, wouldn't turn at all. It searched out on slow go, speeding up only when a random piece of rock showed up in its sights.

Slowly Cargo began to build up an image, taking the batwing from full back to top go and letting out the sails. That should flush him out a little better. Only it was the kind of move Ghoster hated. Where in hell was Plato? Or didn't she see the mirage? Maybe she had even lost her fix on him. Except for their maze link, the batwings were as nonexistent to their own side as they were to the other.

And then, before he had a chance to complete the picture for the maze, a flare went off high and behind them. Cargo laughed. The mirage bolted like a stupid deer, overshooting the batwing that had rested so carefully concealing position.

The mirage moved up the speed scale well past the masking point and approaching top go. Plato, it had to be Plato, was hard on his tail, chasing him like a hound at a fox hunt.

Every nerve taut, Cargo waited and counted off the seconds. The mirage was ahead, up and ahead, veering off to turn the angle of the attack back on Plato.

That's when he pounced. The batwing sprang into the mirage's trajectory without warning. As Plato overshot the approach, Cargo turned in close.

The maze was full of rainbows. Ghoster was in his glory, targeting while they were dancing vac at top go. The mode showed him all Eyes, a blaze of colored light.

The explosion filled the void with burning luminescence. Cargo closed his eyes, but even behind the lids he could see the mirage burn. He'd been on vis too long, had kept the blast shield of his helmet up and the canopy on clear so that he could track without instruments. He had forgotten and damned himself while still trembling with the rush of danger. The maze trembled with him, going into a positive feedback series. It had been programmed to stimulate adrenaline levels as high as possible.

"What the hell is going on out there?" a voice came over the chatterbox.

Cargo flinched to hear it used, to see his invisibility destroyed. And by Fourways, if he identified the voice correctly. If anyone should know better it was the person who had trained them. "Mirage sighted and destroyed," he reported briefly.

The next message came from the *Horn*, recalling them all. Cargo swore. He was ready to go on, to take on the next mirage out there. If there was another out there. He was hot and high and deep in mode. He didn't want to come out and face that other universe again. Here he was perfect, cool and invincible. Here he was a single mote of focused energy and it felt good. He wanted to fight. He did not want to return.

In the end it was the maze itself that forced the issue. Being a machine, even if off the scales with artificial intelligence, it was still not alive. It didn't care about feelings, only orders. An order from the mothership would be obeyed even if the pilot was dead, if the maze could manage in a straightforward and unimaginative manner. Returning was something it could do in an emergency, and Cargo felt it whirling through logic programs to define that situation. When he knew it was close to cutting him off he gave in. It was worse to be cut out of the maze suddenly than to have to go back home. There had been plenty of excitement for today.

By the time the airlock had gone around the second time, Cargo was over the height of the rush. Three-B's, adrenaline and coffee had combined to slam energy into overdrive when it was needed, but now it was draining out of him with the sweat that soaked the neck and back of his flightsuit. He felt wrung out but good. He'd gotten the mirage, and that was something to be proud of. He and Plato together.

Now all he wanted was a good hot shower. He unlocked the canopy and it lifted overhead. His legs were cramped and filled with pins and needles when he climbed over the edge of the cockpit and rested his weight on the inset rung. A crew member guided his feet downward and made sure he didn't fall. Being taken care of. It was his privilege for killing the mirage.

He didn't take off his helmet and break the final connection with the maze until he was standing on the deck. It was like being cut off, alone and half blinded. Cargo always needed time to adjust to coming out of mode, to get over the pangs of grief of being merely human again, instead of human and Akhaid cybernetically augmented with the very fastest and most advanced level of AI. He always felt a little stupid and slow those first moments, but at least he didn't throw up. He'd known more than one classmate, when they were learning to drive Kraits, who had been obviously, odorously ill more than once.

He peeled the gloves off his hands and flexed his fingers. That cooled him down somewhat and got the blood moving.

By the time he'd stashed the gloves in his helmet, he had already gone through the first stage of returning from mode. The deep exhaustion didn't hit until the second stage.

A crew member came up with a readsheet on the batwing. He printed it after barely passing his eyes over the first words. A shower, that was what he wanted, and clean clothes that didn't stink and a couple of hours sleep.

Bleary eyed and intent on those few but pressing needs, Cargo didn't notice Fourways crossing the deck. "I want you in my office in ten minutes," he said brusquely.

Cargo acknowledged by rote, because he'd been saying yes, sir and no, sir for so long that he didn't even think about it anymore. It wasn't until the first lovely splash of hot water hit his back that he realized he hardly had time to get wet. He cursed under his breath in Romany and washed off the surface layer of grime and sweat before he got dressed. Hair still wet and near dripping, he managed to show up in the hangar office less than thirty seconds late.

Plato was already waiting when Cargo slipped behind the celo screen that separated the office from the rest of the hangar. Fourways looked up at both of them and grunted. He didn't ask them to sit.

"Now can you tell me the meaning of those pyrotechnics we saw out there? Or were you just celebrating New Year's early?" Fourways' tone sliced through them like cold steel.

Plato said nothing. Cargo had hoped she would explain, but it wasn't her place. It had been his idea, and he had been responsible for the kill. Plato had just followed his lead.

He took a deep breath and settled his eyes on a pink spot on the wall a little over Fourways' head. "We saw the enemy and engaged before we were discovered, sir."

"There was no order to engage," Fourways said so softly that the very mildness was a more serious threat than outright anger would have been. "We don't know how many mirage-class craft they have, but the thing is new. We were to observe and gather data. Your explosion gave us nothing to work with. We don't even know how much ordnance they carry."

Cargo exhaled carefully. "They can't mask at anything above low go," he offered.

Fourways sneered. "Nothing can. I want you both to think about something very carefully. You are not Krait drivers any more. You are in the Second Directorate, and that means our priorities are subject to the First Directorate. Intelligence comes first, second and third. You aren't here to play hero. If you want to do that we can transfer you back to Group Seventy-nine this time tomorrow. They've got a few openings, I hear."

"I do not want to transfer, sir," Cargo said immediately.

"You'd better think about it," Fourways said. "I'm not sure I want a pair of hotheads, who still think they'll get ahead by being blast happy in my unit. I'm not sure I want you in the Directorate. Dismissed."

Cargo turned and left before he could hear one more word. He hated to acknowledge that part of the reason he was so angry was that Fourways was right. It was something that had come up every day on Vanity. They weren't paid to make fireworks any more. Besides, the black ferroporcelain shell of the batwings wouldn't take the violet silhouette of a spearcross to mark the number of kills.

"You know," Plato said quietly when they got back to their stateroom. "On Paragon they believe there is one right and one wrong, only one way to be. I Walked to find out if I agreed with them, with all the teachers and everything, and I decided I didn't. So I left. Now, here I am."

She tried to chuckle and was not successful.

"Fourways is just an asshole, that's all," Cargo said. "Let's go eat dinner. I'm starving."

Plato agreed, but without enthusiasm. Cargo understood her reluctance. He didn't want to see the rest of the unit either. He hoped Ghoster would be so busy with Steel that neither of them would have time to bother him. Or maybe the Akhaid would decide that what they did was perfectly normal, and there was no trouble involved.

Besides, Cargo was hungry. Everytime he flew, Krait or batwing, or even early on in training on the survey route, he finished every task famished. It didn't matter how much he'd eaten before, or that he'd had a snack not twenty minutes before they had gone. At this point, even if they were serving boiled shoe leather Cargo would enjoy it.

Just the thought of food, of the good smells of rising steam, made him feel better. It was impossible to stay miserable too long when there was a good meal waiting. Perhaps, he thought wryly, that was the Rom speaking. Before he had known the Bishop, a good meal and a good song, a blanket, a pillow, a suit of clothes and his freedom were all he desired in the universe. At least the good meal part hadn't changed.

"So you screwed up playing spooks and reverted to your savage old habits, huh?" Stonewall asked when they entered the crowded wardroom.

Cargo wanted to slam him, but his situation was bad enough without a few days in the brig, besides. Then, strangely enough, Stonewall smiled. It wasn't his usual unpleasant grin, but a full and friendly invitation to some hilarious and private joke.

So Cargo ignored him instead and concentrated on his dinner. It was a fairly good imitation of coq au vin with garden peas and salad. The *Horn and Hardart* had just been reprovisioned, and he meant to take advantage of it as long as the good stuff lasted. There would be enough dinners when he would want to be distracted or would miss entirely anyway, if the schedule here was anything like the *Torque*.

"You know," Stonewall said slowly, "if I could get a proper mint julep in this place, I would buy the both of you one each. I really and truly would. Matter of fact, maybe I'll give you my marker on that for later."

"Stonewall, would you mind telling us why this sudden rush of sympathy?" Plato demanded, stony eyed.

Stonewall's smile grew even brighter. "Well, Miss Plato, the thing of it is, you all are walking around like you was whupped puppy dogs. But the fact of the matter is that you were only acting pure and natural. Besides, everything every matte vet has said is that everybody does that a few times. Gets aggressive. Forgets that we're in the Peeping Tom business now."

"And why should that make you pleased?" Ghoster asked, more curious than worried.

Stonewall laughed. "As whupped as I seen these two look, I think they are never going to forget what business we're in now. And I won't, either. I'll never forget how bad they got chewed out for purely natural actions. So, the way I figure it, they took my whipping for me. I guess I've got something to be grateful for."

A couple of tables away Fourways was sitting alone. He

made no attempt to join the rest of his unit. He knew perfectly well it was a bad idea. But he heard Stonewall clearly, and he was pleased. Things were working out better than he could have imagined, and faster. Which was the only way to win a war.

Chapter

9

Cargo had never been to the Trustee Palace on the Collegium, although he had heard plenty about it from Two Bits and Angel. What they had said paled by comparison to the reality. Cargo had been in a lot of nice places in his life; the Cathedral residence and the Master's House at St. Alban's, his undergraduate college at the Delhi-Cygna Institute, the Lladogo Mansion to visit the collection and the Marble Lounge at Timothy's which loomed in his memory as the best.

He'd only been five when they'd gone to Timothy's, reputed to be the best jewelry boutique on the playground world of Luxor. His mother had taken him. She had dressed in glowing pink that rustled and had spoken Indopean with a cultured accent, a lady and a valued customer. The salespeople brought out trays of diamonds and rubies, large and liquid and glittering in their secret hearts. Rafael's eyes had gone wide at the sight of those sparkling things. The vision of them filled his world and became large, like the constellations over an unlit field. His mother talked and patted him on the back. That was his cue.

Just the way they'd practiced at home, Rafael had pretended to choke. His mother called for water, for a piece of bread, for a doctor for her darling, while she pressed her linen handkerchief over his mouth. The handkerchief had been drenched in Obelisk, the most fashionable expensive perfume of the season, and the little boy thought he was going to pass out from the smell. Something hard slipped into his mouth while a beautifully dressed young lady hurried over the rich carpets with a crystal glass. Rafael drank the water obediently.

142

The stone went down the way his mother told him it would. It didn't hurt at all. His mother, in great distress, rushed him out of the Marble Lounge as soon as he stopped coughing.

The emerald he had concealed was worth enough for the family to live on for ten months, including a light yacht and a new, super luxury set of clothes for all of them. His father lost the rest in one night in a casino on Luxor.

Rafael was perfectly content. His parents had let him stay up late to watch an adult cartoon channel, and they'd let him eat all the peppermint-chip ice cream he'd wanted. It was his very first theft.

Remembering it now, the whole of Luxor seemed tawdry, gaudy and appealing, but not truly glorious—which could not be said of the Trustee Palace.

The place was not remarkably large, but the proportions of the central reception dome were perfect. The floor had been inlaid with a floral pattern in cut granite, so perfectly polished that he was afraid to step on it. Delicately fluted columns surrounded the central chamber and stretched deep into the corridors leading off the main hall, resembling a forest of stone. With all the colors represented, white and black and deep green, pink and purple and amber and wine, it was even more amazing that the whole of the place breathed together in an overwhelming atmosphere of tranquility.

It suited the importance of the Trustees of the Collegium. Cargo was not alone in his awe for those special beings who were entrusted by the entire government to enforce the Pax without referring back to the center of power itself. At the fringes of the universe, the Trustees held unalterable sway. Even here, in the center, on the Collegium itself, their opinions carried more weight than any Minister's or Delegate's. The Trustees were the unwavering center of the Collegium, their leadership and their morality. And he had just entered the inner sanctum of that power.

Cargo stared up at the dome, carved of marble so thin that it was translucent. Under that dome the Collegium Accords had been signed, the first Akhaid Delegation received, the original Cardia Truce negotiated. It wasn't hard to think of the Bishop in these surroundings. In fact, Cargo realized that the old man fit here much better than he had ever fit in the Residence on Mawbry's, with it's heavy, carved furniture and slightly worn carpets. He must have wanted to be recalled, to come back to this quiet reception dome that was the center of the civilized universe. Cargo wondered idly how the Bishop had managed, after being a Trustee and a player in the great game, how he could have survived being retired.

The soft sound of bells flooded the space, and Cargo pressed back against the wall. Even though he had business here, he didn't want to intrude, to disturb the massive calm. The bells continued. A woman with a shaved head dressed in a gold drape glided across the floor and was gone. Cargo touched the place where the Ste. Maries-de-la-Mer medal lay against his skin. He didn't believe in all this, but it still affected him deeply.

From the shadows under the colonnade he watched the Bishop's approach. He hadn't seen Mirabeau in nearly four years, and he suddenly realized the Bishop looked old. Well and truly old, his skin dulled and gray and pulled like crinkled celo over the bones. The carriage had not deteriorated; the Bishop moved smoothly with the grace and gravity of authority. Still, there was a slowness in his step, a frailness in the birdlike set of his hands that made Cargo afraid.

He had seen his father die, lying in a puddle of blood outside a cheap Spin Street casino, a far distance from the elegance of Luxor. Sonfranka had already been dead by the time he had come, a porcelain doll that had shattered. And Two Bits, the only one who remembered his name as Django Yeglesis, had disappeared completely and not even left a scrap to bury. All that was left of him was his name engraved in the Wall, and only one of his four legal identities at that.

Cargo had seen many people die, but he had never seen anyone wither with age. Most of the people he knew never lived that long.

Gently, with the grace inherent in the history of the dome, Cargo left his position in the shadows and crossed the open room. He timed it so they would meet in the center under the opening overhead, in the pool of butter-colored light on the otherwise cool floor. Then, in the midst of ceremony, formality that dominated the Palace and the whole Trusteeship, Cargo faltered. He faced Andre Michel Mirabeau, Bishop and Trustee of the Collegium, but he saw only the pained and ancient eyes of his father.

Dojo Yeglesis had only given him flesh. Mirabeau had pushed him, forced him out beyond where he thought he could

go. It was fitting, Cargo decided, that in the end it was Mirabeau's name he used. Besides, it simplified matters. The
Trustees could do just about anything they pleased, but not
even that power could give the Bishop a nephew who honored
him. Much as Cargo told himself that it was easier and perfectly correct, he tried to ignore the pleasure he felt as the old
man inspected him in the late afternoon light.

"Rafael," the old man muttered. "I take it you had no trouble getting time off, what do you call it, to come down?"

"Liberty," Cargo answered. "No, no problem at all." He
suppressed a smile and saw the ghost of another on the
Bishop's features. He has assumed the old man had made
certain there would be no trouble even before he had received
the old-fashioned printed invitation with the engraved Lion of
the Trusteeship surmounted by the cross.

The Bishop led him out of the elegant dome room through
a corridor no less formal or historic. It wasn't until they
reached the office that the Bishop appeared to relax. The room
was cream and brass, a decided contrast to the Cathedral Residence. Cargo perched on one of the delicate leather-uphol-
stered chairs and was surprised to find it comfortable and
stable as well as obviously antique.

"The room was swept this morning," the Bishop said.

Cargo started. "I didn't know you bothered with house-
keeping," he stammered, uncertain as to what was going on.
Maybe Mirabeau was senile as well as frail.

The Bishop snorted with something like exasperation. "I
can't believe I'm hearing this. You have just spent months
being trained in stealth on a supersecure base, and it never
occurred to you to be concerned about listening devices."

Cargo laughed and leaned back in the chair, which seemed
able to take his weight. "Right. Only I thought that it was easy
enough to get readings off any brittle material. Not just celo.
Hell, all they have to do is point a high-orbit directional at the
dome and they'd hear every word."

The Bishop's face darkened. "I am aware of that. We are
not in the dome for that reason. I suppose you know about the
PLFN reading the first negotiating session from the marble.
With very expensive equipment no less. I have always wondered where they got that long-range directional. But I didn't
invite you here to speculate. I thought we could talk like old
times, find out how you're doing in the batwing business, if

you like it. I worried when you told me you were making the change."

Cargo shook his head. "Same old Bishop. You know, if I didn't know you so well, I'd almost believe you. So, I like the batwing a lot, right? I especially love the part when they find the second birth certificate. I suppose you know more about that than I do."

The Bishop did not sit. "I suppose I do. But that doesn't mean that I don't want to know what's going on. What gives you the impression that this meeting has anything to do with anything, except that we're both in town?"

Cargo detected the twinkle in the tired gray eyes. Mirabeau had trained him and enjoyed playing this game. Luckily, so did he. "Cream puffs," was all he would say.

The Bishop raised his eyebrows in surprise. "I have to give you a score on this one. You win. What cream puffs?"

"Cream puffs. We always had them when there was something to celebrate. And sausages and cheese and healthy food. Only there isn't anything here to eat at all, so I figured we were getting together for a policy meeting. That, and you always made sure that we understood that a summons on the official stationary was official."

The Bishop looked positively merry. "You're right, but you don't score. You owe me the Packard now. I expect delivery by the end of the decade."

Cargo stared at him in alarm. The Packard was an old joke. He'd promised the Bishop a racing yacht when he'd gotten out of juvie. That was more than half his life ago. And to produce the thing by the end of the decade would take nearly half his pay for the rest of his life.

"Oh, I don't expect you to do it honestly, of course," the Bishop relented. "Just acknowledge where you could do some homework. The fact is, the chef here has a heavy hand with pastry. There are no cream puffs in the entire Collegium District that are worth eating. Power and good food are inimical enemies. The greatest soldiers in the universe have always come from cultures that produce plain boiled meals and disapprove of garlic. Unfortunately, this correlation carries over into government as well. The more powerful, the plainer the food. I believe the Prime Minister lives on green salad with only lemon juice for dressing. On the other hand, it is the one indicator that makes me believe we can win militarily, if we must."

"Wait a minute," Cargo interrupted. "First of all, I don't know why you're saying this. I thought you'd do anything to prevent a military solution. Unless you've changed your stripes."

The Bishop stood like a statue, staring out the window into the garden below. The light filtering through the shielded celo glowed around him like the halo in some ancient religious painting. Cargo thought he looked like one of the strong and crazy desert saints, John the Baptist perhaps, or St. Jerome.

"I'm telling you this because I know the Cardia worlds. I've lived there. I miss the cuisine, the fresh crab in dill sauce, the five-hundred ways to flavor chicken, the delicate layers of puff pastry. There was one dish I have never had again, a fish stuffed with baby vegetables and baked in a crust of puff pastry. And when it came out the pastry was perfectly golden and the fish cooked but firm and the vegetables tender. A dish that defines civilization."

Cargo closed his eyes against the glowing cream walls, the rich chased brass slab of desktop. The sensuality of it was overwhelming, planned to be so, to make him hear what he wanted to hear. The Bishop had been a diplomat for longer than he had been alive. Mirabeau knew how to say something without saying it, delicately so that no blame could stick.

Now Cargo felt the familiar cold in the pit of his stomach, the cold that spread to the extremities and lay there like bricks of ice. The Bishop had given him a non answer, the kind he'd heard only once or twice before.

"What is it you want me to do?" he whispered.

He felt the Bishop's hand on his hair in blessing, the dry palm with no weight at all and all the mass of the Collegium itself.

"I know you have the courage of your conscience," the Bishop said in the same voice he used for prayer. "I know you are no coward. The problem is, how does one decide what is right and wrong. You have your orders, your duty. These things are important to you. I made sure they were, that you believed in duty, in honor, in all the things your people cherish and those they reject. I made sure. Now there are times I doubt I know what is right and wrong myself. There is enough wrong done on both sides, and enough goodwill, too."

Cargo's mouth was dry. He wanted to shake his head, to get up and bolt out of the deceptive office, the lulling snare. But the chair was deep, trapping him in soft layers of leather. The Bishop was old, was standing in the fading light like a saint, was facing away from his recognition.

It was not the Bishop's fault, he reminded himself sternly. The only trouble was that the man was too good. For someone who had spent so many years in this Palace, he was insanely committed to absolute good and evil, to serve the one and eliminate the other no matter how much it cost him. That was not the way the universe worked. No one knew that better than Cargo. Absolute good and evil meant nothing next to staying alive, next to Plato, next to the simple loyalty to his friends, his team. In the end, all the words only meant that; the final loyalty to one's own, the few small beings who share a life. It cut across place of origin, ethnic group and even species most of the time.

But he owed the Bishop. Mirabeau had kept their relationship pure, had never brought up the fact that Cargo owed a debt greater than he could ever repay.

It had all started with Angel and the yacht. Angel was three years older than he, already sixteen and married and experienced. So when Angel said the Belle Sidon was on no-way security, Rafael believed him. Loads of yacht owners didn't bother to pay for more than the number code on the door and a second one on the ignition. Only for someone who had access to a vac suit, knew something about how chips were set in a board and had a little nerve, those codes were as easy to break through as butter. Sure, most owners had the sense to at least have the lock print-coded—the best did a chromoscan on three levels and insisted on retinal patterns before ignition—but that cost a bundle.

C.L. Wong was a cheapskate. His reputation was famous on at least seven habitats around the Collegium circuit. The only reason he had Belle Sidon at all was that it was cheaper to run his own spacerig than to take the public liner; that, and because Wong was more paranoid than he was tight. Aunt Anna, a respected *phuri dai* who had been a great *boojo* woman, in a fit of fury when Wong refused to pay for his two son's readings, cursed him in front of the ofisa. She wailed in her high voice, thin as the wind, calling down the *mule* of her ancestors to haunt C.L. Wong. And, she said, her eyes glazed with fury and prophecy, Wong would die on the Arkadias Line packet run.

Aunt Anna had called on that fate because it was the worst she could think of. All the old people were afraid of dying on the packet run, where their *mule* would haunt all space and be spread across the solar wind. They were terrified.

The only person who believed Aunt Anna, including the great *boojo* woman herself, was C.L. Wong. Rafael had heard only indirectly about the curse, and about how Wong had bought the Belle Sidon the next day. Angel had told him, and Angel was a true *chal*. So it was only a fitting and just revenge to steal the yacht when the man was under a curse, after all. Besides, he was too cheap to invest in even the most elementary security. Perhaps, Angel joked, he relied on the fact that even *mule* feared his temper and his sons. Both of them were training to go into the family business, a business that would make the Rom look like Space Scouts.

Slipping down past the Last Lock to the stored suits was easy. The boys had done that more than once in preparation. Most kids on Mawbry's liked to go out and watch the ships come in. Nor was it difficult to jimmy the plates once they were out. Rafael had done it every Friday last year when he'd taken Uncle Tommy's rig down the Collegium with the other Romany *shavs*, to spend the weekend profitably selling flowers in front of the bars and pleasure houses. Uncle Tommy had insisted that the boys break into the rig as quickly as he could get in legitimately. It had been a great game.

So stealing the Belle Sidon wasn't much of a technical challenge. They would have gotten away with it, too, Cargo reflected, if the port authorization hadn't been spot-checking drivers. There'd been a number of accidents in the moorings lately because owners were getting lax and permitting youngsters to operate small private yachts. Naturally the authorities had to do something.

The bored harbor assistant who found them underage to be ferrying a three-hundred-tonne craft didn't know he'd stopped a theft in action. He just assumed that the kids had permission from the owner, as so many had, and it was just one more matter of forcing a citizen to take responsibility for endangering public safety.

Naturally, C.L. Wong had thrown the book at them. He went on the newsline with citizen-action complaints about the "young hoods" of Mawbry's. By then, the juvenile proctors had discovered that none of the boys had ever been to school, had a proper apprentice id or a social-service account. While the court sentenced and the social-welfare office tried to figure out where the records were wrong, Rafael was suffering the worst days of his life.

Mawbry's was by no means a poor habitat. It was as liberal with its thinking as with its wealth, so the whole idea of Juvenile Hall was that the youngsters were either emotionally ill or victims of social prejudice and psychological pressure, being quite malleable. They had no place in their philosophy for just plain bad kids, and there were more than a few in juvie. Perhaps they were the minority, but they were the ones who weren't afraid and who ran the residential cottages. And they'd hated the Romany boys who owed allegiance neither to their gangs nor to the various social-benefit segments of the habitat.

Rafael had learned to hate the night. After lights-out, when the supervisors had left and the boys were alone, the older and meaner ones would make their demands. At first, it was little stuff—cigarettes and money. After a week it was a loyalty pledge to the Bad Hands. The gang leader, a thick-muscled youth of seventeen, had held a sharp-filed spoon to Yojo's back and begun to carve. Rafael had been afraid when he had smelled the blood, seen it dribbled out over the table to the smooth concrete floor.

Later his mother said it was the Gitano in him, the rage. He jumped halfway across the open space between the table and his chair, flew toward the gang leader with his fingers curled like claws. It hadn't taken the gang members more than two minutes to peel him off the leader's back and get the restraining web around him.

The next morning it was reported as a "psychotic episode," the gang leader explaining in his best voice how such a horrible thing could happen in their cottage. The social-welfare worker sighed and added a notation to Rafael's record, muttered something about a transfer to a more supervised treatment facility.

Thereafter, every night for a month the gang bound him with the net that clung to his skin and pajamas and the concrete walls. He never knew what it would be—cigarette burns or rape or being left alone. Those weren't as bad as the times the leader came in with the "crazy sheet," the soft plastic bandages used to tie someone in a psychotic attack, and held the thin strips over his face until he passed out.

Not being able to breathe haunted him. Cuts and burns didn't hurt nearly so much as the desperate attempts of his body to find air, the searing acidic feeling in his chest and throat as that need was denied.

The Bishop had saved him from that. He owed the Bishop something more than his life, perhaps his sanity. He knew he couldn't survive in the gang cottage much longer. The thread that connected him to reality was already beginning to ravel, and most of the time he welcomed that oblivion. One day he had been in the cottage, terrified of sunset. The next day he was in the Bishop's residence at the Cathedral. It was a miracle.

Perhaps, Cargo reflected, it wasn't entirely that he didn't believe in miracles as that he had already experienced a major one. Two didn't happen in any person's life.

He still hadn't figured out why the Bishop had taken such an interest in his case, in the three of them. They weren't any better than most of the kids in juvie, and not appreciably worse. Perhaps it was their lack of records, the fact that they hadn't attended school or job training and weren't registered for the public dole.

Of the three, Cargo had originally thought he'd prefer apprenticeship. It was an insult to make a Gypsy read. Besides, he'd tried school once or twice for a day at a time. When the teachers found out that he had no background he invariably found himself the butt of cruelty, different only in degree from the nights in the detention cottage. The Bishop had other plans.

In five months of tutoring, Rafael had made up nearly six years of schoolwork. He was far ahead of Angel and Yojo, who had always been better than he was at things that counted. They had lighter hands and more creative tongues. More than that, he found that he enjoyed what he was learning. Most of all, he had loved pure mathematics.

Only in the still times with the Bishop could he admit why the discipline appealed to him. Mathematics admitted no lies. Rafael found that he loved the one place in the universe where there was such a thing as the absolute, provable truth. Beautiful and true, it was also useless in any traditional way, and he loved that too. Almost everything else, from literature to computers, could be seen as learning to lie or steal better. Angel did see it that way, actually, and went on to a great success in breaking banking codes before he was located by C.L. Wong's sons and killed. That was Angel's decision. For himself, he had thought he was free of the threat of juvenile hall, of the court snoop who said he was nothing but justice fodder to keep the wheels turning. If he grew up to be a scapegoat, he'd have achieved something.

Damn, he hated the social workers at juvie. They were a lot more tolerant of gang members, who they had studied and understood, than of a culture nearly as alien to them as the Akhaid. Well, to be honest, not nearly so alien, but equally unknown.

Cargo had never questioned what he owed the Bishop, only how to repay that. Always before it had been easy. Be a good student, work hard, get promotions. Do Gaje things like tell what you think is the truth and don't steal, but the Bishop realized that these were Gaje ideas and so was willing to sigh and shake his head and beg them not to do it again, ever. Most of the time Cargo had managed. He had not stolen anything— well, nothing worth anything anyway, since the yacht. And he hadn't yielded to temptation to commit fraud, even when God had put the opportunity in his path.

It had been six years ago, in his last year at school. He'd gone to the local mess mart for a soy and salt, which was more politely known as a hamburger, when the beverage machine got a case of the hiccoughs and spilled hot coffee in front of the counter. Rafael had nearly wept for losing the chance laid so baldly in front of him. A faked fall, plenty easy enough, and running complaints of back pain and—voila—a nice insurance settlement.

But he hadn't done it. To this day he wasn't sure if he was more proud of keeping honor with the Bishop or ashamed of his stupidity. That had been the most difficult until this moment. The old man hadn't protested when he had opted for fighter training instead of a desk job on reliability testing, had even come out to the ceremonial parade to embarrass him since, as he was *marhime*, his mother would never come.

Now, in this too lovely, cream-colored haven, the Bishop was asking for something. Not a commitment, not yet. But a thought and the beginning of a thought that might lead into dark places hovered around his mind.

For once it was no Gaje thing the Bishop asked. Not to kill. Only the Gaje killed. The Rom lived to laugh and tell stories and sing the ballads late at night at a party with plenty to drink. The good stuff. The part of him that had been called Django until he was thirteen knew the Bishop was right. This killing was not his business. It would make him very happy to leave it alone, to return to the kumpania and the old ways. Then he remembered he could never return to the kumpania, which was why he had chosen this way in the first place. The *kris* had declared him exiled, and so, he had decided to become a success on Gaje terms if he couldn't do it as a *chal*.

As Cargo—the Gaje persona he had laid over himself like a veil of brightly stained celo—the Bishop's words horrified him. Mirabeau, the great statesman, was asking him to betray his friends, his comrades, his oath.

He remembered Old Piluka saying *"Yekka buliasa nashti beshes pe done grastende."* With one behind you can't sit on two horses. He used to wonder what that had meant. Now he understood all too perfectly. Now he had to choose which horse to ride. The thought made him sick.

"There's something I want to show you," Mirabeau said quietly, interrupting Cargo's thoughts.

Cargo nodded and rose. He could at least look. He had committed himself to nothing so far. The old man motioned for him to resume his seat and took a place on the matching sofa. Cargo didn't see him cue the lights to dim or the screen on the far wall to drop.

As the first images flashed in the layers of the screen, Cargo knew immediately that he was looking at a Krait's live cameras. There was something about the flatness of the image, the jerkiness of the recording that was found nowhere else.

Four Cardia fighters appeared on the scene from Blue/ Above three and split. Cargo noticed there was another Krait out on his periphery. What the hell were they doing vis? he wondered. He had only had that kind of contact with the enemy two or three times in his career, each of them an ambush. So that's what had to be going on.

Two gomers made straight for the Krait. It wheeled so hard that he couldn't pinpoint the enemy. Using the exhaust to threaten, maybe split them, only these guys weren't buying it. Coming out of the roll they were ready and defensive.

"Eyes," Cargo muttered under his breath.

The Krait tacked Yellow/Over eight and around, widening the angle of attack for position. The gomers scissored around him, and the Krait twirled in a perfect 180 to get guns down them. It was the Krait's best move, and Cargo whistled. Whoever was doing this was good. He couldn't have pulled out faster or positioned better himself.

And then, before he believed it was possible, the two Cardia craft were gone. Eyes had it. There was the greenish telltale streaking behind, hardly visible in darkness. Dancing vac.

The two gomers who had been off harrying the other Krait were on him. Anger filled him, rage pumping through his veins as he followed every evasive move the pilot made. They weren't playing fair, and he hated that. The situation had just been made for one on one. But you die for thinking dancing vac, you die because if the enemy doesn't kill you the maze will. And the other Krait, his wingman he guessed, had appeared on the far side of the other two.

It was touch and go. He wondered why more Eyes weren't fired. Out, probably. Or else his buddy didn't have a clear shot. For this angle it didn't look like he did, either. Hard to say. Eyes like Ghoster would know, would be able to figure some way to slice the target. Luck if nothing else. Ghoster had a lot of luck.

And then one of the enemy craft blew. No telltale. Or perhaps it had come from the wingman. There. Suddenly the glitter of a charged-particle beam filled the screen. Brilliance flared white and burned his face, his eyes. He blinked rapidly against the glare and the black-violet dots blazing against his retinas.

All his training forced him to attempt to see what was happening. All his instincts screamed at him to throw his arm over his face, block out the blinding light. He couldn't move his arm. It was taped down to the seat; now he was in the Bishop's office and the battle was far away—

Then the light cleared. The gomer was gone. So was the other Krait. Cargo stared, then felt the room get cold. Dark endtape filtered through the display as he tasted the bitter dregs of his lunch churning in his stomach. He hadn't recognized the tape until the very end, hadn't recognized Two Bits' bright yellow-orange craft until he had seen it blown.

Automatically he went into the deep controlled breathing he used coming out of battle in the maze. He had learned it in first-level training, and the habit had become instinct. If it bought him some time to frame his words, it was because none was needed to confirm his thoughts.

"I don't know why you showed me that," he told the Bishop quietly. "Especially when you want me to play the traitor."

The Bishop's eyes went very wide, a look so pure and innocent it speared Cargo against the soft leather seat. He shook his head as if Cargo had wounded him somehow with those words. When he finally spoke it was in the very slow and thin voice of an old man. "I didn't think that was what I was asking. And I showed you this to help you. Because I know how close you and Yojo were, and that the investigation was hard. That's all."

Cargo turned away. Before he had been more than positive. There was nothing in the universe that he had done that could have hurt Two Bits. He'd been certain of that. Somehow he hadn't remembered the heat of the light as the particle beam took out the enemy. He hadn't remembered that it had filled his whole world, every sense.

"I didn't," he protested feebly.

The Bishop stared at him with a compassion that was great enough to kill. "The tape was inconclusive. the panel said."

Cargo wanted to hide from the kindness in those gray eyes, and from the word "inconclusive." It was a word he knew very well, and seeing the tape had only made it more clear. The Bishop didn't know he had been cruel. Cargo saw it in his face, in the terrible and perfect love there. The Bishop hadn't known because he hadn't understood. The old man knew nothing of Kraits and particle beams; he had only sought to reassure Cargo that there was no guilt as he had proved it.

"It was an accident," Cargo whispered so softly that he wasn't even sure he had spoken aloud. "He shouldn't have come so close, that's all, he got in too close. You can't make the calls vis. It wasn't made to work that way. Not in so tight. Not on vis. And he did always do that anyway. You know, Two Bits always liked to get up real close. From that angle it's hard to tell, impossible. Ghoster couldn't have seen him. I couldn't have."

"Are you sure?" Mirabeau asked. "It wasn't in the picture at all. It's a sin to take more guilt than you deserve, you know."

Anger poured through Cargo and his answer was as cold as the wind of Vanity. "I am very sure. I've spent two years of my life training to fly combat and four more doing it. I've got credit for more than seventeen kills, a couple of them vis. I know how it looks when the charged particles get hold of them, and I know the difference between one and two. And, oh yes, I know all the equations, how much energy here and there and how much reaction and mass. As well as you know about sin."

The Bishop collapsed inward, his celo-thin skin pulled more tightly against the bone and his whole being going hollow. He sank down into the sofa in slow motion, as if he was too weak even to submit to gravity. His parched and burning hand searched out Cargo's, and squeezed so hard that he threatened to break the fingers. "I didn't know."

The anger drained out of Cargo onto the rug. Only the emptiness remained, and the knowledge that he was responsible for killing his best friend. "Oh, God."

"I am sorry," the Bishop said, those intense gray eyes staring into his soul. "Forgive me. I didn't know."

Lost in the Bishop's unrelenting gaze, Cargo found the place where he and Mirabeau were the same. The infinite and deadly compassion he feared so in the Bishop invaded him, and for the first time he understood perfectly what the old man intended. Like a rock standing against the storm, Mirabeau stood only on his faith.

There was only one way to forgive his foster father. Only one way that counted. "Tell me what you want me to do." He pronounced the words slowly as if he saw into the tangle of fate in which he did not believe. *Cross my palm with silver.*

Chapter

10

Leaving the Trustees Palace, Cargo walked out into the controlled environment of the Collegium like a blind man. Aimlessly he wandered through the imperially white streets, the faceless monuments of government offices looming on either side. He wanted to get away from them. They were unreal in the same way the Bishop's request was unreal, the same way it was inconceivable that he had killed Yojo. The thin light had the washed-out look of a dream, and for a moment, Cargo believed that he would wake up on the *Horn and Hardart* next to Plato.

Time and place distorted, the way he always imagined it out manifold in the Other Six. Instead, he walked through the strangeness and tried not to see it.

The world had not changed. Only he had. In an hour, maybe a little more, he had become some different creature. The metamorphosis wasn't finished yet, and there was still pain. He wasn't sure whether he was going to end up a fragmented splice-life experiment or a butterfly and didn't really care. Somewhere from the back of his numbed mind came the information that in the classical world the butterfly was a symbol of the soul.

He turned away from the white monsters with their dead and noble statuary into a side street. One ran into another, into the network of alleys that made up the second Collegium, the city where beings lived and worked. In its crackled web that interpermeated the official presence of the capitol were pink geraniums set out in flowerpots on scrubbed tile steps, high-gloss celo recently recoated in a fresh pale-green layer, hand-lettered signs stuck into trees and attached to light posts stating that a female red-point Siamese kitten answering to the name of Muffin had been lost in the neighborhood three days ago, and would anyone who saw her call this code.

He did not participate in this life around him, but it reassured him to touch it at this fragile distance. Here, in the neat alleyways of the Collegium, it was possible to believe that there was no war, no hunting and killing going on in the sky. That they were all safe from the demands of honor and the tangled conflicts of loyalties, of different versions of right and wrong. All of which he could see were true even when constrained to choose only one. That was the difficulty.

The residential district gave onto a neatly kept block of shops and restaurants, a neighborhood parkade that served sandwiches and beer around the rows of brightly colored games. It was very far from Spin Street, from the bustling of the hard-edged entertainment palaces there. Suddenly Cargo felt as if he had woken from a disrupted sleep. Around him people went about their business—three youngsters dropped tokens in the games, a woman about his own age with the ubiquitous badge-chain of a Collegium employee dangling around her neck bought expensive-looking cheese wrapped in green fabric. The woman looked at him, noted his uniform and dismissed him. A group of what appeared to be friends, or at least coworkers, sat in front of long yards of beer at the sidewalk tables. They didn't notice him.

Humanity surged around him and lived, touching each other and being part of this place, this alley, this neighborhood. He was a stranger, and the life here didn't touch him at all. He was anonymous in his regulation haircut, hidden in a life that these people rejected and then no longer even saw. He had become a symbol, but he had ceased being a man.

Suddenly he longed for the noise and tawdry glamor of Spin Street. There at least he had an identity, if only that of customer. There he was accepted and at home, could find others who didn't look through him when he appeared.

Quickly he turned and made his way to the end of the block with the green and purple pillar indicating a public chutestop. The chute was cleaner than the one on Mawbry's, and he was only three stops on the express from his destination.

By the time he disembarked at the Spin Street exit it was dusk. Streetlights were already on, and the variously lit pleasure palaces and dives seemed harsh and inviting against the softness of an atmospheric sunset. At least it was brighter than Vanity and more calm. No violent wind ripped down the single street, which was already filled with people in various uniforms of the armed services intermingled with those in the equally distinct uniforms of the services of the street.

"Cargo, is that you?"

Cargo wheeled around. In the sunset Stonewall's blond hair was almost roseate, and his height threw a shadow half a block long. He was standing with two strangers in front of a place that was no different than half a dozen others, with a pair of illuminated dice in the window. Slowly he approached Stonewall and the strangers.

"Now Cargo, I've just been bragging on you, how you can win eight-deck khandinar like nobody I've ever seen. I told these good buddies that they have never seen the likes of you, and that all the times we played I never did catch you cheating. Now, they think if you're cheating they're going to catch you, and if you're just lucky they're going to clean up. So what do you say to a game, one or two?"

Stonewall definitely had some annies in him, Cargo judged. The two strangers both wore the shiny wings of Krait drivers and patches that identified them as with the Shard Falcon group off the experimental vessel, *Freen*. Both were human. That was good. He'd never quite figured out how Akhaid bet, but he'd never been able to win much from them.

He thought about saying no. He wanted to see Plato, sit down and tell her about the Bishop and the choice the old man had given him. And he didn't want to tell her, didn't want to put it into words. He could hear her voice, mocking and slick, sliding over all the reasons he had to listen to Mirabeau and consider his point carefully. He wanted to talk to Plato. But he wasn't sure he was ready just yet. It was easier to sit down and play cards, gamble only money instead of things that mattered.

He heard himself saying sure, he'd play, and joining them in the smoke at a scarred leather-covered table with a bored house dealer. Over in the far corner he saw a Mah-Jongg game led by a traditional lady-master whose whole right shoulder and arm were covered with a magnificent dragon tattoo. His estimate of the place went up considerably. He idly wondered if one of his companions were a professional gambler dressed in the uniform of the Shard Falcons just to lull him in the game. Not that he really had anything to worry about—he'd had his share of games with professionals and his share of wins. And he'd been thrown out of more establishments than he could count, on six worlds, for winning too well, which was a very private source of pride.

He looked at the seven cards in his hand. All red. Not bad. He rearranged them, thought a minute, then leaned back and watched the opening rounds of betting as if he were simply a spectator. People gave too much away in the first rounds. It never hurt to start conservative, dead in the middle of the heat. Now he was sure Stonewall held at least two aces, and that the woman from the Shard Falcons was down low and all black. The dealer noted the bets on the table tab with total disinterest. Cargo rearranged the cards with one hand, always keeping the other in plain sight on the ancient leather.

With a controlled flicker of emotion, he hesitated over the discard, threw two cards and accepted what the dealer gave him. Nothing registered on his face, but he wasn't even thinking about that. He was fully immersed in the game, in the ice-cold equations that, coupled with a ferocious ability to count cards, had insured a winning streak that had lasted since his sophomore year in the Faculty of Probability. Various possibilities and combinations came to him. He computed the odds in his head, a trick he'd learned when another player started reading his tab with a reflecting cigarette case. Very funny.

Deliberately he threw the first hand. Strategy. Lull the new players into thinking he wasn't all as good as Stonewall said so they'd up the odds. He had never taken a first hand in his life and never would, not if he could help it. His father had been knifed after a perfect first-hand play in a high-stakes game.

In the second hand he made it appear to be luck, then he threw the third. At that point they had consumed only a couple of beers, which didn't count, and two plates of greens, which did. Cargo had taken a share of the annies like anyone else, but had palmed them into his pocket. He didn't use annies when he played, and he didn't like to waste good stuff just because he didn't. They'd keep.

Time was gone and all space had shrunk to the size of a card table. Focus was everything. Even the Bishop's request faded behind the order of play. The stakes had gone up, high enough to attract the attention of the dealer and to ward off the good-timers. Professional companions didn't disturb serious games. No percentage in it. It wasn't until the ante was over five high that Cargo started to clean up consistently. It wasn't the money that mattered to him. Money did not really exist, and he didn't mind spending it. The concentration, the display of pure skill attracted him as the stakes rose.

In the background, the other games were still going on, but they were distant. Losers leaving various tables drifted by and watched the tension in the four khandinar players, presided over by a dealer who had taken on the mixed persona of Dracula and the King of Hell dressed in formal black and wearing the regulation gloves. The Mah-Jongg master with her tattooed shoulder and arm came over to watch, one professional to another.

Cargo didn't notice. He was in the game the same way he had been in the maze with Ghoster, so completely experiencing the mode that other life paled and disappeared. He didn't notice when Ghoster found his way in and recognized his partner, and then stood and watched as Cargo took pots big enough to keep them all in Spin Street for a year. He didn't even notice when Plato found him, although he did recognize some change in the atmosphere. He thought it was luck, which he didn't believe in. He would have been relieved to know it was simply the subliminal effect of her perfume.

It wasn't until four A.M. local time, when the rest of the place closed down, that the game was over. Cargo handed his credit over to the dealer to let the unbiased professional observer credit his account with the winnings. They weren't massive. He'd won more on other occasions. But they weren't trivial, either.

"What I'd like to know," Stonewall said as they left the place, "What I'd really like to know is how you do it. I mean, why don't you cheat and do it easy?"

"I don't have to," Cargo answered. "I did my thesis on the probabilities in eight-deck khandinar." He abruptly broke away, as if embarrassed by revealing even that much.

A throaty laughter caught him from behind. He wheeled and was caught nearly off balance when he recognized Ghoster.

"How did you find me?" Cargo demanded.

"I smelled you in the Other Six."

Cargo smiled. He'd heard that plenty before. "Don't give me any of that metaphysical crap," he said companionably. "How about some greens? I got a pocket full of them."

Ghoster laughed again. "I will take them. You don't need them. You need to find Plato, who is probably asleep in the Mission Court Hotel, which you will now be able to afford. I told her not to worry about the price, that you wouldn't even notice it by the end of the night. But don't turn on your official pager. That's what we came to warn you about. We've all disappeared so Fourways can't catch us too soon."

"What?" Cargo demanded, coming out of his card-playing haze. "What about Fourways?"

Ghoster took the annies for Cargo's hand and tossed the two largest into his mouth at once. Then his ears went flat against his skull. "Nothing," Ghoster whispered. "Nothing at all, like the wind of Vanity, always screaming and never saying anything. Like out in the Six."

"Just tell me," Cargo pleaded, hope nearly gone. The two annies weren't the first of the evening, to judge from the Akhaid's overdramatic speech. Besides, Ghoster never talked about the Six except when he was wiped.

"Hide," Ghoster said. "Don't let anyone know where you are. Plato will tell you. I don't want to be there so I'm getting gone."

Cargo shook his head and checked the local tourist-assistance display for the Mission Court Hotel. It was located three long blocks off Spin Street towards a more respectable district and probably every bit as expensive as Ghoster had said. He glanced down the street. It was as nearly closed as it ever would be. The bustling mob of liberty-happy merchies had died down to a thin trickle of washed-out beings, half staggering under the gentle illumination of the soft yellow lights. One or two coffee shops, invisible between the more brilliantly highlighted cafes and bars and casinos and arcades, were still quietly busy.

Off-duty prostitutes sat around the high counters drinking steaming coffee from humble white china mugs. From outside the transparent layers of celo he could see them leaning over, telling one another a joke or a story, or inquiring about a working night. Then there would be a serious answer or they would all lean back together and laugh. Cargo couldn't hear what they said through the thick display window or smell the thick coffee in their mugs.

From the way they had kicked off their shoes under the table and leaned over when one spoke, he caught a glimpse of their camaraderie. Not so different from his own group, he thought. Except that he envied them at this moment of the early morning; that they were all together and coming home out of the cold jobs while he lay somewhere out in the unknown. For a moment Cargo was tempted to join them, to wrap his hands around a hot mug and inhale the homey warmth of the plain light and the plainer waitress.

In a darkened storefront two young children were wrapping up for the night. A can of flowers stood between them, bedraggled and nearly dead. "Please, sir, would you help the refugees of Major Nine?" the young girl asked, holding out a ragged pink carnation.

"*Sarishan*," Cargo greeted her in Romany and enjoyed seeing the deep-red blush color in her face.

"I'm sorry," the girl apologized quickly. "I thought you were Gaje. The uniform, I mean. And it's dark."

"Yes," he agreed. "It is dark." Then he walked away as if he had been burned and did not slow down until he reached the Mission Court Hotel.

The pager was flashing when he got up to the room Plato had taken. He went over to it and stared, his mind not quite made up to answer. Plato seemed to be asleep, sprawled on top of the blankets, damp tendrils of her hair clinging to her neck.

"Ignore it."

"You're not sleeping."

She shook her head with wry amusement. "Obviously."

Cargo glanced back at the pager once, then shut it firmly away from the moment. Plato's warm skin smelled of soap and perfume and the night. She had never been so beautiful, he thought. He had never seen a woman he desired more.

"Cargo?" she said, reaching out to draw him toward her.

"Rafael," he muttered against her soft flesh, but she didn't answer.

"I'll tell you why Gypsies steal," Cargo said. Plato was half-asleep on his shoulder, and the light from the window had begun to brighten almost imperceptibly, so that he wondered if it really was that early in the morning, or he had simply become accustomed to the dark. Plato murmured, and Cargo felt content.

"We have the right to steal," he said lazily. "See, at the Crucifixion, there was supposed to be another nail, one for Christ's heart, only it was stolen by a Gypsy. And ever since then, God gave Gypsies the right to steal."

Plato giggled and shook her head. Her hair tickled him. "You believe that?" she asked sleepily.

"No. But it's not a bad story."

Cargo decided that he was happy, luckier than most people ever were. Plato fingered the Ste. Maries medal lying against his chest without looking up—something she frequently did. He wasn't sure whether he liked it, and then decided that he did. Nothing was going to be wrong. They were on the Collegium, and time had stopped.

The light in the window really was brightening, casting deep ragged shadows of the table and easy chairs over the floor and stippling their bodies. If he kept his head turned just away from the door, he could manage not to see the pager flashing, waiting for an answer. He could pretend it wasn't there and sink into the universe that consisted of just him and Plato and this slowly brightening room.

Then the pager buzzed—a high-pitched shriek that tore through his senses. He leaped across the floor in two jumps and opened the line before the screech could go still higher. By the time he shut the noise off Plato was half out of bed, disoriented. Then she noticed the pager and made a face.

"Damn him to hell," she muttered.

He had to accept the message—there was no help for it now. But Cargo had the urge to kill Fourways. Plato was already falling back asleep, and he very much wanted to join her. Instead, he printed the pad and cued the dispatch to voice. He didn't want to turn on the lights. Perhaps, if the summons wasn't too urgent or too long, he'd able to return to the warmly rumpled sheets and sleep until the sunlight got in his eyes.

The screen came back with a "No Voice" line in red, top and bottom. That made it worse. Only highly classified code was sent under "no voice," and he hadn't realized that a hotel would be cleared to receive—let alone have spent enough money for—the equipment that would enable them to do so.

He glanced over at Plato. Her breathing came in the deep rhythm of sleep. He wondered what made her choose this place, if she knew all along that Fourways was sending something classified. He didn't like that. Maybe it would be better to assume that she had inquired idly. Even more likely, Cargo considered, that she was from Paragon, from a wealthy family. She probably always stayed at the most expensive hotel, the kind of place where someone far senior to them would normally stay and need to use secure transmissions. It wasn't worth bothering about now.

Cargo swore furiously when he read the message itself. *Report Top Security Office, first shift oh-six hundred.*

He had half an hour. No time for coffee. No wonder the thing had gone off. There had to have been a time lock.

A time lock *and* a "no voice." That was pretty pricy for run-of-the-mill orders to report. Something about the levels of security involved disturbed him, but his head was too full of cobwebs to make sense of anything.

He picked up his uniform from where he had left it, crumpled on the floor at the foot of the bed. One shoe lay directly under the heap but he had to search for the other. Eventually he found it tangled up with Plato's jacket, both of them shoved under the bed. He lost a few seconds wondering if he had the time to shave until he looked in the mirror. What looked back was some red-eyed derelict.

Even shaving and eyedrops didn't improve the image much. What he needed was a night's sleep and a hot shower, and the thought of that much luxury was tempting. It was hard to keep his eyes open. Dressed in the wrinkled jacket, he decided that he looked like hell. He also had only fifteen minutes left.

The hotel was expensive enough to run a scooter to the packet, which was late. He thought very seriously of taking one of the haulers and flying himself in, but the port authorities took a dim view of borrowing equipment. He arrived aboard the *Horn* twenty minutes late.

Ghoster met him at the lift, and Cargo rolled his eyes. Ghoster had managed a perfectly pressed uniform, alert eyes and even a touch of energy when he walked. It was hard to believe that Cargo had left him downworld only three hours earlier.

"How do you do that?" he asked, slightly disgusted.

Ghoster's ears rose slightly and then drooped. "I knew. Before I left. Only you had gone earlier, so I thought if you could stay out of it so could I."

Something about the way Ghoster said it rang false. Cargo didn't know quite why. The Akhaid's face was as unreadable as always, the tone of voice light and bantering as usual. It was as if something had shifted in Ghoster, and Cargo stopped dead in the corridor and looked directly at the alien.

That was precisely it. He had always listened to Ghoster as if the other were a human in costume. It wasn't that Ghoster was lying, but that Cargo perceived the alienness of his partner as a thing apart. Ghoster tried to translate things into equivalent understanding, but there was an essential connection missing.

In the miserably harsh lighting, the softly stippled lizard-like skin of the Akhaid gleamed as though it had been polished. Cargo studied him for only a fraction of a second, but that was long enough to fix the skin, the oversized feral eyes as connected with the intelligence that was too far removed for him to touch in the maze.

As if they had been thinking in unison, both turned and picked up the pace. They remained silent as they headed to the Security Office, past the magenta and blue stripes on the hot yellow walls. Just before the bulkheads merged from yellow to the pink outside the Security Office, Ghoster stopped.

"You're not the only one who forgets," he said simply.

Cargo smiled. He was tired, and whatever had seemed a revelation had to be remembered as the activity of an exhausted mind. Ghoster, although he had managed to attend to more of the cosmetic details, had to be nearly as fatigued. So he pretended that it was nothing. It was nothing. By the time he'd had a night's sleep and had washed the silt out of his eyes, it would be an insult to remember. Instead of saying anything he knocked on the door.

The unit opened softly and admitted them. Fourways sat behind the desk, eyes darting between three screens, and the animation in him made Cargo wonder if he'd eaten a plate of yellows. He indicated absently that they were to sit down and wait until he was ready. "Good," he said briskly and looked up from his displays.

"Well, gentlemen, I suppose you're wondering why I've

asked you here in the middle of your liberty and at this ungodly hour."

Cargo nodded crisply. Fourways must have lost his mind. Or this was an imposter. They were seated, he wasn't raking them over for being half-an-hour late, he was even being somewhat genial. This was not the Fourways Cargo knew.

To their left a briefing field cleared, turned pearly gray and then displayed an n-dimensional graph. Cargo knew enough to recognize the manifold markings, but the reduction was difficult to follow.

"Near the Veil," Ghoster muttered. "From Marcanter there are a few quick corridors through the topography to the Collegium."

Fourways actually smiled. Cargo thought he would pass out from the shock. He would have put down cash that Fourways was missing the muscles.

"Excellent, Ghoster," Fourways said approvingly. "Now, the problem is Marcanter. Always been a problem. You know they nearly didn't go with the Cardia when they seceded from the Collegium. Anyway, it seems that the mirages are based over there, and there's a neat little twist in the manifold that can bring them through either near the Veil systems or near us. There was some debate at the time about the elections there. If they were fixed I can see why. Marcanter is at one of those miserable strategic dimples that we have to take into consideration.

"That, however, is only the beginning of our problem. It seems our VIP has asked for you personally to take him down to Marcanter. After we finish our First Directorate mission, naturally."

Cargo didn't realize he was holding his breath. He understood all of a sudden exactly what the Bishop had been talking about. No wonder Fourways was in such a good mood. Still, something was bothering him. "What mission? Why now?" he asked. "Haven't we known about the quick corridors for a long time? Haven't we even used them ourselves?"

Fourways blinked rapidly. Even Ghoster seemed confused. Of course. They didn't know he knew about the Bishop, about his party's fifteen-year struggle to contact their sister group in the Cardia. They didn't have the faintest idea about how the old man had struggled to put an end to this conflict.

Other pictures flashed on the screen, quickly, one after another. They were the mirages, hidden deep in the ground like the batwing on Vanity. Those pictures hadn't been sent by any constellation or any snoop. This was strictly First Directorate on the flesh-and-blood side. No matter what they said, Cargo was staring at proof that there were still spies in the universe.

"The reason we're looking at it now is because the Cardia celebrate their so-called Liberation Day in fourteen days," Fourways informed them. "They've invited a very senior statesman, Bishop Mirabeau, to a private talk at that time. I believe you know the Bishop. The First Directorate doesn't trust that invitation. What we need to do is wipe out this base. This is where they're launching from, and if we can get these mirages then they won't have advance warning on movements. This is the only military base on Marcanter. If the Cardia have a show of our strength before they sit down with a certain ex-Trustee, there's a good chance they'll be more willing to make a settlement which the Collegium can accept. It's necessary to get rid of these mirages first."

Ghoster closed his eyes for a moment, then opened them. "The others will be taking out constellations, other snoops and listening posts, correct, sir?"

Fourways scowled so familiarly that Cargo took back the possibility of an imposter. "That is on a need-to-know basis only, and you don't need to know anything at all. The reason I've asked you both here this morning is because I wanted you two to run the prelim scout on the Marcanter base."

"Just the prelim scout, sir?" Cargo asked, amazed.

Fourways closed his eyes and grasped the dented sides of the desk. Then he exhaled slowly and looked straight at Cargo. "You'll do a prelim on the base," he said slowly. "After that, you're going in. The First Directorate has set a paper cover team, testing at the factory. Now you're coming on board. Easy. The *Horn* will be stationed here. With your data, using surprise, this team will scatter the mirages. And the Kraits will take the base."

"And the peace mission?" He couldn't help asking.

Strangely enough, Fourways smiled again. This time it was a weary gesture, acknowledgment of something he'd prefer to forget. "Bishop Mirabeau might have been a Trustee and he might still pull a lot of strings, but even that doesn't guarantee accurate information all the time, does it?" he asked.

Cargo held steady. He'd never known the Bishop to be

wrong before. He'd spent enough time in the Bishop's study —both of them discussing and repeating various turning points in history—to suspect that whoever had decided to attack Marcanter just before Mirabeau was due at the invitation of the Cardia peace faction was not exactly helping the Bishop's cause.

Fourways' eyes bored into Cargo. Both of them forgot that Ghoster was there. "You know, I've tried every way I could to tell if you were so high up on the hot list because of Mirabeau or because you deserved it. I never trusted politician's favorites. Usually they're chosen because they'll kiss more ass than they'll kick. I thought you were different. You seemed to be the genuine article, and I know I damn well made you prove it. Only now I'm not so sure. You come in here listening to whatever rumint the geeks are creating this month, and you're ready to blow us all off. What I want to know, Mr. Rafael Mirabeau, is whether you are loyal to your team and your group, or to that collection of liars, thieves and con artists that you dignify as your fine diplomat ancestors?"

There was nothing Cargo could say. He was stunned, physically unable to open his mouth or make his voice work. Fourways was beyond him. All along he had thought of the commander in a very different light, and he had been wrong. Cargo didn't like to think of himself as that blind, that unable to perceive the layers below the surface. He had always thought of himself as Sister Mary's son, with the *boojo* woman's uncanny knowledge of the depths of an individual's being.

"I am waiting, mister," Fourways said. Cargo thought he seemed vaguely sad, and that unsettled him even more.

"I just want the truth," he managed to croak.

Fourways shook his head. "The truth is that whatever idiotic story your Bishop Mirabeau got could as easily be Cardia disinformation as an honest overture. I may not like Bishop Andre Mirabeau—not what he stands for, not his party, nothing. But we're here to protect him whether we like it or not. So you like it. But that doesn't mean you have considered all the ramifications of the base down there. A batwing base. Did it ever occur to you to question where they got their stealth designs? You know, Cargo, you're not the only one around here who has any sense of honor."

"I didn't mean that, sir," Cargo said softly. "I'm sorry my

manner insinuated that. Exactly what data are we to gather in the prelim?"

Fourways leaned back and began to tell them. Cargo tried to keep his attention on the task, but under it all he was too aware of the fact that he had had the chance to impress the commander, to bring him over. And he had failed.

Chapter

11

They broke back into the manifold three days later. Being outmanifold had been comforting this time, more because of Plato's constant presence than the mountain of paperwork they were buried under. Stonewall summed it up very neatly when he arrived late for a card game. "When I hit the Wall, I'm gonna get to the Pearly Gates, and St. Peter's gonna ask for fifteen copies of a three-twenty-two form for admittance, two medical certificates, and then send me back because I didn't fill in line thirty-seven of the secondary harp-requisition order form."

At least, Cargo thought, he and Plato were on the same sched. Plato had bought a reproduction of "Point of Tranquility" when she was at liberty on the Collegium that adhered to the metal bulkhead and made the tiny stateroom more personal.

Besides, they had taken on fresh provisions on the Collegium, so pears and mandarin oranges and mangoes and sliced apples appeared at every meal. The last night they remained outside the manifold, the chef produced something that he called Black Forest cake. Cargo had enjoyed it thoroughly until he overheard a couple of Krait drivers talking on late recwatch.

"Damn glad that stuff didn't get served at *our* mess," one said. Cargo thought she looked like a schoolgirl, not a pilot. Much too young. Or maybe she only looked very young because she seemed so scared.

"Well, one of these days," her companion said. "I prefer it to the black rose."

The younger pilot shuddered.

Cargo turned away, his stomach churning. He knew the story of the black rose. It took up exactly one paragraph in the text on naval tradition that had been required reading in OCS. It had fascinated him. During a short period early in the Collegium's history, when pirate attacks were a serious problem, those who went into individual combat with the pirates were given a black rose the night before they entered embattled space. In later years the Black Rose became the Collegium's highest award for heroism.

Different ships had different customs, but no one had informed the batwing about the captain's own interpretation of the tradition of the Black Rose. Black Forest cake indeed. Cargo decided not to tell the others. They all knew perfectly well that the raid on Marcanter was not exactly a training run on Vanity. Still, he didn't like the idea that the chef and the captain had practically written them off. The fear made him cold, fear that there might be more in the plan than Fourways had told them in the three separate briefings he had held: to give them all something to do while they were outmanifold, he had said.

Now, as the *Horn* emerged behind the fifth planet in Marcanter's system, Cargo lay panting under the restraining web in the cockpit of the batwing. As soon as they were fully established in the manifold, he and Ghoster would slip away into the dark. He didn't want that moment to come. For the first time since he had first driven a Krait, he wanted to back down, run away. Even the web clinging to his face was preferable to what lay out there. What Fourways had asked.

He'd already taken four Three-B's but he reached gently into the pill patch and swallowed four more. The web accepted the gradual movement as nonthreatening. Maybe, Cargo thought, if he could get deep enough into the maze he wouldn't notice the web. And the maze would take the fear, would look only to ways and means of accomplishing the objective. Locked with his mind, fully geared in mode, there would be a distance from the emotions. They would freeze in the absoluteness of maze thought.

Just as he was about to make the transition, a buzzer went off, alerting personnel that they were reentering the manifold. Normal space once again, outside of the Other Six mathematical dimensions through which things oscillated to create the fundamental universe. Cargo couldn't care less—just so long as he didn't feel anything—that there wasn't any jerk or tension to make the web go rigid.

This time the helm got through it elegantly. There wasn't even a hint of transition when the alarm pitch lowered, indicating full stabilization back inside the Old Four.

Automatically Cargo stripped the web from his body and tossed it out the hatch. Helmet fastened, he descended into cybermode like falling into a black hole. He wondered vaguely if eight Three-B's had been too many, and then he was immersed in the maze.

The maze was brighter than he had ever experienced it. There was a clarity that had eluded him before, and within that clarity he sensed Ghoster through the membrane more sharply than he had ever expected. The calm logic of the maze distilled his thoughts so completely that it was possible to contemplate Ghoster removing his web, entering the mode, with a rich and close sense of singularity that had always caused pain before. The membrane and the maze kept the personalities apart; it was the merging of purpose Cargo experienced, and it gave him a feeling of omnipotence. A feeling that he knew was dangerous, but still seductive.

At the edge of his awareness, he realized that the alarm had stopped. In the unrelenting lucidity of the maze he was more than prepared when the batwing hooked the track and began the roll. The airlock closed and cycled around him. And then they were dancing vac again.

Marcanter was visible, a white, brown, red and blue globe hanging like the fruit of temptation at the down nine. The maze quivered with his desire as it angled the batwing toward the planet. From this distance it was deceptively serene. No hint that the Cardia mirages and a sneaking death lay hidden in the folds of those billowing clouds. Vis was excellent.

Ghoster's thoughts caught him subtly, reminding him that the mirages were as silent as they were. That their major protection was to keep the white clouds always in full view in the hope that any black, mirage-seeking vac would show up against the screen. They sure as hell wouldn't show up on instruments. The maze transmitted the last with a sense of recoil, as if it had some instinct that it had been insulted.

Slow go, he thought into mode although his hands sweated from frustration inside the strapped-down gloves. Slow go, which would mean hours of soft, near drift so that the constel-

lations wouldn't pick up the batwing from spectral emana-
tions. Top of the mask mark wasn't as high as he would like.
That part was still primitive, the fight or flight response held
so tightly in check that it was physically painful.

At least they were at the advantage, he reminded himself
sternly. He and Ghoster had surprise. No one was looking for
them. None of the Cardia dreamed that a carrier, much less
something the size of the *Horn and Hardart*, was drifting
behind a bulk of rock barely outside their orbit.

The maze questioned the thought and Cargo banished it
immediately. Instead, he visualized the approach he, Ghoster
and Fourways had decided would keep them covered best.
Slow go to constellation level, and from there no go at all.
Marcanter's gravity would draw them down, and it remained
to the maze to keep the position steady. They had already
decided to come in over the largest watermass on the planet,
which was less well patrolled and had far fewer censor bases
than any comparable continent. From there the mission would
really begin, and somehow Cargo, for all the terror pounding
in his chest, felt almost light-headed with happiness.

Fourways had chosen him because he was Romany. There
could be no other reason. None of the others on the team—
not Plato or Stonewall or Steel or Glaze or Fourways himself
—not one of them could steal a mirage from under the
Cardia's nose. From the base itself. Only the person who had
had the guts to steal C. L. Wong's yacht had any chance of
success. As Fourways had said so dryly, Cargo was experienced.

Around him the blackness changed subtly. They were clos-
ing slowly on the placid form of Marcanter. On vis, off to one
side, Cargo caught an anomoly that snagged his consciousness. The stars blotted for a moment and then reappeared. Not
daring to turn the batwing, he squinted out into the dark, trying to make out the shape and shadow of whatever was moving. No doubt it was a mirage, but he had lost it vis. And the
maze insisted that it never had been there in the first place; he
questioned whether he might need to visit sick bay and a psy-
chiatrist.

There in the dark, dancing vac, he knew them. He didn't
need to spot them on vis to feel them out there, the mirage that
barely existed on the outside of awareness. They surrounded
him and then paraded past, one by one, gliding majestically as

if they alone owned the night. They never noted he was there.

"Do you want to know the secret to being invisible?" Old Piluka had asked him. *"Do you want to know how to steal like a true Rom, creeping like the first dawn? Because it is very easy to be invisible."* Old Piluka had laughed and held a belly so large that he had no lap to hold his grandsons on. It was the night before Djanjo went out with his cousin, Angel, their first time alone.

"The secret is what the Gaje don't see. They see a rich person or a poor person, they see a threatening person. But they don't see the person who is part of the scenery, the bartender at the bar, the workingman running the crane, the person who walks in one direction with his face set. And that is how you must be invisible, as the Rom always have been. We can be whoever it pleases us to be."

The old man had been wise, and had been very rich too. Cargo had profited more than once from his lessons. He didn't remember his grandfather very well, he had poured a bottle of scotch on Old Piluka's grave when he was only seven. But the voice and the words stuck, sometimes taking on the aspect of the Bishop. Now they wore the original semblance, as if by preparing to steal he had come back to his people and the *marhime* had been lifted. That was stupid. Only that the knowledge was in him, bred into his genes.

It was not precisely that time did not exist in the maze. Rather its function was somewhat different, as if it had become a dimension of space. Ghoster had told him that when they were in mode they functioned outside the manifold, in dimensions that had been compressed in the birthing of the universe. All Cargo cared about was that time became maleable, expanding to suit his needs dancing vac in the middle of a fight, or contracting a long voyage into a single point of experience. He didn't notice the long hours pass as he and the maze together directed the batwing through layers of watching constellations. The batwing slipped in, invisible to all of them, her contours and honeycomb structure hiding her sedate approach.

In the maze he had not gone glassy, losing the peak of concentration. Rather, as the maze returned him to a fuller command of the situation, Cargo felt refreshed and serene. He was at the top of his form and he knew it. They were close now, close enough to make out the patterns of the clouds, that were not pure white at all but tinged slightly pink.

Ferrous materials. No wonder they had hidden the mirages here, Cargo thought. The maze agreed. The ruddy shade of some of the landmass bore it out. Good strategy, although Cargo never made the mistake of thinking the Cardia command was stupid. The beings who did that got to the Wall very quickly. Still, he was impressed that they had realized that the clouds could be "raked" and the particles aligned to haze out almost any ELint device in use. No wonder the pictures Fourways had shown them had obviously been taken by living spies, the spies the First Directorate insisted it didn't have.

But the cloud mask worked both ways. Those on the surface couldn't see what was out in space and had to rely on snoops and constellations for their safety. And, once below that layer, even a Krait would be undetectable. The clouds worked like a natural chaff layer. Under them, any searching device would immediately blank out against the raked-iron particles.

Wisps of atmosphere came up to greet them, and they entered endo under such quiet control that there was no burn to speak of. Better that way, Cargo figured. The maze agreed. Both had been trained to avoid any conspicuous display. They entered the cloud layer only moments later, and the maze panicked. All instruments were out, registering crazy banks of nothingness against the ferrous backshield.

Cargo clamped down with his mind on the confused machine. He knew where they were, in the chaff layer. He would bring them down out of it, orienting to the large watermass that he and Ghoster had agreed was the best approach. The maze babbled away. It didn't trust a human pilot's instincts above its own instrumentation.

Cargo ignored it and focused his senses as he had in orientation training so very long ago. Three directions, each described as a color: horizontal blue, vertical red, intersect yellow. All he had to do was keep himself open, aware of the gradual shifts in the gravitational field provided by the planet. That, ultimately, was the way he wanted to go, just like following running water.

The maze resisted. It couldn't sense the gravity except as a reading, and all the other readings were insane. The machine balked and almost refused to be handled, trying to direct Cargo's interest back into the vac they had come from.

Cargo made the images he had learned in prelim training and had never had to use before. He showed himself to the maze—entered it, and then expanded until the maze was only a small part of his brain. He was in control. The maze had to accept that a sentient being was its master. It had been programmed that way under all the layers of artificial intelligence architects' distrust of humans and Akhaid both. Silently Cargo cursed those beings who trusted the judgment of a rummage-sale heap of silicon, DNA and electron boards over the rational argument of the sentient brain.

The maze pleaded once more for control and then gave in. Cargo had no time to pursue his victory. They were in enemy airspace, in the middle of a ferrous cloud, and the wind was building.

Thank God for the winds of Vanity. They had taught him to recognize and ride a storm. Even the most developed of the Cardia worlds lay under open sky, and around him Cargo could feel the faint stirrings of a baby thunderhead. Through the membrane he could feel Ghoster's answering excitement.

The pressure changed rapidly, high and low interchanging, moving and swirling into each other. Low-pressure pockets appeared, and Cargo fell into one. The batwing plummeted down, obeying only the law of gravity. Cargo whooped once before they caught an updraft and rode it out.

The thunderhead glowed sullen red as Cargo ran before it. He could see the lightning flickering through the cloud, the shadow it cast on the dark boiling waters below. It filled him with energy—electrical changes that he had learned about in proper and civilized classes but experienced as a creature of flesh.

Then Ghoster's thought came through the maze. *Down,* it said, not in words but in images filled with impatience and fear. Cargo acknowledged. Ghoster was right. The longer they stayed near the clouds the greater the chances of someone catching them vis, a black spot against the pink, red and rust of the thrashing sky.

The descent was steady and assured. Cargo drifted the batwing down on the currents like the bit of floating silk she appeared to be. Endo, riding atmosphere, he could keep the engines at nearly no go. Except vis against the coming storm, there was no way to detect them as they came within sight of the teaming whitecaps on the violent sea.

The batwing rode so close to the surface that the swells could be seen clearly from the canopy; and it appeared that the larger ones might even dampen the layers of clear celo with spray. Cargo gave the maze direction again. Over the water, he was without direction which the maze instruments could provide. This far under the clouds the instruments were able to function on only a limited scale, but that was enough to find the landmass they were seeking.

Marcanter's modest southern continent lay well off the shore of the larger grouping. Isolated from any population centers it was an ideal location for the mirage base. The only difficulty lay in penetrating the defenses around the island continent and landing the batwing where it wouldn't be seen.

He had at least an idea for the first. Fourways had gone over it with them in the multitude of briefings when they were outmanifold, and Cargo and Ghoster had refined it in their free time with some assistance from Stonewall, Steel and Plato.

Essentially, the strategy was primitive: stay as close to the ground as possible. They couldn't read what they couldn't see, and no device could see the flat no-profile presented by the batwing against the background radiation reflected from the surface, especially not when it hugged the contours of the earth. The western side of the continent offered the best cover. A range of ragged young mountains enclosed half the boundary from nearly five kilometers in down to the sea. The mountains had thrown up an archipelago of tiny, uninhabited islands that spread deep into the eastern ocean and that very well could have telltales on them. In fact, Cargo would be surprised if the whole archipelago weren't a minefield. So the trick would be staying over water between the islands, and then down low between the peaks of the mountain range. It called for some serious piloting, but nothing that the hills and winds of Vanity had left to chance. He knew perfectly well that there would have been unpredictable thermals all through the hills, and in that moment of choice he welcomed the challenge.

He could feel Ghoster's echo through the maze, as if the Akhaid had only been waiting for him to accept. They had been undetected so far, but Cargo forgot that this was the pullout point. No such thing existed for him. Only the wailing of the challenge called him, the exhilaration of exercising his own skill to the utmost.

Cargo flew as he had in the mountains of Vanity. The maze—fully under control—was relegated to a function in the back of his mind, following orders before they were fully formulated. That was what it was for. Maze walking was only for dancing vac, out there in the uncharted territory where anything could go wrong. Here, surrounded by air and water and great shaggy islands rising straight up from the sea, here was a being permitted intrinsic authority over the maze. And here it only obeyed.

The high islands rose like spikes from the harsh gray surface of the storm-worried sea. Cargo thought the batwing steady, practically skimming the water in the labyrinth of the archipelago. Obligingly, the maze provided him with complete charts. He imaged the course between those islands as a brilliant red line. The maze acknowledged and together they flew. Cargo nudged the maze closer to the protective rock walls, and it responded in true mode as a part of his own body.

The islands packed thicker as they came closer to the mainland. Slightly above, almost lost in the silhouette of the towering mountains of the western coast, Cargo thought he caught the dark flecks of mirages heading north. Only vis, he reminded the maze. The only way they'd ever see them.

On the verge of entering the mountains, Cargo saw another black shape emerge from the pass. Even in vis, only there was no way he could miss it this time. The mirage passed close enough that he could see the shadow it cast on the mountainside. He thought the maze back, hiding quickly behind the peak of an island, hoping only that the mirage driver was as thrown by the identical shapes of their craft and was maybe expecting company this time of day. That was the best he could expect.

He clued the maze to word-communication. He had to talk to Ghoster, to use words for safety and precision. "Revise plans," he thought in cybermode. "Land on island, then transport to base."

The only response he received was a faint interrogative, which he answered with a brisk laugh. The islands were extremely close together. They would find some way back. It was better to improvise ahead than follow a plan that has become trouble, Old Piluka had said. Cargo could sense that

Ghoster was in no mood to improvise and ignored him. Ghoster only knew he was Rom, but Ghoster didn't quite appreciate what that meant. Not yet, anyway.

The maze alerted him to a long stretch of hard-packed beach. As good a landing place as any. Cargo thanked the maze, forgetting it wasn't due any courtesy, and visualized the landing.

The maze brought them in smoothly, the batwing rolling down the beach as the storm overcame them and broke above. A great sheet of water poured down as Cargo began his final out-check. From inside the cockpit they could hear the hiss as the rain hit the superheated surface of the batwing craft and turned to steam.

Cargo was still in mode when he heard Ghoster turn on the chatterbox. A strange echo filled the batwing as he heard Ghoster's voice and sensed his meaning through the membrane. He had to force himself to concentrate only on the words. Enough Three-B's and getting out of mode was really painful.

"What are we supposed to do now?" Ghoster asked. "We're down. How do we get to the mainland, with a storm and all? What the hell did you expect, a miracle or something? Dammit, Cargo, there's high seas out there."

Cargo snorted. "Swim. You know how to swim, don't you?"

"I'm not even about to open this hatch with that storm coming down," Ghoster replied furiously. "You think I'm planning to swim in that sea? You're worse than crazy. You're out of your sweet-turtle-dung mind, you know that. You're so gone in I don't know what direction. You think we're going to swim all the way to the mainland in this mess and climb ashore and infiltrate the base? I think you've been watching too many spy shows, that's what I think."

Cargo tried not to laugh. "I don't expect us to swim to the mainland. I figure they've got a storm watch going, and we'll get picked up. We'll bury our clothes—how they gonna know where we came from, right? And if we're picked up drowning nobody's gonna expect us to talk. Now, will you release the canopy so I can get out?"

Ghoster hesitated. "Getting half drowned wasn't exactly what I had in mind. Besides, why do you have to get out now?" he asked sullenly.

"Because I'm dying to take a piss, that's why," Cargo snapped.

The hatch opened, and they were both immediately drenched. The sea was washing up around their ankles when they got down. "It's gonna wash away the batwing and us," he complained nonstop, another whine added to the noise on the beach.

Cargo made short work of his more personal business, then rolled up his uniform and stuffed it under a large rock.

"You ever thought of how they're going to find us?" Ghoster demanded. "If they can't track a batwing, how are they going to find us out there? We're not exactly a carrier-size target, you know."

"You don't like the water," Cargo said very slowly. "Why Ghoster, I think I have found out what you're afraid of. I never figured you were too much of a coward to take a little swim. I'm shocked."

Ghoster's ears were plastered to the sides of his head, but he stood his ground. "I still want to know why they're going to pick us up when they couldn't get the bat," he insisted sullenly.

"Because," Cargo said, already past the end of his patience, "they will be looking for us. I figure they have storm patrol like we do with infrared tracking. And the bat is infrared absorbent. Doesn't show with the mask on. Without the batwing, you and I show up just fine, two bright red sparks in the middle of that nice cold ocean."

Ghoster looked at the water creeping closer to his knees than his ankles now and looked as if he were going to be sick. Cargo waded out next to him. "Just think of it this way," he said reassuringly to the Akhaid. "You can't get any wetter than you are now."

Ghoster nodded miserably and followed Cargo out to where water got deep. There, he grabbed Cargo by the shoulders, refusing to let him step off the shelf and relax against the rain-driven swells.

"One last thing," he shouted above the storm. "What's our story? If they pick us up, what's our story?"

"The truth," Cargo yelled before a particularly large wave broke over them, washing them apart and carrying them off on its own.

• • •

It was dry. That was the first thing Cargo noticed. Dry and warm. Then he tried to move, and the pain came from everywhere. He couldn't even locate it. His skin, his muscles, everything ached intensely. Even breathing made him feel like he was doing violence to the lining of his lungs and bronchial tubes.

"How are we this afternoon?" asked a soft voice with a strange twang in Indopean.

Cargo wondered where he was for a moment. The accent wasn't familiar. Then it came back. He was on Marcanter. He muttered a curse in Romany and tried to open one eye.

"You shouldn't use that kind of language," came back in Romany, and then the voice switched to Indopean. "We will assume the shock overcame you, and that you aren't an ethnic separatist. Besides, half the group here is betting that you're all the novo stealth unit and got caught in the storm. They tell me that those things handle like pigs in atmosphere, so we're not holding you on charges. At least not yet."

He was able to see pretty well. The woman who was speaking didn't look like a true *chal*. Half, maybe. But what she said cautioned him not to inquire further. Besides, she wore a white coat that screamed doctor from a distance of at least two hospital lengths, and the patches on her left shoulder made him suspect that she was probably a flight surgeon.

He grunted suspiciously. Of all classes of beings, at least among Gaje, the one he hated the most was doctors and flight surgeons. When he was in training they were the enemy, even more than the Cardia pilots. They could ground you and looked for every excuse to do so. And he would swear they enjoyed running every Krait driver in the Nav through a full physical twice a year, just to keep themselves in trim.

The doctor laughed. "You're a pilot?" she asked.

Cargo tried to shake his head and found it wouldn't move. For a moment he worried that he was paralyzed, but he had never heard of the body moving and the head staying still. Then he realized that he was wearing a heavy collar that pressed around his neck and held him tight.

"What happened?" he asked in a panic.

The doctor walked over and patted his hand in the eternally patronizing medical gesture. "Don't worry. You'll be all right. I'll even pass you to fly myself in a few days when the muscles finish knitting."

Cargo wanted to cry in frustration. There were too many things he needed to know, and the damned doctor was keeping them back on purpose. Just to torture him. He was sure of it. They were all alike.

He could barely follow her as she walked to the door. "Wait," he croaked out. "How long?"

She smiled enigmatically. "Don't worry. The storm hasn't let up yet. You haven't missed any action." Then she was gone.

Cargo wanted to nurse his anger in comfort. Visions of securing doctors with their own IV tubes and subjecting them to every blood test in the known manifold was just the beginning of a fitting revenge. Cargo knew that, given sufficient time and hospital food, he could complete the scenario to his satisfaction. That luxury, however, would have to wait. He had no idea how much time had passed, and he couldn't afford to spend anymore being idle.

Cautiously he pulled back the sheet to assess the damage. The evidence was not pretty. His skin was more mottled purple fading to green than its proper honey color, and there was a large swathe of bandage around his left shoulder; however, there was no indication of broken bones or internal injuries. Thank God there were no tubes sticking into him.

Mostly, he figured, he'd been pretty banged up. From the soreness in his shoulders and throughout his respiratory system, they might have pumped out some seawater. Any danger from that was now long past, and the only problem was that it was painful to breathe. That would have to be ignored.

Gingerly he eased his legs from the soft sheet to the floor. His head throbbed violently, and he thought he was going to be sick. For a moment he panicked, wondering if he had a concussion or a skull fracture. Then he told himself firmly that it was doubtlessly some miserable chemical the medics had injected. That was the way they got their excitement at work. Didn't matter what side you were on, even what species. Ghoster had told him that Akhaid doctors were the same. None of them had any decent feeling at all.

Cargo decided that getting out of wherever he was was not only necessary but a fitting revenge on the medical establishment as well. He stood up. He wanted to crumple back into bed and rest. Maybe for once, purely by the odds, they were right this time.

Then he understood that his thinking was fuzzy. He had forgotten where he was—that this was Marcanter and he had infiltrated the hospital. They didn't suspect anything so far. The hospital had to be part of the base; the complex was the only thing on this wretched continent.

Obviously they had given him some medication, or he would have seen it immediately. And the Three-B's he'd taken before leaving had made it worse. They didn't interact well, even when taken in reasonable doses. But it was reasonable, he told himself firmly. There was no way to guarantee that he could get more down here. No doubt the Cardia used them; basic mode technology hadn't changed that radically even with the extreme improvements in response. That was the area they bothered with anyway, how the maze flew the machine, not how the mind controlled the maze. That had been considered established just before the Luxor shooting and the Cardia secession. The Third Directorate, who had for reasons unknown parted with some shred of information on this subject to make his task manageable, were firmly of the opinion that the Cardia was more intent on increasing production of almost every weapon system. They wouldn't screw around with a cybermode system that worked more than very well.

Great. Now he was thinking instead of standing. At the moment that didn't count as progress. He forced himself back on his feet and began all over again. One foot in front of the next. Push off the wall. Make the legs carry the weight. There was nothing wrong with them, except for the fact they hurt like hell. Cargo was not really fond of pain.

Three more steps and then back. That was better. Some of the problem was just that he was stiff. A few good hard bumps would do that. As he walked around the room he found his muscles loosened a bit and the worst edge of the pain faded. It was still there and he knew he wouldn't be able to run, if it came to that, but at least he was mobile.

The next problem was clothes. He'd left his own on the island. He checked the locker next to the bed. The medics hadn't seen fit to issue him any. Not even a bathrobe to go over the disposable paper pajamas folded in a neat stack on the top shelf of the locker. Reaching to get them down was almost more than the flimsies were worth, but they were better than nothing. Besides, he had to seem a lot better if he was going to sweet talk any medic into issuing him clothes and maybe even a passport out of the hospital.

Once dressed in the paper pajamas he found the head. There was a stool for a possibly badly injured person to sit on while taking a shower, and Cargo availed himself of the opportunity to rest. At least the place was well equipped for hygiene, and after a shower and shave he peered in the mirror. A few strategic splashes of icy water brought more color to his face. If one ignored the swelling and discoloration on his left cheek, he was near passable. Maybe shaving hadn't been such a good idea. He hadn't realized that the bruise was so multi-colored. At least he felt better. The heat of the shower had eased the worst of the muscle aches and had quieted his head a bit. It wasn't a concussion.

So far as Cargo was concerned, the reflection passed muster. All he had to do now was walk. He managed across the room better than he expected, keeping quite steady and not holding on at all, until he reached the door. Then he stopped to wonder where the nurses' station was and if they would grill him and send him back. For a moment he was more frightened of them than of the grilling he would doubtless receive if he was caught.

The absurdity of it struck him and he laughed exactly once before the taped shoulder and side, to say nothing of his recently pumped respiratory system, protested violently. He was in. Well in. No one questioned a pilot downed in the drink. Even naked he could claim the suit had filled with water and started to drag him down. No one bothered about a flier afraid of drowning. Everyone was afraid of something. The important thing was that his presence wasn't questioned.

Fear of drowning made him think of Ghoster. He wondered if Akhaid patients were on a different corridor, or even a different floor. He wished it wasn't so reasonable to separate the species in hospitals so that specialized equipment didn't have to be duplicated. That was all medical disinformation. The real reason, he was absolutely certain, was that the doctors didn't want to bother walking any further than they had to. It was easier to group the patients rather than spread them out all over the hospital to socialize.

No, his thinking was still fuzzy. He wondered again what they had given him to mix so badly with the Three-B's. Didn't matter. The first priority was clothing. Then finding Ghoster.

If he was lucky he'd get something for Ghoster to wear, too. Assume their new identities. Best of all was for both of them to be themselves, only slightly changed. Fourways always said that. Cover should be as close as possible. That way you don't fuck up.

He only prayed that the First Directorate had gotten it right, or else he and Ghoster were both dead. If any of the stealth drivers knew the factory test team they were in bad trouble—well, he could always say there had been a second test group, or even a special team to demonstrate for the politicos. That would even work at home. He hadn't been trained by old Piluka for nothing.

He decided to chance the door. He nudged it open a few centimeters. That brought no response so he decided to try the whole way and step into the corridor for good measure.

He found that his room was located near the end of the hall. Not quite all the way down near the visitor's lounge, but well out of the direct line of the nurse's station. There was only one nurse on duty there at the moment, and he seemed absorbed in something on the desk. Not that Cargo trusted that. He was sure they had telltales all over the place. Medical types never trusted anyone, and with good reason.

Sounds came from the lounge, which was half concealed behind a turn in the hallway. The far end held several high windows, through which Cargo could see it was still day, and that the storm had slackened off to a gentle drizzle. He headed in that direction, hoping that some inspiration would come before he had to confront his first Cardia beings—not counting the doctor, that was, but doctors were generic enemies.

Cargo entered the lounge as if he belonged. The three people draped over the furniture were pilots. All wore shiny silver wings. Cargo smiled sheepishly.

"You one of the guys from the factory test group they pulled out in the storm?" one of the Crafters asked.

"Yeah," Cargo said. "It was pretty bad."

"We keep telling Command that these things weren't made to fly in red storms. How come you didn't get better stability before you signed off on it?" another one, a woman with very blond hair, complained.

"I don't even think they've ever seen a red storm," the first one chimed in. "And try and explain the Scorpions were hardly designed to fly endo, let alone in a lot of weather."

"Handles like a pig," Cargo agreed instinctively and the others assented in chorus. It was almost too easy. "They took away my clothes," Cargo tried to bring the conversation closer to his own situation.

"Ah, yes," said the one who hadn't spoken yet. "You are in the ward of the famous Dr. Locke. As in lock and key. As in she don't trust any of us in her sight, let alone out of it. She's got at least five of us here, and you don't think she's gonna just let you out, do you?"

"But we've got to get out," Cargo pleaded in near desperation. "We've got work to do."

"And don't I know it," the woman said.

Looking at her more carefully, Cargo noticed an extra layer of ornamental stitching on her collar. A ranker, more than likely.

"So, you ready for some action?" the first man asked.

Cargo grinned. "Ready as I ever was. Only I need clothes to walk out of this place. Damn, first day I'm here the meds know me. But what are you here for?" he demanded, suddenly suspicious.

The blond woman laughed. "We're here to pick up a few more fliers, mister. You did come down to do some real work, right? Well, it looks like we got ourselves a target just waiting for the picking, a great big carrier that isn't even gonna notice us sneaking up all around. Very nice. But we're a little short on personnel. That's why we requisitioned even you test turkeys. I'm trying to find a couple who might be ready to ride."

Cargo hardly dared to breathe. "Well, if I had some clothes and the nurse was looking the other way I'd be happy to prove that Marcanter isn't the only place where real stealth jockeys get their hours."

"What rank you have?" the taller man asked. "You mind being a lieutenant j.g.? Only thing I think we got that fits."

Cargo's eyes went wide as a wadded flightsuit was tossed across the lounge. "You do this often?" he asked in amazement.

This time there were no smiles. "On Locke's ward, all the time," the first man said. "Only way to get people out of here. Don't worry, she's got a rule. You get out, she'll clear you to fly. Isn't easy, and we haven't won yet. You've got to get past the nurse, the duty guards and be back in the ready room before Dr. Dungeon'll sign the papers."

Cargo blinked rapidly. This didn't happen. This was luck, a kind of luck that didn't even exist.

The woman smiled. "Move fast. This is standard procedure. Only way to get my group to strength before we start hitting the scrags, right?"

Cargo made it back to the room and changed. Excitement made all the difference. A shuffling, pained patient had been walking around the halls earlier. A visitor between shifts exited after looking in on a friend. Happened all the time.

He didn't dare ask about Ghoster until they were on their way to the ready room and Cargo saw a group of Akhaid coming out another door.

The woman nodded thoughtfully. "If your partner is getable, they should have got him. We'll rendezvous with a few other groups before check in time. You ready?"

Cargo breathed in deeply, appreciating the fresh, overheated and humid air of Marcanter. And nearly collapsed coughing.

"By the way, what's your name?" the woman who seemed to be in charge asked as he got his breath back.

Cargo thought quickly. There was still one name left, and no doubt the First Directorate had used it. "Kore Verdon," he said slowly, tasting the name in his mouth. "From Marcanter, born in Grafton."

"You don't sound like you come from there," the tall man said.

"We moved around alot," Cargo improvised and shrugged.

"We don't have until the end of the universe," the woman fumed. "What's your sign? I'll log you in when we've got time, which probably means after we get back."

"Cargo," he said with not a little pride. "Call me Cargo."

Chapter
12

"Rescued like shit. We got washed up. On the rocks!"

"This isn't time for that, Ghoster," Cargo warned. He kept his voice low, but still could feel the eyes of half the hot shack on them. The place was too cramped for privacy no matter how low they talked, and Ghoster didn't seem to be in any mood to be reasonable.

"You hear this guy?" Ghoster yelled out to the whole group. "If I wasn't dumb I'd have quit, you know?"

Around him he saw heads turn. The gray-washed walls were a somber change from the endlessly varied magenta-pink-yellow-blue-violet of his own service, but the expressions on the faces were identical. No one quit. And no one yelled in the hot shack either, not when an enemy carrier sat nearly on Marcanter's neck and doubtless ready to swoop down and annihilate them all. Them, their families and all the people most of them had known all their lives.

Cargo turned his back. He didn't want to look at a whole group of Marcanter batwings staring at him. A group. He'd put down money that someone would come to his defense. Or something. And in less than a few hours he was going to bring one of their precious Scorpions back to the *Horn and Hardart*.

Fourways was crazy, he decided. It was one thing to shoot down a mirage. It was a target, that was all—a projectile made of scrap and ceramic and a few DNA boards. He had never signed up to kill people he knew, to look them in the face and know their features and shoot them. He couldn't think like that. Fourways had his psyche profile. He should have known that.

This bunch wasn't any different from his own team. Knowing that intellectually wasn't the same as wondering if it was the blond woman or the tall man he'd killed. It just wasn't the same. It was Gaje, that's what it was. It was something beyond a Rom to do.

He had been raised to lie and steal, to assume roles and make people believe the most outrageous stories if it suited his purpose. And it had made him feel superior, the way it always made the Rom feel superior, to forget the things the Gaje could do. Because in the end it was always the Gaje who won, who ruled everywhere. Akhaid or human, Collegium and Cardia, they were all Gaje, all of them. In the end that was all that mattered.

There was no place to hide. He couldn't live in the middle any more, where as *marhime* he played at being Gaje and hoping to be taken back as a vrai Rom in the end. Nothing was left to pretend.

The Bishop was right again, as he always had been in the past. Cargo understood now why the old man had opposed his choice from the beginning—but he also knew that Mirabeau had not comprehended why he had needed it. He had to try to become the ultimate Gaje warrior in order to find out that that was no more real than the world he had left. In that moment he knew that he was no longer the Gypsy *shav* his mother had raised, or the fighter pilot Cargo, or the Bishop's protegé. He had come free of the restraints of thought and time and saw the moment in perfect clarity as if from a great distance.

He said nothing. The decision was in him, a thing that happened of its own accord. Around him people got coffee from a large urn that scented the entire shack, but hardly covered the odor of flesh and fear.

Someone thrust a disposable cup in his hand. He could feel the heat through the thin lining. The liquid was closer to mud than what the Bishop would accept after dinner, stuff so thick and bitter that it was duplicated nowhere else except aboard carriers like the *Horn and Hardart*. He drank it and the homeyness comforted him until he remembered where he was and who the people surrounding him were.

"Don't worry about it," said the tall man who had brought the coffee. "Some people just weren't champions in the breast stroke, right? So don't let it get to you. You both had a bad time. Now there's something more important to do."

Cargo nodded. He didn't trust himself to say anything at all. He didn't want to look at the tall man, hoped the other would forget to tell him a name or sign so he could believe that they hadn't really met.

"By the way, I'm Mike Allen," the tall man said quietly. Cargo's hopes died. "Tem asked me to tell you, we're keeping loose and lone. You've got Early Bird. I'm your backup."

"Thanks." Cargo raised the cup in a mock toast. He had no idea what Allen was talking about. Only a lifetime of training kept him from worrying. He could fake it. He could fake anything at all. Like Old Piluka said, it was a matter of saying yes to everything and then doing as you damn well pleased.

The woman joined them. "I'm Tem," she said, sticking out her hand. "And it's a good thing we picked you up when we did. No singles around here at all. Screws Loose's got a full roster. Anyway, I just put you down on my team. We brief in twenty minutes." She nodded to a discreet gray door. Cargo sipped his coffee and tried to will himself to relax. Not that it mattered if he couldn't. Tension about the mission was reasonable enough.

The muttered stillness of the hot shack was pierced by a siren screaming through all the tones of the audible range. The gray room was close to empty by the time Cargo was able to look, and he followed the rest out onto the concrete flats. No different from the bat cave on Vanity, he noted quickly as he ran for the nearest Scorpion.

Pure reflex drove him. Information had already been read into the maze before the alarm had even started. He had to rely on it. The pill patch wasn't on his sleeve, and for a moment Cargo panicked, thinking that he'd left his supply back on board the ship. Then he found a discreet pocket near the collar with eight Three-B's. He swallowed six, leaving the last two in case he was out longer than anticipated. The regs suggested only four, but no one went by the rec dosage. Not when all the charts and briefings were held in the maze. Every level would be in use.

He picked a Scorpion and climbed in, one far enough back in the order that he should have a little time to watch those ahead of him. Around him the flares lighted the group so that everything was clear in black and white and gray. No colors at all, except those of flesh, and even the warm tones of skin were bleached and darkened by the lighting. Mechanics became the universe and everything living was gone.

He groped for the maze and couldn't make contact. Sweat broke on his forehead, the cold sweat of terror, of a bad dream. He had dreamed this more than once when he was in school: sitting down to take an exam in a subject he had never studied, playing in a band where he didn't know the music. Recognizing the dream, he tried to convince himself that he would wake up and it would be right.

Ghoster broke in on his concentration and threw a helmet in his lap. It was silver gray without any markings. Gingerly Cargo put it on. Suddenly he didn't know anymore if the Cardia used the tri-level maze connections, if the missing helmet was the only thing that had kept him from control. It didn't fit like his own helmet, made him feel again like a rookie who hadn't checked out in training, who could be thrown out any day. That had been a real nightmare, too, banished after the shiny wings had been pinned on in a ceremony whose only use was to embarrass him to death.

The Three-B's, he told himself sternly. Without the maze connection the drug was heightening all his perceptions, all his fears and intuitions. Which was useful in mode but dangerous outside. And he still was outside. Fear nearly became panic as he realized just how different the Scorpion might be. A strange craft takes a long time to learn. There are manuals to read and carefully graded check flights that tell you exactly how the beast moves. And the Scorpion was so unknown that he was still outside the maze.

But it looks so familiar, he told himself in amazement. If he hadn't known he was on Marcanter, didn't have the stiff neck and still painful bruised elbow, he would have sworn he was back in Vanity in a batwing.

Outside the open canopy a tech knocked twice on the earpiece of his helmet. Cargo looked around and signalled to latch. What would happen if he couldn't get its maze into operation before it was time for him to enter the relay? What if he couldn't even tell the mirage to get on the tracks?

As the techcrew in gray uniforms set the locking pins on the canopy, Cargo felt the maze close around him. At first it was the same familiar maze that he had always known. Then it opened out, drawing him under its layers. In depth it had a different texture, a different feel. And he was in deeper than he had ever been before.

There had never been any words for the mode. It was a state of thought that could only be accurately described to those who had experienced it. But the maze Cargo knew—any maze—had been interactive. He and it and Ghoster together had manipulated their mutual environment, had merged into a single consciousness where each retained individual identity. This time he was in so deep that mode itself was like the dark sea that had closed over him in the storm, and drowning in it he could for the first time appreciate Ghoster's fear of water. The whole experience was both closer and more global than flying had ever been.

Neither time nor lineality mattered. He understood threat and the carrier lurking beyond the next planet. They had been lucky, the maze informed him. There had been an ally aboard, or else the hulk would have slipped into their space unnoticed. In the back of his mind he wanted to turn around, run, tell the commanders on Marcanter that this was a peace mission. That Andre Michel Mirabeau had come only at the express invitation of members of the Cardia government.

The maze reacted with something like a startled burp. It didn't understand. Nothing in its programming had foreseen turning back, not for any reason. It invaded Cargo's mind even more deeply, impressing on him the need for speed, the quiet importance of their mission and firm reassurance in his own ability.

Via the maze he knew where his own team was stationed in the outgoing raid, precisely what their responsibility was. The Scorpion was armed with only three charges. That was all the excess mass the engines could carry. All the rest was taken up with Peeping Tom devices, the very best ever built—things that even the Collegium hadn't thought of, let alone duplicated. Something that gave readings underground. Another that recreated images from fragmentary data. Cargo was struck with a new fear. The Scorpion acted and reacted exactly like the batwing. It *was* a batwing on high recce, right down to the number and power of charges it could haul around.

The maze, interacting at an instinctual level, glowed with pride as Cargo recognized the design. They were only three months old, the maze informed him, and Marcanter currently housed all of them. The maze was almost childlike in its need for admiration and its complete self-centering.

Frustration welled through him, threatening to overcome

even the maze. It started to break and reform, fitting around his thought until it stabilized again around him, forcing him to conform. Of all the stupid, crazy things. And he had to be trapped in a Cardia maze that could not communicate with the *Horn and Hardart*.

They could take base now. It was that simple. The Cardia had been losing too many fighters. The mirages were surveillance craft and they had been gathered at Marcanter for a single task. Cargo didn't get it from the maze alone. There was another source of knowledge—a slight but nagging ache in the data bank, where the pain was the knowledge, too. With the data the maze had supplied, Cargo realized that one good strike could wipe out Marcanter, and without Marcanter the Cardia rebellion would collapse in a matter of months.

The Cardia strike command was committed to a major strategic victory before the general staff reapportioned funds. The mirages and the midge fighters were new programs and could be cut from the budget if they weren't shown to be effective very soon. Two members of the general staff insisted that ground troops should be moved into the disputed territories and force the Collegium to fight on land, something the Collegium was not really equipped to do well. No, the superstrike group had to prove its worth and then some to save its own hide. And so they had come up with Operation Early Bird.

Early Bird was the soul of simplicity. As Cargo understood it from inside the maze, the thirty-four extant mirages were to infiltrate to the inner worlds of the Collegium, it was hoped even to the Collegium Center itself. For an invisible craft this shouldn't be too difficult. There they were to knock out the early warning systems and contact the home command. Midges would come in once the warning systems were inoperative.

Primitive, Cargo thought, but it would work. Would have worked, he amended. No matter how sophisticated their facilities became, surprise was still worth more than machinery. No matter how much accuracy and range any system had, once it was forced to vis you were back with living skills and abilities again. No matter how much technology was at hand, fighting wars hadn't really changed much since the days of the linen biplane. The sacred double "s" of supplies and surprise that had worked for Alexander and Napoleon were still crucial.

And inside the plan was something else. The Cardia command that had set up project Early Bird was afraid of the peace faction in the government. The threat of financial cuts was the first real show of power the opposition party had made, and without strong countermeasures it looked as if the Cardia might actually consider the possibility. Especially since the opposition leaders were now telling the flimservices that they would have a surprise package to hand the people in six months, maybe less. Just before the elections, if things went well.

Cargo wasn't sure where this wealth of information came from. Not from the maze alone, that was certain—not unless the mode imprinted more than straight data. Which he couldn't entirely rule out, although it seemed more like something out of a late-night chill show.

And then the truly hideous part overcame him. Not only couldn't he communicate with the *Horn and Hardart*, he couldn't even make contact. He was going out to raid it, and there was no way now that anyone would ever trust a Cardia mirage. He was caught, swept along in a wave that he knew would drown him. The thought was sheer terror.

As he faced the complete meaning of it the maze relayed their clearance to the track. He couldn't resist, not this far ahead. Steadying the magnolox on the track that would build enough velocity to launch the ungainly mirage off Marcanter wasn't going to blast the *Horn*. It was only a small part of a task, one part that he had done a million times. There was nothing threatening, nothing even aggressive in the smooth speed of the forward pull and the glorious freedom when the track released.

And they were dancing vac, thrust exo in a single righteous glide to the void. The maze joined him, exalted as ever a being was surrounded by the cold. He couldn't sense Ghoster apart from the mode, from the single merged entity they had become. But not entirely one. He knew Ghoster's alienness, was aware of it but not feeling the distortion it usually brought. This maze was different, new, and Cargo reveled in the glory of it, in the power of the Scorpion extending under his disciplined control, in the precision and grace and liberty he felt when he and the mode became a creature completely reborn.

The greatest and worst secret was in the first moments of

thrust, hurtling into the embracing darkness. The secret was the being itself, a thing beyond the parts that made it. Four parts, the human and the Akhaid and the craft and the computer, all smoothly integrated in the maze. And all dancing vac, what they were born and created to do. Nothing else mattered. It was cruel that to keep this joy they had to pay with death. And Cargo saw clearly for the first time that that was the price of these moments that only his own caste ever shared. They were willing to die for the moment, and more important, they had contracted to kill for it.

And it was worth it. If this were the last moment of his life, Cargo knew he would die happy.

Around him, shadows against the void, he could feel the others dancing with him. There were no readings, not even in the maze, but it knew where they should be. There he sometimes saw a flicker of darkness against the dark, a secret answer to the autonomy of the maze. Their power and number filled him with strength, with love. They were his enemy and he was going to battle with them and they were his dearest friends of less than three hours' acquaintance. And his joy and his sorrow were so great that the maze and the very manifold twisted around him in a frozen salute, a leap, a gyration in torment.

Sneaking up on the *Horn* the Scorpions had only three charges each, but there were enough of them and the surprise was great enough. They could blast the carrier down to subatomic particles between them. Plato and Stonewall and, hell, even Fourways would be no more than a flutter of starlight before they became part of the dark forever.

The maze followed his thought. He could feel the reflection that was Ghoster, hearing him, feeling his understanding interfaced in mode. An idea drifted up from the depths of the maze. Cargo didn't know where it originated, whether it was from Ghoster or from the hidden twists in the programming itself. Or if it was some strange body-reflex of the machine-body which had a no-mind that entered into all their calculations. This, however, showed the touch of real genius.

All he had to do was blow too soon.

Time became warped in the maze while Cargo considered at something square the speed of light. Silent patrols were sent out, members of the batwing team in constant surveillance before their hit on Marcanter Base. Waiting for him. Cargo and Ghoster together knew the entire patrol route and schedule, and the maze had it translated and useable before they had even decided on a course of action. Although his instruments couldn't pick up a patrol vessel, knowing one should be in the vicinity would be enough. All he had to do was blow one charge impotently into space, blow it big enough and bright enough that the *Horn* couldn't possibly miss.

With a gently teasing feel, the maze sorrowfully regretted that the three charges in the Scorpion's battery were insufficient for Morse code. Cargo wondered fruitlessly, afraid, what that was. He knew he was putting off knowing until they reached the point where someone should see them clearly.

Ghoster!

His desperation took hold of the maze, shaking and threatening its integrity. He filled his mind with his partner's name, willing the Akhaid to come to his aid. He had made a decision. Ghoster would have to carry through, bring it off. It was Ghoster whose mind was as indelibly tied into the weapons systems as his was in navigation and control.

The maze, threatened more by his distress than any outward hostility, released its own calculations of success. Only the maze had no idea of what he was really doing, what his goal was. His whole chain of thought was completely opaque to it, a region that the machine-mind couldn't comprehend because those who had created the software hadn't thought that way. They had never confronted the endless night and their own deaths imminent, or the necessity of killing friends no matter what side they were on. These were not things that anyone in a safe office in a design group considered. They were undone, left out, and so the maze was helpless and afraid, trying to reassure him as best it could. Success, success, rang in his mind.

Under it he felt Ghoster, slipping closer than they had ever been, close enough so it hurt. In front and behind him, within his field of knowledge, came flooding the thing no human dared face in the Akhaid. They were more than alien. They knew the Other Six. The dimensions that for Cargo had been only mathematical symbols and a method of transportation became solid, real. He thought he was insane. Surely this was what the crazies saw when they were being carted to the nuthouse. Them and the saints, all the saints on the calendar. In horror and revulsion he withdrew and curled in on his own perception, cherishing it.

Ghoster remained with him. The contact became more tenuous perceptually and stronger in his logical mode. No problem, Ghoster assured him. He and the maze could handle the shot. They'd get up real close, so that the Cardia team wouldn't suspect a thing, get it off and warn the *Horn*.

Cargo tried to acknowledge and pull out, but the maze held. It had melted together in its own terror. There was nothing anywhere in the mode to keep him from Ghoster's disturbing mind, from Ghoster's superimposed realities strung together dimension on top of dimension to a place where time no longer existed. It made Cargo sick. He could taste the coffee soured in his stomach, and he grabbed on to that physical fact.

Around him he saw the flickers of darkness, the Scorpion legion going out to challenge the carrier. They seemed farther away now, and he couldn't make out so many. Obligingly the maze provided data; the Cardia formation was going lose, breaking into individual invisible units, each with a particular target.

And they had a target, too. The maze was very pleased. The no-thing that refused to register followed exactly the course predicted. Ghoster was calm. Cargo quivered with him through the maze and it was the Akhaid who kept them both iced.

Was it Stonewall? Fourways? Please Ste. Maries let it not be Plato, he prayed by rote although the words were meaningless.

The maze was pleased to have a target. This was something it could do. This brought safety, and safety was comfort to the beings. It was firm and ready, telling Cargo not to worry: that it was going to eliminate the threat.

That was when Cargo realized he had to be sensing the maze from Ghoster's point of view. The whole mode had broken down, had forced them deeper into each other's minds than it was sane to go. No choice. Maze malfunction. Too many Three-B's.

Ghoster. He could feel the Akhaid mind cold and clean and focused on the target, directing a single charge with an ease that Cargo could only applaud with awe. Ghoster was in his glory, completely in charge, competent and without equal.

Cargo could feel it steady, the thought following through
neatly, instructing the maze carefully at top go. And he didn't
understand it at all, not until the release of the energy.

No.

He tried to stop it. When he understood, he thrust all his
concentration on holding back that single bolt. But Ghoster
had already struck. The maze, needing to reassure its beings,
had finished the processing before Cargo even began to try to
pull it back.

Eyes wide and staring, he would have been blinded if the
maze hadn't darkened the canopy against the explosion. Even
then, Cargo wished it had forgotten.

Directly in front of him a batwing blossomed into a multi-
hued explosion. Like a superspeed Easter lily it glowed pristine white, a fountain of sparks rising and collapsing back on
themselves. The universe was born and died in that single
moment and then the batwing was gone.

Cargo wanted to cry but the crying wouldn't come. The
maze didn't understand and Ghoster didn't understand, and
for himself it hurt too much and wasn't real enough. Not yet.
It was just a machine, a waterfall of brightly colored starlight
—that was all. He couldn't acknowledge the death or the killing. At least not yet. He wanted to forget it and himself.

The chatterbox remained obstinately silent. No break in
silence. Sending any message located them for the enemy.
Which enemy?

Numb, Cargo followed the maze's instructions. Where to
go. Stay between Tem and Mike Allen, people who weren't
any different from Stonewall and Plato. He could still feel
them around him, the mirages moving unseen in the dark,
approaching the carrier *Horn* that stood out like a second
moon. A great pregnant beach ball, a tiny secondary, that's
how the carrier looked through the filtered canopy. It shone
with reflected light a pure, nearly white that could have been
natural. There was no burn on the outside of the *Horn*. It had
never entered atmosphere, had rarely engaged as a primary in
action. Its big guns and very bulk had saved it from being
harried by the smaller craft that came out after moving targets.

And then the *Horn* blossomed. A garden of brilliant
flowers in all the hues of the visible range bloomed around the
single vessel. They had gotten Cargo's message. The Kraits
were deployed.

He had never realized just how gaudy they were. The cocky defiance that had chosen the color scale had never reckoned with the fact that, en masse, they looked exactly like a cheap Spin Street professional ready for business. If he hadn't known their capabilities he would have laughed at them. Instead he rested deeper in the maze, knowing that this was Ghoster's best part. All the alien wanted him to do was steer.

They were invisible, he remembered, with one charge gone. The Kraits couldn't see them, couldn't get a fix in mode for the Eyes to lock on.

Carefully he began to direct the maze, drawing, nudging their bearing slightly off to one side, slightly "down," edging away from where the Kraits headed to seek out their invisible enemy. The maze rebelled. He could see the orders in his head, images of the other Scorpions in position waiting for the kill. They were real, solid in the maze, needing his protection and his aid.

He ignored it. Ahead of him Cargo saw the Krait teams splinter off, four fighters to a team, searching cautiously for the intruders. Fourways must have briefed them, told them how batwings operate in the dark.

The maze tried again to present images that would lure him back to the others. This time he could feel Ghoster in the maze, the essential alienness of his partner unmistakable under the computer-urged images. There was no emotion from Ghoster. Instead he caught a strange undercurrent that flowed with the programming of the maze itself. Protect. The Scorpion was Cardia. Protect own life first. Fight Kraits. Kraits are the enemy.

That was Ghoster's panic. The maze's panic. It didn't belong to him. Cargo tried to clear his mind from the mode, imaging a cool mountaintop, untouched by any being at all. The maze cooled in response, confused. It didn't know where his mountain was, couldn't find it. He began thinking in Romany, telling the maze things that he had thought he had forgotten in a language it couldn't follow: about the bargaining session when his mother argued with Sonfranka's family about how much to pay for her and what other responsibilities they would take. She was a fifteen-year-old virgin and showed signs of great talent as a *booja* woman—very desireable merchandise and they were determined to drive a hard bargain. His mother had ended up paying a premium over the going price, along with providing the wedding dress and dinner besides.

Ethnic language not in database. The maze protested loudly. It didn't like language at all, preferring the image series it used to steer and aim by. But if there was a language instruction it was Indopean, Atrash second, along with maybe seven or eight of the most common ethnic languages. It didn't understand Romany, couldn't even identify it.

Cargo wasn't displeased. He had bought maybe one or two whole precious seconds, enough time to make a decision. He already knew that it was not possible for him to fight the Kraits. His only hope lay in being captured. They would bring him in, escort the Scorpion into one of the large hangar decks on the *Horn and Hardart*. And then his mission would be over and rated as something of a success besides. Only it wasn't going to be easy.

Through the maze he could feel Ghoster's protest. With all the concentration he had developed and all the strength of mind he had honed, Cargo pressed down on Ghoster. The Akhaid was afraid, was reacting by rote. Cargo formed the image of the Scorpion being taken into custody—formed it and held it steady so that it achieved a degree of solidity in the maze.

Behind the shielded layers of celo, Cargo looked out and concentrated on watching reality. The Kraits were going in vis; they didn't have any other choice. That much warning, at least, he had given them. A brilliantly colored team of four separated, opening up like a flower in bloom, like the throat of a hungry fishing bird or a snake. They were using each other, the vivid electric yellow and pink, as markers to flush out the intruder.

It was beautifully done. Three of the four took positions on the three axis. They even matched on the old color-code yellow-red-blue to describe space with no local vertical. The fourth played chase, crisscrossing the grid at top go as the other four rotated around. They danced it out, fast and whirling, each sure in its own moment where to go next and when to turn.

From the center of this search pattern a darkness appeared, floating inward toward the center. Now the Kraits took opposite sides and ran head-on parallel. In one pass they identified the mirage.

The Scorpion driver, no idiot, knew he'd been flushed. He must have wanted to run for it, to pour on the power and bring the mag to top go. But whoever was in that machine was too well disciplined. He cut whatever go he had, keeping the mask well up so that the Kraits could only find him by analog and vis. He wasn't crazy enough to give them a spectraprint as well. And he took his time.

Cargo could almost see the Scorpion drifting, the maze cutting in at the last moment to line up the shot. And when it came it was perfect, the kind of kill they talked about in hushed voices on the rec deck for weeks. The pink Krait opened like fireworks and then disappeared all at once as if it had never been.

It took nerve, Cargo had to admit. Especially when the next shot took the Scorpion midships, a tearing ragged thing that was neither clean nor careful. Disabled. The yellow Krait turned away after the attack run, not loaded for a second shot. Ghoster's disgust read through the maze with piercing clarity. In his estimation any Eyes who doesn't set up two shots was asking for the Wall. Then a half-flash not quite in but not quite out of the visual range and the yellow Krait became a twin to the pink.

Only this time the fireworks were even bigger, as the blue came around and fired blast after blast into the Scorpion, tracing back on the mirage's own firing trajectory.

It must have been the explosion that had shown them up. Against the fireworks of exploding ships and trigger charges, the black shadow of the Scorpion was a clear silhouette against the multicolored background. And the attack was classic, coming in blue six. Just where every Krait driver knew to watch his tail, where every Eyes called to remind them. If he'd had time to curse or scream Cargo would have. As it was, he tried to run.

Chapter

13

The Krait was right on him, bearing down on him at top go, and Cargo was running. He tried evasive, using all three axes, a quick cut to starboard yellow and counter in starboard red. The Krait stayed with him. This one was damned good. Like he had been before he'd become a batwing.

There wasn't time to think dancing vac. There was only action and reaction. Cargo opened up the separation, trying to widen the angle. It took all the brains and courage he had not to bring the Scorp all the way up but to run slow under the mask. At least that way there wasn't any spectraprint bleed of the kind that made Eyes very, very happy.

He could feel Ghoster targeting, ready to shoot the Krait the same as he had the batwing. Cargo stuttered mentally, shaking the Scorp from side to side as if it were a sick and crazy thing totally out of control.

Ghoster's resistance ran through the lines. Cargo couldn't fight him anymore. It was all he could do to run, to keep the Krait from making them a very nice picnic for the Eyes. Stutter and slide, back and under as far as he could go, doubling over his own trajectory from a different axis. Damn. He didn't want Ghoster to shoot, didn't want to think about another Krait driver gone. Friendly fire?

He instructed the maze in a rapid flat spin. It balked. Cargo pushed harder and the maze tried to resist. If only he could talk to the Krait, to the *Horn*. He was out in the middle of the night wearing the wrong uniform and he couldn't even tell his own side who he was.

He imaged the spin stronger. It had saved him well enough

when Two Bits went to the Wall. He brought that moment to mind.

The maze stalled in confusion and Cargo understood and cursed it. The Scorp didn't handle in a flat spin endo. In atmosphere its flat-body design would bring it down like a rock. So the maze refused to comply. Simple.

Kraits, hell. He wished he had a couple of designers and programmers out there. Then he wouldn't have any trouble shooting. Damn desk jockeys didn't think and were too high-nosed to ask.

Two full seconds had passed. A second Krait cut at a skew angle "over" them, yellow axis. So they were all out hunting vis, making their own backdrops. Soon, very soon, two more little bright fighters would be there and then even getting captured would be impossible.

Purely on instinct Cargo pushed once more at the maze. This time he pictured a star roll, the craft rotating 360 degrees on two axes, very fast. From slow he upped speed to top go as the maze responded and began to flip the Scorp around, pulling high enough gees that Cargo recognized the first signs of impending blackout, the darkening along peripheral vision, the long tunnel ahead, the narrowing not only of vision but of thought as well.

And then a single blast hit. The Scorp's cockpit strained against tearing apart as the charge hit on the baffles that camouflaged it in radar. The star spin shattered out of control. Cargo thought out to the maze for damage assessment, but the computer mind had been too traumatized to respond. It gibbered at him, repeating primary procedures.

Cargo swore and garnered what he could while the maze regained its composure. There was still plenty of pressure in the cockpit, and he couldn't make out the fatal hissing indicating an atmosphere leak. So far so good. The instruments in front of him glowed dull red, unblinking. According to the readout he was fine on fuel but was leaking relay fluid along the port rudder.

No wonder the maze was a mess. Without the relay medium it couldn't control the craft. And there was something else about the relay fluid that Cargo remembered from an early maze engineering class in ground school: the fluid was part of the maze matrix itself, charged biobits fed in living solution. Which meant that whatever capabilities the maze had were strictly what was not printed in DNA. Which wasn't much.

He tried to think into the maze again, but it still jabbered away mindlessly. The fluid leak was steady, and at exactly the same rate at which the maze was losing its mind.

Cargo pulled the heavy webbing strap releases around his arms, freeing his hands to take off his helmet. Not that it hadn't kept his head in one piece and couldn't still do so, but he needed to break the connection with the maze, break it totally and finally, or the thing's insanity would penetrate his own thought.

Breaking contact with the maze cut him off from the chatter. It also cut off most of his options for control. With the relay leak there was a good chance that most of the mechanicals were out as well, which meant he was stuck as far as possible on the stick. He'd never used one before, except in check-out and training runs. That would have to be enough. If the damn thing worked. If the Cardia hadn't done what the Collegium designers had been debating for years and left the thing out altogether. An antique, someone had said. When you've got the maze you can't use anything else.

They hadn't taken his position into consideration. He had never imagined a time when the maze was gone. The maze was instruments and air and light. And it was crazy.

Under his right arm as part of the hand secure system, the stick was locked on a code he tapped out with his fingers on the secure pad. The whole section came free. Cargo decided to check outside.

He'd lain quiet enough. One of the Kraits was still in the area; the other had probably written him off as useless and had gone in search of other prey. He lay low, not daring to breathe for fear of hitting the stick and sending the Scorp into gyrations that would alert the Kraits. Better play dead. An old Romany strategy anyway.

Around him explosions went off one by one, silently. There was no screaming death in the vac, no rush of engines, no blasts of ordnance shrilling in to their targets. There were only the colors and the lights. Cargo felt deaf and removed, as if everything he saw was unreal. Like all the times he had flown a Krait before, all coming back on him, there was no pain and no dying until he returned to the familiar precincts of the carrier. Only then the damage showed. Beforehand, during the worst, it didn't even have the pseudoreality of the evening news where they dubbed in a soundtrack for the civs.

He kept quiet. The Scorp's lights, which had always been shielded from bleed, were completely off. Cargo had even turned back the intensity on the status boards, so there was hardly enough red light to stain even a fold of his flightsuit.

Strange that it was all vis. Usually they went out and released charges at ranges that transformed even the largest and most strangely shaped carrier or merchie into just another point of light. Here they were so close that he could almost make out the living forms under the bright celo canopies of the Kraits.

He wondered what Ghoster thought of all this, and it took a moment to realize that he wasn't going to get any answer. He opened the chatterbox, but nothing came out. Opaque. The thing might not be dead, but without the maze there was no way Cargo could fix it. It was the maze that had linked them too closely together, and without the maze they could just as well be half a galaxy away. No, it was worse. No matter what the distances, there were ways of getting communications through. Except to his back seat, at least until they came inside.

Cargo turned to watch Kraits and Scorpions engage each other in strange-looking encounters where one partner was invisible. Over all, sitting with what appeared to be the quiet detachment of a carved Buddha, the carrier *Horn* stood removed from the battle. The carrier had been warned in time and, so far at least, none of the gomers had made it in close enough to take a shot.

Hand on the stick, Cargo nudged it back slightly, trying the manual maneuver he had practiced often enough in the past. The Scorp lurched raggedly and then the go went. The black craft died.

Slowly, as if breathing for the first time, he sniffed the air. There was a perceptible difference. Not much, not yet. He'd never checked out in the Scorp, but from what he could see it was the identical twin to the batwing. Which meant the survival radius was about seventeen hours.

Fear, even terror, were not new. Cargo had felt them every time he'd flown, every time the magnetictrack engaged the base and shot him out the belly of a carrier or upground from a batwing cave. He'd known it even worse in juvie with the net thrown across his face, and earlier when his cousin Angel flicked a knife in his face and requested his assistance at this heist or that con job. Knives worried him, and cling webbing, and the beautifully moded weapons every Krait and batwing carried.

Beyond all those, he was intelligent enough to fear space. It was the kind of fear that the Bible spoke about, that the Bishop explained was also awe. Space deserved awe, just as the sea had commanded the respect of sailors for as long as the oceans held power. Even now there were those who drowned every year because they didn't recognize that a wild thing, although it seems tame, can turn, can revert to its natural state. He respected the vac like that, like an animal he had trained to hand but which still had teeth and claws and the instinct to use them.

This fear was something new. He had lived with the vac a long time but he had never faced the legends, the off-smelling air and the lightheadedness that were precursors to oxygen deprivation. There was definitely more than just a tinge of something in the air. He could smell his own sweat and terror clinging to the atmosphere. The circulation system was either dying or dead.

He paused to wonder if Ghoster was still alive, or if the silence that the maze imposed hid more than lack of communication. Ghoster's air could be gone, or he could have died of acceleration in the star. His underbelly could have been cut by flying debris when they were disabled, or it was even possible that the shot had hit directly into the Eye's space, cut off from Cargo in the maze.

Unthinkingly his left hand groped for the medal lying next to his skin, the bit of luck Two Bits had left him. If there was any luck in the manifold he was going to need every shred of it now. He could almost envy those brilliant fountains of sparks that exploded so quickly. Even the batwing they'd hit, whoever it was, had never seen it coming. In truth, there was just revenge.

But Cargo decided, just momentarily, that there wasn't going to be any revenge. His *mule* were heavy around him and wouldn't let him die, not this way, silently drifting off, unable to signal distress. All his *mule*—his father and even Son-franka and old Piluka—all of them were with him and they clamored against his skull, insisting there was an answer. He had always been the clever one. This was just another riddle, and he had the key. All he had to do was open it up.

There weren't so many flashes of light outside anymore. He couldn't sense the Scorps around him, couldn't catch sight of a shadow that blotted out the stars for a moment and then moved on. The Kraits seemed tighter together, banding into an eye-searing array of color as they pulled back to the *Horn*.

That was the key, he realized. The *Horn*. The silliness, the lightheaded lack of attention to details had hidden it from him. He felt like a sleeper who had suddenly been shaken to consciousness. How the hell was he going to get into the *Horn*?

The maze usually controlled communications, but it had been reduced to a jabbering idiot as the relay fluid leaked out biode after biode. Cargo considered attempting to make it function at least that far, even strapped his helmet in place so the bridge package was in milocontact with his own altered biodes. That, with the Three-B's still floating around in his system, should bring him back into symbiosis with the maze. He flinched mentally, not wanting to enter mode again if it meant going subject to a crazy maze. That could mean the Wall. But so could the stale air that hung around him.

Cargo had been in mode hundreds of times. Every time he entered he was greeted with a cool acceptance, a neat locking of his own mind into the whole three brain and hardware link. It was clean and precise, a crisp falling into place and then a clearing of the senses, merging with all the abilities the maze had to offer.

The pain came unexpectedly, jarring him from steady concentration. The maze was overheated, as if the loss of subunits had forced others to work overtime and were functioning at half melt. It was not possible.

The maze did not acknowledge him. He was in it, completely submerged in the mode, but the maze drew back. The usual coils that reached into his mind, his imagination, and obeyed were missing. Gently he thought himself out to that truncated machine. He was aware of it, running abbreviated checklists over and over at superspeeds.

Out he thought at it, imaging the open space between the Scorp and the carrier, picturing the microwaves that would carry his thoughts to one of the four large antennae on the *Horn and Hardart's* skin.

At first the maze didn't even bother to stop running the

landing list, as if the Scorp would ever land on firm ground again. Cargo kept up, frustration and fear building up into a great gust of pure energy that he shot through the unsuspecting maze.

Slowly he felt it turn and recognize him. No longer an intelligent creature, artificial as it might be, this thing was retarded and mute. He gave the instructions again, but the maze was only confused.

Maybe Cardia mazes were different, he thought. He wished he could feel Ghoster through the membrane, know if he were alive and conscious at least, if not lean on him for help with the broken computer. There was no trace of the Akhaid in the system. Doubtless, Cargo decided, he had done the smart thing and removed his helmet, getting out of the way of whatever the maze was going to come up with next. It might be pierced and bleeding, but there was no doubt that it was still powerful.

He could feel it waiting for him, willing to do what was required if it could only understand. Cargo thought. Maybe.... But he didn't know anything about the internal workings of the Cardia batwing. He didn't imagine it could be that similar to the batwing. At least not unless—

And then he was quite sure of it. Whoever had leaked the rest of the information over time had leaked the plans for the batwing, too. Oh, maybe not the same person, but another plant in the hierarchy. That was the only way it all made sense. The Cardia hadn't had batwings before, hadn't had any stealth technology. How had they learned to use the honeycomb structure, the ferroceramics that coated the batwing's skin, the mask to keep the infrared profile down to a zilch.

And the shape and feel of the two in flight was identical. Cargo knew dispassionately that he and Ghoster were the only beings who had experience in both. If it hadn't been for the internal markings and the different names, he would have sworn it was the same machine. And if there was plenty he didn't know about the batwing, there was more that he did. He hadn't wasted too much time on Vanity. Studying the manuals had been infinitely more interesting than listening to the everlasting wind.

So there was one chance and he was going to take it. On the batwing the microwave communication unit was located directly forward of the first passive receivers. Cargo pictured the diagrams as he remembered them from Vanity and instructed the maze to contact this particular port on this bar.

Hesitantly the maze began to search out the correct port, the outcast antenna. Cargo held back any elation as the maze brought him in contact with the primary transmitter. Gently, almost gingerly, he guided the computer to turn on the flow circuit and hit the scope.

Too much at once. The damn thing recoiled, nearly retreated, while Cargo tried to reassure it. Safety. This is safety.

It hadn't gone far and he was able to coax it back. This time he had to avoid the overload. Obviously the thing was missing more than half its high-level programming, but which half and what functions remained intact Cargo couldn't tell. No time to speculate on it, either. Instead he gave very clear instructions to the maze to complete the connection for the unit to function. He prayed to Ste. Anne that he had remembered all the details correctly.

The feedback inside the maze told him he had hit home. Now for the scope. The main targeting subscope could be connected to any system on board. Cargo instructed the maze first to connect it to the transmitter, and then waited until it reported all clear to explain exactly where to aim it.

Ahead of him on the *Horn and Hardart* the hangars were opening and admitting the first Kraits on deck. From this distance they looked only like little dark windows, but to Cargo they signified all the pleasures and warmth of home. Sweat trickled down his forehead and into one eye, blurring his vision. He reached up and wiped some of the moisture off his face, but with the vent out the humidity was coming from his own body. Lethargy crept into the desperation, a heavy and purely physical lassitude that he knew was brought on by the overripe air and heat.

He fought it, but it had teeth and fought back. He hardly had the energy to think, let alone raise a hand and remove the miserably hot and heavy bucket from his head. No, that was the link to the maze and they were almost there now. Just a little further, and a little longer, he promised himself. Then he could sleep forever.

With the last of his will, Cargo returned to the maze. It had connected the now functioning transmitter with the scope. Now. All he had to do was send out to the *Horn*, something,

something. The only thing that came to mind was a distress call.

"Now I will say that was surely a dramatic way to get in," Stonewall drawled. "I do admire the fact that you came back at all, given just how friendly and all those Marcanter pilots were to you all. And how you were from Marcanter in the first place, fancy that. My, my."

"Stonewall, didn't your mother ever teach you if you didn't have something nice to say, shut up?" Cargo demanded through gritted teeth.

"And it seems like you haven't even suffered any truly permanent damage," Stonewall continued. "You're just as much a bastard as you always were. I was sure hoping that that crazy maze had scrambled some of your brains and rearranged them to make you a nice guy. But you don't even have the decency to turn purple."

Cargo sat up in the sick bay bunk. He remembered being semiconscious when an Angel team had towed the crippled Scorp in; and needles; and that no matter how many times he told them he was fine and just needed a shower and some fresh air, they insisted on filling his system full of junk that took care of any awareness he had.

That had been yesterday. That much at least he had gotten out of the medic of the morning, who had been debating with the records clerk about the advisability of a solid meal. He had interrupted the corpsman with a rather brusque order for toast, an orange, fried eggs and two jelly doughnuts. Milk, no coffee. Once he had the man's attention, he asked about Ghoster.

"There's nothing wrong with either of you now, except for your judgment," the medic had said.

The man had barely left when Stonewall arrived.

That he was alive was the first thing Cargo noted. Stonewall. Then it had to have been either Fourways or Plato—he refused to think about it further. Let them tell him.

"Why don't you fill me in on what I missed?" he finally asked when it seemed like Stonewall was not disposed to play roving reporter. "And why don't you sit down?"

Stonewall shook his head and leaned against the bulkhead, which had to be about the only wall on the whole carrier that had been painted plain white. The only chair in sick bay was painted white too, and one leg had a serious ding near the

foot. Little chance it would survive anyone over the age of ten
using it too long. Or maybe it was there to pull over as an
extra table. Hell.

"You know, that's how we knew those mirages were coming. Someone blew away a batwing. The Wall loves ya, you
know." Stonewall's eyes were on the ceiling, on the white
curtain between the beds, anywhere except on Cargo. "We
took a beating, you know that. I'm gonna catch the bastard
who tipped them off and then I'm gonna nail him to the Wall.
One thing to know what's going on. Another thing when people don't come back. People you care about, you know? But
there are times I have my doubts about you, Cargo, I surely
do. There are times I think you're the bastard I'm looking for.
More than once I was on your trail, and Fourways called me
off, said, 'Lookee here, Bishop Mirabeau, big Trustee, hands
off, no-no.' Well, I'm giving you fair warning, Cargo. If
you're not who I think you are, I could like you real well, but
when you blew Scatter to the Wall you lost all my sympathy. I
just figured I'd warn you."

"Scatter?" All Cargo could think was that Plato was alive,
and at the moment that was all that mattered. He didn't worry
about Stonewall. Hell, he was as ready as the big Earther to
kill the bastard who'd warned the base. "I thought Scatter had
gone. And since when is this your personal campaign? I'd as
much figured you for the gomer as you did me."

"Then you thought wrong," Stonewall said with a hint of a
grin tugging at his mouth. "Scatter's my opposite number,
Akhaid. I want you to tell me why you had me figured, you
know?"

Cargo didn't want to play games. There were more important things, like where was Plato and what the hell was going
on and how did they know the Cardia base had been alerted.
Instead he played along with Stonewall. Rule one: if you want
the goods, play the game. So he detailed Stonewall's behavior, his too-intimate knowledge of intelligence, his familiarity
with the Directorate and procedures, methods of surveillance
that he had shown in the early days of their training. "I just
thought you were a fast learner at first," he said. "But there
was too much. And, finally, the way you went after Bugs for
no good reason, it seemed to me like someone trying to cover
up."

Stonewall's eyes went back to the blank ceiling. Both were

so silent that the rush of air in the filtration system seemed a noisy imposition. Finally Stonewall spoke, his voice very low and soft and heavy with sadness. "I do admit I am amazed. I never thought you were the observant kind, my friend. And what you saw you did see, I will concede. But you got it figured all wrong. Damn. If I'd known I might have talked to you about it all, but that's all past. Thing of it is, Cargo old buddy, is that I'm from the Fourth Directorate."

Cargo closed his eyes. He wanted to scream from the sheer insanity of it all. Totally upside down. Romany. Stonewall was counter-intelligence, and Scatter was Fourth Directorate too. It made perfect sense, everything except one fit. And as he lay with his eyes closed sensing Stonewall standing over him, he could even see the other. "And Bugs?" he asked. "Why?"

"Bugs is one of ours," Stonewall said. "You notice I say is. One of the best undercover types we have. You saw her every day for ten weeks and she could sit down in that chair and you'd never know it."

"So she never committed suicide?"

"No." Stonewall shook his head and this time Cargo's eyes were open to see it. "Scatter and I, we were hoping to flush out the agent. Make him or her think that we thought we'd caught one and then get careless. You know? Only whoever it was never did. Until you started shooting, buddy. Scatter was my partner, my teammate like the rest of you will be in the matte and black ten years from now if you survive."

"Well you're looking at the wrong one," Cargo told him coldly. "Maybe you'd better check out Steel, or Fourways even. But it isn't me. Besides, did you get a look at the Cardia mirage? They call it a Scorpion. Anyway, it's dead on the batwing, like someone stole the designs. Think about it. My class, the bunch of us who were honest pilots once, we came aboard four months and two weeks ago. You think we could have gotten those plans out and the gomers could have built a fleet of these things in four-and-a-half months? Pure and simple arithmetic. Your bosses have been looking in the wrong place. Maybe they don't want you to look in the right one?"

"Fourways may be a bastard, but he isn't a traitor," Stonewall said. "And the only reason you're here and not in the brig is because your precious Bishop is on board."

Cargo deliberately turned his back. "Tell Plato I'd like to

see her," he said coldly. "I don't have anything to say to you. Ever."

Stonewall had been leaving but stopped halfway out the door. He grasped both sides of the hatchway and stood motionless, waiting. Then he mastered himself and turned back in again.

"Plato's on the Wall," he said softly. "She was some lady, she was."

Cargo turned back abruptly to face Stonewall. "What do you mean? I thought you said it was Scatter in that batwing."

"It was. He took Plato's craft. And when the attack alarm went off she didn't have a shield or spit to zip up and wear. She went down to the Krait barn and got herself playing sub in a regular team. I am sorry, Cargo. It's rough."

"When?" he asked, meaning the formal memorial.

"Eighteen hundred. Dress gray. She wasn't the only one who's gonna live on the Wall because of today, buddy."

But Cargo wasn't listening anymore. He was back in the Mission Court Hotel, with the scent of her in his arms and the winnings in his pocket. She never did tell him if she found any of the meanings she had Walked for. And now she was dead, and he wondered if it meant anything at all. Doubtless Plato would have found some reason, and without her all the meanings blurred, too.

Cargo loosened the collar of his dress grays as soon as he entered rec deck six. The memorial had been no different than the ones he had attended on the *Torque*, when the captain had read from the little book of "approved for all uses" homilies. That was all. Then the list of all the names that were, that very moment, being engraved on the Wall. It was the only burial they would have.

No different from the *Torque*, except this time he wasn't a Krait driver—and while Ghoster still stood on his right side, Stonewall had been on his left. He had tried to ignore Stonewall, to think instead about what Plato would have said. She'd have told Stonewall to shove it with the spy mania, would have appreciated the special prayers the Bishop had offered in his private Mass even though Cargo was sure she had no particular faith.

The rec deck was crowded. Even with the doors of the lounge open onto the ball court, almost every available standing space was taken. Yet for such a mob the silence was overwhelming. Only an occasional sharp breath, a muffled scrape as someone shifted to find better footing, the soft liquid sound of amber spirits being poured into glass, broke the absolute stillness.

The crush didn't stop Cargo. He knew his place here, and everyone else knew it, too. They pressed even closer to let him by, across the room to the bar where he picked up a full glass, and then back again to the far wall where a table had been left standing. He saw Fourways and Stonewall and sidled around past them to where Ghoster stood at the edge of the table. Already there were five, six people standing on it, most of them flashing wings. Maybe they thought it was strange to see a batwing at a Krait driver's ceremony. No matter. It was essentially unchanged just as they were, just as Plato had been in the end.

Damn, she'd been something. He told himself that he was proud to be here for her, glad to have known her while he had. It didn't stop him thinking that maybe he had been right after Sonfranka to keep to women who would never matter for more than a night, two at most.

It was Ghoster who held his drink, Ghoster who assisted him up on the table and squeezed his ears to his head in true distress. Like the others, he leaned against the wall a little looking out over the sea of heads. People were still drifting in, packing into the foyer in front of the lift. He could see from this vantage point that they were pressing into the bank of African violets that adorned the entrance. African violets. It was when he had pulled Ghoster out of them drunk that it had all started in the first place, maybe a year ago now. A very long time.

Someone on the table nudged his elbow. "It isn't going to take any more," she said.

The lift opened and the commander of the Krait operations group, chief of all Krait attack teams on the *Horn and Hardart*, got out. He was given space, too, to walk to the bar and take a glass. The crowd parted as much as possible to permit him to walk to the table, but he remained in place.

All the little noises stopped, the random throat-clearing and shoe-shuffling. "Like the maze," he heard a whisper from near his feet and knew without looking that it was Ghoster.

Yes. Like the maze. Focus, the complete clearing of the

mind, the perfect concentration that channeled force into form. Through the maze.

Cargo looked at the glass and used it as a focus. Trained by hundreds of hours flying in mode, he concentrated on all the anger and hurt and loneliness he hadn't even had time to feel. And when he had the image clear—when the liquid became the maze, the rich biode environment—then he released it all in a single, violent swing.

The glass hit the wall with a satisfying crash. Other glasses hit at almost exactly the same time. All those on the table were now empty-handed. Only then did the Krait skipper climb up on the polished bar and raise his glass.

"To every driver who ever died in battle," he said, throwing his glass.

Then one last person, a representative of the group as a whole, climbed up on the table. She wore the shiny wings of a Krait driver and had enough battle chips around her collar that Cargo thought she must have started flying when there were no Crafters and no war.

"To life," she said.

"To life," the whole mob roared back. And the sound of crashing glass was everywhere.

"Te avel angle tute," Cargo whispered in Romany for Plato, for Beatrice Sunday of Paragon. *May this be before you.* How many times had he whispered it for his father and Sonfranka and Two Bits, for all his *mule.*

But when he climbed off the table he wasn't thinking of sorrow. He left the rec deck. It was time for all the others, those who had lost friends and buddies, to get drunk and play children's games and laugh. Time to banish the forbidding spirits of the dead, time to change the luck. Cargo didn't want to see that.

He was Romany and Gitano, and he was filled with the need for revenge. As he took the lift down to his quarters he held the Ste. Maries medal and prayed for the first time in years.

Dear God, please let me catch the bastard first. Let me have him. He hadn't realized he had been so intent until he reached his stateroom and took his hand away from the cheap metal where the images of Ste. Maries-de-la-Mer was imprinted in his palm.

• • •

Three boxes took up almost all the space in the center of the stateroom and the chair and desktop besides. The largest was for clothing, bulk items, mementos that would be sent back to Paragon. Underwear, toothbrush, the half-filled container of shampoo, the things no one would want and yet according to regs could not be simply thrown away made up the bulk of the package.

The second-largest box had been filled and sealed long ago. That had been the easiest to put together. The contents of her classified file—batwing and Krait manuals, *Horn and Hardart* emergency procedure charts, class notes from Vanity and the previous week's daily security brief—didn't move him at all. With only a few exceptions—the notes, perhaps, or the battered Krait tape—they could have been the contents of anyone's files. They could have been his own. The classified seals along the sides and across the bind ribbons made it look only more ordinary and less threatening than the more personal articles.

Worst job on the ship, they called it. And the greatest drawback to rooming on the roster. A roommate's last job was this final clearing of the fragments of a person's life. When there was more than reasonable friendship involved, more than one being had been advised to keep the change of quarters unofficial precisely to avoid this one final task. Actually, he found that as long as he avoided the third box and the second desk drawer it wasn't too bad.

The third box about the size of the smallest desk drawer was for the most personal items. So far it contained only a holocube with a formal portrait of Plato, Beatrice then, in the horribly ancient robes of a university graduate. That, and the shiny wings she hadn't worn since the day she'd been given the new ones painted out matte black.

The door opened and the Bishop came in without announcement. Cargo started, then remembered he'd left it set on "admit" in the vague hopes that someone would interrupt him. Actually he'd rather thought it would be Ghoster, or Fourways on the outside. He'd never thought the Bishop would come down to his quarters, to the cramped lower decks where the junior officers lived.

"Rafael." The Bishop lay his hand on Cargo's shoulder gently, then seated himself on the bunk. Cargo was surprised, not so much by the subtle courtesy as by the fact that the

Bishop would realize that while even a former Trustee of the Collegium could sit on the carefully pulled blankets with perfect security, a batwing lieutenant found in the same position would be merely sloppy. One of those stupid things that were part of not just the indoctrination of military etiquette, but a form of group acculturation as well.

Cargo removed the classified box from the one straight chair and sat down facing the Bishop. The ex-Trustee looked even older than his ninety-seven years. While he was not wearing a clerical black jacket, his tunic was a sober gray-and-purple plaid, terribly correct for paying a mourning visit. He should have realized the Bishop wouldn't travel without all the necessities.

"I've heard they're looking for the being responsible for warning Marcanter," the Bishop began.

Cargo snorted. "Then you heard wrong. The Fourth Directorate's already picked out someone to blame and you're looking at him. And if you really want the truth, at this point I don't care anymore. I mean, what are we really doing here anyway? What does it mean? Why should I care whether this coalition wants this government or that, or a monopoly on export-quality fissionables?"

The Bishop blinked and smiled sadly. "So much to pay for wisdom," he muttered.

"You're the one with the conspiracy theories and the rest of it," Cargo lashed out.

The Bishop nodded slowly, once, permitting Cargo's anger. Then he looked down and began to speak, no longer the Trustee, Andre Michel Mirabeau, Bishop of the Church of Rome. He was only an old and tired man who needed to explain. "I never told you much about the conspiracy theory," he started softly. "You didn't want to listen. You didn't want to know how I felt about the military, this rancid excuse for a war. I'd managed to get you a safe job, but you loved the Kraits. I couldn't keep you away. I'm not sure I even wanted to, not when I saw that it was the flying you loved. It's a pity, a true and great injustice, that our species has historically reacted with its greatest inventive genius to the business of killing people. I would have thought that challenge, or at least profits, would do that—but the record stands. Anyway, that's not what I wanted to tell you."

Cargo's eyes flashed, but he tried to hold the anger down.

The Bishop appeared defenseless and beaten, and that in itself was sad.

"The Akhaid are very different from us," Mirabeau continued. "Their biology, their maturational process, their reproduction, in short the survival of their species, is completely different from ours. They see different needs, perceive an entirely alien set of values. It isn't a matter of trust, it's a matter of seeing."

Cargo couldn't listen to much more. "You know, I've lived with an Akhaid for nearly four years now. I'll admit I don't understand him, but I don't understand being Eyes, either. I can't figure out why he got in a Krait with me and trusted me to handle the thing until we got back. Not to get us blown up or run us out of fuel or forced down on some rock we couldn't get off of. I don't understand how anyone can sit there and trust another being to make those decisions. You were a legate, but I've met Ghoster in the maze nearly every day of our working lives. You know what the maze is like? Do you really think I could be mode with an Akhaid and a computer and not know the differences? I'm probably more aware of them than you ever were. Do you know how it feels to confront a being who is actually seeing the Other Six, and what's more you can see a glimpse of them too through the maze? It's a form of insanity, and there were times I really thought I was going to lose my mind."

The Bishop sighed and shook his head. He hesitated a long time before he spoke as if weighing Cargo's words carefully and preparing a counterargument as he had when he had lived in the Palace of Trustees. "I accept that you know certain levels of Akhaid experience more thoroughly than I could," he finally said. "But that doesn't mean you are competent to use that base to extrapolate an entire sociopolitical policy. Even on those terms of intimacy, you would hardly be the ideal subject for this kind of analysis. I submit that your partner Ghoster is most likely the same. But I don't want to argue with you. It isn't why I came."

"Why did you come?" Cargo asked softly.

Heavy silence filled the space between them. "To you now? Or to Marcanter at all?" the Bishop inquired.

"To Marcanter," Cargo supplied, the words tumbling out of his mouth before he could retract them. It frightened him. He'd never asked the Bishop anything like that before. Mirabeau lived in a different world now, a world where everything that was not spoken was a secret, where policy was soft and shifting to fill different expediencies. All his life he had been an instrument of that policy. Even the Bishop's adoption of him was part of the ultimate plan.

It took the old man's presence in his cramped junior stateroom to make him understand. Mirabeau had had plans for him. And he had tested the Bishop not as a mentor but as a father. But still the Bishop had come to him, accepted his decisions, acceded to his demands such as they were. Andre Michel Mirabeau was willing to take him as he was, had not cut him off when he had entered Krait training or even when he had gone to Vanity.

Now the struggle was over. He would do whatever the old man asked. Doing and not doing had made no difference, except now the Bishop had become truly old. And Cargo understood that his age had nothing to do with years alone, but with years of disillusionment and shattered plans.

"I came here to tell you I'm sorry about Beatrice," Mirabeau said softly. "And to tell you that I've arranged for you to have a little time off. Maybe to go to the Wall. To recover a little before the next step."

"But you didn't answer my question," Cargo said quickly, before the sadness the Bishop had tapped overwhelmed him. There was only a fraction of a second left to divert it.

The Bishop smiled. "Politics," he answered. "The Cardia are divided and the antiwar faction has gained a good deal of power recently. Or should I say again? They requested me as one of the preliminary negotiators because I've been part of the Collegium opposition since before the Luxor Incident."

Cargo focused on this to the exclusion of his other feelings with the concentration that was trained in the maze. Every moment the Bishop stayed was one more moment that he could hide. "But why now?" he asked.

"Funny," the Bishop said. "There have been chances like this once or twice before, and something always came up. Once one of the negotiators was found dead on the way. Looked like perfectly natural causes—cardiac thrombosis, almost impossible to predict or prevent. Another time there was an attack on the ship, forced the team to retreat. Like now."

"So you're not going?"

The Bishop smiled. "I'm going. I'm too old to get frightened by something like dying. And I wanted to ask you to take me."

"I thought you told me it was already arranged. I thought you had specially requested me."

"I did," the Bishop said slowly. "I did. But I didn't ask you. I'm asking now."

Chapter

14

He had never been to Hangar Twenty-One before. No one on the *Horn* had. The Chief Petty Officer had ignored it in general, and told anyone who asked that it was currently storing spare parts. Now that Cargo had clearance to enter, he hesitated before the door. Not that he could change his mind. The time for that was long past. He could savor the freedom that he had known for only five short years for a few seconds more before he became the Bishop's son again. As if he had ever been anything else.

Only a few hours, he thought. *Just the flight there and back. That's all.*

He didn't hear anyone come up behind him, didn't notice any other being until he felt a hand on his neck. Not a human hand, but one that was cold with glistening scale plates.

"Ghoster? What are you doing here?" he asked as he turned around.

The Akhaid was completely at ease, a kit bag in one hand and his helmet in the other. "You don't think I'm going to let you go alone?" he said smiling. "Plenty of room on a dip ship and your Bishop doesn't mind the company. Besides, having already been on Marcanter, I'd like to see some of it. What can I tell anybody when they ask what it's like? Tell them all about the insides of the hospital, maybe, or the hot shack?"

"You could always lie," Cargo suggested helpfully.

Ghoster only snorted and made a face. "What are we waiting for?" he demanded, and pressed his authorization into the lock.

There was only one craft in the middle of Hangar Deck

Twenty-One and it was the most beautiful thing Cargo had ever seen. Not beautiful like a Krait or a batwing, which were about the harmony of design and purpose, of speed and courage. This was the symbol of the Collegium, and its beauty was of power and authority and ancient tranquillity. The hull had been burned the deepest violet, the wreath-around-the-atom symbol of the Collegium tastefully counterburned in yellow and flanked by the lion emblem of the Diplomatic Corps enclosed in the triangle of the Trusteeship and surmounted by a cross indicating that this was the Bishop's official vehicle.

The shuttle had an oversized personal yacht design. Cargo figured that it could probably carry twenty in relative comfort, and perhaps twice that number could be squeezed in in case of an emergency. It reeked of wealth and good taste, both of the Collegium and Andre Michel Mirabeau personally.

"Your Bishop likes to travel in style," Ghoster said.

Cargo agreed and they entered the craft. It was more luxurious inside than out without sacrificing either perfect taste or official presence. The bulkheads had not been burned, but had been painted a soft blue that was perfectly matched in the carpet. Over the carpet was an antique rug with a medallion and flower pattern in complementary hues. The cream-colored leather chairs and sofas were designed so that the acceleration harnesses were completely hidden. The desk was as obviously antique as the rug. Cargo ran his hand over the warm, polished teak.

"Come over here," Ghoster yelled.

Cargo went. Stowed carefully in the tiny galley were trays of hors d'oeuvres shaped like flowers, a mousse shaped like a fish with a small jar of green sauce and two silver bowls heaped with caviar.

"I haven't had caviar since Vanity," Cargo muttered.

"Me either."

"I didn't know you liked it." Cargo was shocked. Ghoster almost never liked human food, with the notable exceptions of coffee and anchovies. On the other hand, the bowls were near to overflowing and there were several packs of crackers in the drawer. A small snack wouldn't be missed, and the caviar looked like the highest quality Vanity pink.

"You don't think the Bishop will mind?" Ghoster asked as he bit into his second serving.

"Not at all," Cargo said, swallowing quickly. "He'll never know."

"Do you approve?" the Bishop asked from the hatch. Cargo and Ghoster wheeled in unison. Cargo thought Ghoster was rather overdoing it, trying to scrape the eggs off one of the crackers and back into the bowl.

"Excellent," Cargo said making no excuses at all. Old Piluka had always said that when caught red-handed, the only thing you could do was brazen it out. "The crackers have too much onion flavor, though."

Mirabeau chuckled. "I'm giving a reception here tonight after we land. This is my official residence and office, after all."

"Then how are we getting back to the ship?" Cargo asked quickly. The Bishop hadn't said anything about the transport not coming back.

"That was all agreed in the preliminary to the preliminary. They're going to loan us an old-style shuttle for as long as it takes."

Cargo sprawled on one of the sofas and licked the ends of his fingers. "A clunker, you mean. Do we get to stay for the festivities?"

The Bishop was smiling merrily now. "No, I'm afraid not. I'd like you to, actually, but we don't want any military presence to scare off the faction at this stage. They may be large and powerful, but they're still a minority. By a slim margin, I'll admit, but no need to compromise them. Shall we be underway, then?"

Cargo nodded briskly and settled into the pilot's seat, which was made of the same elegant cream leather. There was something he didn't like about that. It made him feel more like a chauffeur than a pilot. He took out two Three-B's and swallowed them quickly. A transport like this didn't have anything near the maze any military craft did. He supposed the only reason it used a living pilot at all was snob appeal. For ordinary shuttle-work the maze could handle things perfectly well alone.

Ghoster was looking around for the second seat, which the transport didn't have.

"Please come here and sit with me," the Bishop said from one of the deep sofas. "It's been a long time since I've had an opportunity to practice my Atrash."

Cargo thought that Ghoster was just a little reluctant to join him. Well, who would want to sit and make small talk with an ex-Trustee and the Collegium's secret negotiator? If Cargo hadn't known the Bishop since he was fourteen, he would feel tonguetied in Ghoster's position, and Ghoster wasn't exactly what Cargo would call glib or an extrovert.

The trip down was uneventful. After the initial launch from the carrier, the maze more or less told Cargo to get lost, so he had wandered back to where the Bishop uncovered a hidden stash of caviar and the three of them feasted until the approach bell rang melodiously.

Cargo returned to the pilot's seat. They were nowhere near the western continent he had penetrated as a batwing. Auolia, one of the three prime cities on Marcanter, was located in a lush river valley on the most densely populated continent on the planet. Diplomatic privilege, even under cover, still commanded the most preferential treatment. They were whisked through the orbit pattern and directed to land on a private lick inside the government compound. Then the Bishop had to wait until a red carpet was unrolled to the steps of the transport before he could depart.

"That custom started because assassinations were so common," Mirabeau said, pointing down to the strip of carpet. "So if some head of state or the like was murdered the blood wouldn't show and people wouldn't panic." Then he stepped down and greeted the five Cardia officials standing in the receiving line.

After the honors had been done and the Bishop spirited away for some official function, an Akhaid in an officer's uniform came up to the transport. Cargo invited him in, not quite sure what to make of it all.

"You are both invited to take lunch with the Eighty-Seventh Transport Division of the Quartermaster's before transfer of one of our vehicles to your possession for your personal departure from Marcanter."

Cargo and Ghoster looked at each other. Mirabeau hadn't mentioned anything about Cardia diplomatic hospitality extending to them. Besides, a Transport Division of the Quartermaster's? That sounded insulting. Cargo whispered as much under his breath with as much Vanity slang as possible. He didn't want to insult the offer in return.

"You crazy? Quartermasters have the best food," Ghoster

replied rapidly, and then turned to the Cardia officer and accepted for both of them with a number of long-winded and flowery phrases.

At least, Cargo thought an hour later, no fault could be found with Cardia hospitality. He and Ghoster had been given a sumptuous suite to wash and rest in while their clothes went through a clean-and-starch cycle. Then they were escorted to a feast at the Officer's Club that he was certain could not be surpassed by whatever official function the Bishop was engaged in. All the food was not only beautifully prepared, but had been provided fresh and whole, a rare and expensive treat. There were human and Akhaid delicacies alike, things that for all his years at the Bishop's table Cargo had never tasted. Wild mushroom pie and sharp yellow cheese on red apples were his favorites from the banquet.

Afterwards they were taken downstairs for drinks. Here were gathered an assembly of junior officers, and while none of them were pilots they were all veterans of the bars. And from the bottles stacked up for display, the place offered just about everything—and what they couldn't import from the Collegium had been counterfeited.

"Try this," someone said, handing him a glass.

"I've got to fly in a couple of hours," he refused regretfully. "But my partner would probably enjoy it." He hoped he wasn't destroying all chances for a successful treaty by refraining. He took a glass of iced coffee as a polite backup for the toasts that followed. More than an hour had passed before he noticed that he couldn't find Ghoster in the crowd.

Cargo remembered the African violets. It would be worse to pull him out of the bushes here, shaming the entire Collegium. Maybe, Cargo prayed softly, he had gotten back to their suite before he passed out. Just so long as he wasn't lying in public drunk or annied out of his head.

The Akhaid who had invited them accompanied him across two streets busy enough for a downtown and up the outside steps to the apartment where they had been given room. Cargo burst in the door and looked around. The light was off. There was no one there.

No, Ghoster, don't do this, he thought irritably, wondering where his partner could have ended up. They only knew one other place here. Back to the official transport.

Cargo sighed and reluctantly allowed the Cardia officer to

accompany him. He was certain the other had orders not to let them wander around by themselves and he could understand and respect that, even if he was embarrassed by possibly having a witness to having to drag Ghoster away from public property.

There was no sign of his Eyes as they made their way back to the lick. Cargo insisted on going slowly and searching any likely hiding places. Ghoster liked to crawl into cool, shaded places when he wasn't sober. Cargo only hoped he was back in the transport because there was no place else for him to be. Not unless Ghoster had gone off on his own in the complex, the consequences of which Cargo dared not even contemplate.

The transport sat glistening in the lick. A couple of diligent ratings working under diplomatic license had already washed the dust of burn and landing off it. Cargo approached the locked door slowly.

"I don't think he's in there," his companion said uncertainly. "Maybe some guys took him drinking down in the UnderBar. That's the fun place. I should have thought to check there first. Would you like to go over now? Or maybe we can go to the office and I can call. That'll save a trip."

Cargo shrugged. "Let's first see if he's in here," he said offhand. "He might have come back for the caviar."

Then, with a sudden premonition, he jumped and avoided a gripping scaled hand shot out to restrain him. He had his authorization in the lock and his head through the door before the Akhaid had quite recovered his balance.

Somehow what he saw in the halflight of the interior didn't shock him as deeply as he would have suspected. Ghoster was curled up under the maze panel of the Bishop's transport, and he wasn't sleeping. Cargo didn't need any advanced lessons on munitions to recognize that whatever Ghoster was doing wasn't meant for anyone's health.

He dove for Ghoster with both fists as his partner ducked further under the maintenance panel. Ghoster threw up his arms to block his face and tried to kick. It was ineffectual. There was no room between the pilot's chair and the maze housing to fight. Cargo tried to drag Ghoster out to where he'd have more reach. Under the repair station he wasn't able to throw a punch.

"Stop right there," a voice commanded.

Cargo and Ghoster both froze, then turned to the door. The

Cardia officer who had accompanied Cargo held a sonic wand pointed in their direction. Ghoster got up and dragged Cargo with him.

"Over there," he told Cargo, indicating one of the deep leather-covered armchairs. The wand followed his movements too precisely to be ignored. Cargo sat down on the chair and tried to look comfortable while Ghoster tied him with the safety straps. It was a lot like the restraints in the batwing—both arms strapped to the supports, only this time the buckles weren't placed under his hands. He made no move to resist. He was too stunned. It took no genius to figure out that Ghoster had been wiring the transport to blow, and from the setting on the clock that still dangled exposed, it was due to go up around the middle of the Bishop's little reception.

"So you're the agent," he said, his voice flat with unwanted knowledge.

"It's all right now," Ghoster said to the other Akhaid, who handed over the sonic wand and left. Ghoster waited until the door slid closed again, then he lay the wand on the desk and settled himself on the sofa facing Cargo.

"I can't believe it," Cargo said blinking.

"Things are not exactly what they appear," Ghoster said softly. "That being helped me because he is in the Cardia radical-right faction. They can be useful, but they're pure turtle-dung anyway. I didn't tell him what I'm really doing."

"And you're going to tell me." Cargo's voice was heavy with sarcasm.

"Of course I am. We're still partners," Ghoster replied pleasantly. "You see, I am hoping that this will be the last thing you need in your Walk. There are some of us—not a particularly large group but enough to keep things going—who know perfectly well that you humans use this method of Walking, killing each other over nothing, to achieve your full potential. It is a drastic solution, in my opinion, but it appears to be necessary for your species. So those of us who choose to take the most difficult Walk ourselves find that we can do that and help your people at the same time."

"Help us?" Cargo asked. He was totally confused and wasn't sure he was tracking. This could as easily be an auditory hallucination brought on by fear or sensory deprivation, he told himself. Only he hadn't been deprived long enough for anything to happen and he'd known fear close up more than once and had never hallucinated. Especially not like this. He didn't think he could make up anything quite this irrational.

"Of course," Ghoster said. "The crazy thing is that your species pretends to dislike the very thing it needs. If you need to survive a killing situation for several years in order to mature to breed, I should think you'd just admit it instead of pretending that you have all kinds of other reasons. The obvious ones seem good enough to me. Anyway, because of these crazy fictions, you've come close to ceasing hostilities any number of times. I don't know how you managed to produce a fully mature adult group in your history, since you insist on pretending that you really prefer peace. We're trying to help."

Cargo understood, and the knowledge made him feel very, very old. "Were your people responsible for the Cardia rebellion in the first place?"

"Yes. And the Luxor incident, too. Naturally."

"Naturally. And you personally told the Cardia that the *Horn* had arrived and hid the diplomatic amnesty that had been extended?" Cargo asked more for form than information.

"That isn't all," Ghoster said, almost complaining. "Remember when I saw that first batwing? When I got so drunk? And convinced you that we ought to become batwings? I got those guys drunk enough that night to write out plans and drawings for me, plans I said I was going to use to convince you that you wanted to fly them. So in effect I gave the Cardia stealth technology. Well, just the infra-red mask, really. They already had the rest."

"Why did you do that?"

Ghoster nodded. "Balance of power. They were behind in that area and secrecy could win the whole thing. Then it would be over and you'd have problems for a while until you found some other reason to fight. Your species has been selecting for millions of years for aggressive killers. Better that you fight each other than fight us. We're always ready to help. At least this way we're sure to survive no matter what you humans have to do."

Cargo moaned lightly. From Ghoster's cultural and physical point of view it made perfectly good sense. Only now he didn't know how to tell this being that what he had done was more destructive than any war.

"I know you are thinking of our friends," Ghoster said. "I could not help it about Plato. I had nothing to do with that.

With your friend Two Bits, I had no choice. That shot was terribly difficult, I'm sure you understand, to get the reflection angle to target on another craft. But he had been watching you and was suspicious of me. I am truly sorry about bringing you pain, Cargo. Even when you need it. I hope you count me as your friend."

Ghoster stood up and reset the bomb by several hours. "I'm afraid I might have to make other plans for your Bishop," he said softly. "But do not be afraid. You have Walked very well, Cargo my friend. And among my *turanpas* you will always be remembered and a young one will smoke *khal* in your name."

"Wait!"

Ghoster wheeled just before the hatch. He studied Cargo quizzically.

"Wait, Ghoster, You said we're friends. We've been through a lot together—couple of bad places, a few good times. Ghost, you know the Bishop was like my father. And you, you've been like Two Bits to me. Like my own brother. Like a *vrai chal*. I'll make you a deal. Trade me the Bishop, this once, and you Walk. I won't come after you, I won't tell anyone who you were. Are." It was the hardest thing Cargo had ever said. The strain in him was not for pleading. He didn't feel like he was begging Ghoster for anything. Only it was very hard indeed to tell the truth of the heart in a language that was not Romany.

Ghoster stared at him for a long time, weighing. "You're gambling," he said softly. "And when you play cards you don't cheat."

Cargo smiled. "I don't have to." He knew how to place his bets. Ghoster might be some kind of agent, part of some misguided Akhaid conspiracy, but Ghoster was also the person he had known in the maze, had gone drinking with and had pulled out of the African violets, was the person who had helped him up to the table when they drank to Plato's memory.

"*Bater,*" Ghoster said. It was one of the six Romany words Cargo had taught him. Then he leaned over and untied Cargo's bonds.

"*Bater,*" Cargo replied when he stood and held out his hand to the alien who was both his best friend and his adversary. *Bater,* may it be so.

•   •   •

The Wall was located in the middle of the Memory Park on Luxor. What had once been a playground was one again, but now of a different sort, more subdued with a little bitter mixed in with the sweet. The Wall itself, two meters high and over fifty kilometers long, was strung out down the middle of a wooded area that faced Luxor's Nile, a river as sparkling and blue as its namesake had been brown and sluggish.

On warm days families picnicked on the river banks and hired horses to ride down the trail overlooking the polished rare blue marble of the Wall. In autumn the entire area was a favored spot for viewing the foliage, and in the winter the Wall itself blended in with the white drifts and blue ice on the river.

There was a walkway in front of the Wall and a neatly raked white gravel bed that separated the place where one stood and the polished and incised marble itself. But the distance was friendly and it was easy to reach out and touch, to caress a name or leave a memento or letter or picture, some relic of their passing. That was the tradition—a folk tradition that just started by itself and was now a recognized ritual. For all those who died in space, for all those whose bodies were never recovered and could never be buried in their home soil, this was the only cemetery they would ever know. And while it was sometimes a sad place, there were always the riders on the high ridge and the sailboats jaunty on the river, the youngsters playing ball and young couples looking for a private place to stammer and blush. It was a place that was very alive.

Cargo chose a Sunday to come, when the engravers weren't working and when the park was full. It reminded him of the stadiat during the season, of the subdued exuberance of the crowd. The concierge at his hotel had a complete map of the Wall and the autotaxi service the whole length of it, although not more than two kilometers were filled with names. Two bottles of Luxor's most expensive Scotch in his hands, Cargo walked the two kilometers comfortably, enjoying the warm spring air and the sparkling honey sunlight of late afternoon.

As he had planned it, he came across the name Yojo Matcho first. There he poured out the contents of the first bottle into the gravel bed. *"Te avel angle tute, Yojo,"* he whispered smiling. If the *mulo* was there, he would certainly enjoy the fine spirits and the comfort of a visit, that someone had come and given him the tribute proper to a Romany *chal*.

Then he continued down, maybe less than a meter more, until he found Beatrice Sunday. He stood and looked at the engraving that held nothing of Plato, not even her name. He reached out and touched it, but it was only stone and foreign. He poured the Scotch as ritual demanded, then fished in his pocket for the gift he had brought. He laid a pair of matte black wings in the gravel and turned away.

As he strolled along the river, staring at the impossibly blue and dancing water and feeling the hollow coldness of his own soul, he saw a Walker sitting on the bank. This one was not starving and blank, but looking into the water as if it had something profound to say.

Without quite knowing why, Cargo went over to one of the sandwich vendors, bought two and gave one to the Walker. The Walker accepted it, then just smiled at him in silence and returned to contemplating the water. Cargo found a place further down, a warm flat rock, and looked out at the golden glints of brilliance sparkling on the river.

He dipped his hand in and felt the chill left from the early spring, but no longer quite the emptiness of his being. All around there were growing things and songs. *"Te avel angle tute, Plato,"* he whispered, and smiled at the whole glorious world.

ROBERT A. HEINLEIN
THE MODERN MASTER OF SCIENCE FICTION

__EXPANDED UNIVERSE	0-441-21891-1/$5.50
__FARNHAM'S FREEHOLD	0-441-22834-8/$3.95
__GLORY ROAD	0-441-29401-4/$3.95
__I WILL FEAR NO EVIL	0-441-35917-5/$4.95
__THE MOON IS A HARSH MISTRESS	0-441-53699-9/$3.95
__ORPHANS OF THE SKY	0-441-63913-5/$3.50
__THE PAST THROUGH TOMORROW	0-441-65304-9/$5.50
__PODKAYNE OF MARS	0-441-67402-X/$3.95
__STARSHIP TROOPERS	0-441-78358-9/$4.50
__STRANGER IN A STRANGE LAND	0-441-79034-8/$4.95
__TIME ENOUGH FOR LOVE	0-441-81076-4/$5.50
__THE CAT WHO WALKS THROUGH WALLS	0-441-09499-6/$4.95
__TO SAIL BEYOND THE SUNSET	0-441-74860-0/$4.95